HUNTRESS

A.E. RADLEY

HEARTSOME
PUBLISHING

Published by Heartsome Publishing
Staffordshire
United Kingdom
www.heartsomebooks.com

Also available in paperback.
ISBN: 9781999702908

First Heartsome edition: June 2017

I lined up my shot. Took a deep breath. And struck the cue ball. It trundled along and clipped the black. The black rolled towards the corner pocket and... stopped a hairs width away from the pocket.

My friend smiled as he took my galaxy smasher. I complained bitterly that it should have gone in. I'd been robbed. He agreed.

"It would have gone in if that wasn't the pocket over the dodgy leg. The table isn't quite flush. I need a thicker book," he explained.

So. Gary, here it is. A thicker book.

When I was growing up my best friend was obsessed with snooker. His parents bought him a second-hand snooker table and put it in the garage.

The problem with the second-hand table was that it had been damaged and one of its legs had been repaired. But it had been repaired badly and was a good inch shorter than the other three legs.

A book was wedged under the damaged leg and the table was... almost level.

My friend would spend all his spare time in the garage. This meant that if I wanted to spend any time with him, I had to learn to play snooker. So, I did.

One day we were playing and I was doing quite well. Which was a surprise because my friend ended up being an award-winning snooker champion and I, clearly, didn't.

In my cocky youth I offered a bet. If I potted the black, I'd get his grandfather tiger marble. If I missed, then I would have to give him my prized galaxy smasher. For the non-marble aficionado this probably doesn't sound as high stakes as it actually was.

ACKNOLWEDGEMENTS

I think I struggle more with the acknowledgements page than I do with the actual book.

The pressure is immense, what if I forget someone? What order do I list people? And, critically, does anyone actually read the acknowledgements page?

On the off chance that they do, here it is.

I must thank my fantastic editors, Jessica Hatch and Cheri Fuller. Between them they have taken a bumbling mess of words and made a book. And they both made the process a pleasure rather than a chore. That's what good editors are all about, so, thank you both.

Thank you to my wonderful wife, Emma. Who listened to me prattle on about CCTV, MI5, being on the run, and narrowboats. Without Emma, there would be no book.

Finally, thank you. Yes, you. I hope you enjoy reading this book as much as I enjoyed writing it.

CHAPTER ONE
MISSING

AMY LET out a sigh and leaned back heavily on the plastic chair of the break room. She looked at the two male police officers in front of her and shook her head in despair.

"She might be dead, you know," she told them.

The older officer smirked and looked away. Probably to prevent himself from saying anything that would upset her further. Since they had arrived, both had been cocky to say the least. They had spoken down to her; mansplaining the rules on exactly when and how to declare someone as missing. The older guy had stood by the door, presumably eager to get away as soon as possible. He leaned against the wall, his thumbs hooked onto his utility belt as he left most of the conversation to his younger colleague, Officer Raj Patel.

"I think you are jumping to conclusions based on very little evidence," Raj told her in a soft tone that made Amy want to wring his neck.

"Why do I pay my taxes?" Amy asked.

"Good one, never heard that before," the older guy said with a sarcastic laugh.

Raj turned around and gave him a look. He turned back to

Amy and tried to look reassuring. He obviously hadn't had a lot of practice. Amy wondered if she should suggest he request further compassion training. Or any.

"Look," Raj said, "I get that you're worried about your friend."

"She's not my friend," Amy pointed out. For the third time. "She's just a customer."

"Do you monitor all of your customers so closely?" the older officer asked, a smirk firmly planted on his face.

Amy turned to look up at him. "She comes here to the motorway services every day, every single weekday morning. She arrives at six-thirty, has breakfast, we talk, and she leaves by ten to seven. She's been doing that every day for the last ten months. Until three days ago, when she didn't show up. Those specific details about your day, you kinda remember."

"Maybe she got a new job? Or she's sick of the swill you call coffee?" He chuckled at his own joke.

"Sorry, I didn't catch your name?" Amy smiled sweetly.

"David Rowe."

"Look, Dave," she drawled his name, ignoring his wince. "I don't expect you to understand, but some people interact with other people in a cordial and sociable manner, and they make these things called friends—"

"Thank you, Miss Hewitt," Raj interrupted in an obvious attempt to keep the peace.

"And there is nothing wrong with my coffee," Amy added.

"Tell that to my tongue," David said.

"No, thanks, you're not my type." She returned his smirk with one of her own.

"Oh, I see." David pushed away from the wall, suddenly more interested in the case. "You were sweet on her."

"Sweet on her?" Amy let out a laugh. "Who even says that anymore?"

David pulled a small notebook out of his pocket and

detached the pen. He looked over the top of the notepad at her as he very slowly flipped through the pages, deliberately wasting time. Amy watched him, fighting the urge to roll her eyes at his pathetic behaviour.

"So, how long had you been in a relationship with her?" David asked.

Amy glared at him. She bit the inside of her mouth to prevent the reply that was on the tip of her tongue from being let loose. After a few seconds, she took a deep breath. "I wasn't in a relationship with her."

"But you wanted to be?"

"No," Amy defended herself. "We were just friendly."

"Friendly." David nodded his head, a sarcastic smile on his lips. "So, can you tell us the full name of this friend?"

"You know I can't," Amy sighed. She folded her arms across her chest and stared at him. He was clearly trying to antagonise her, and she wasn't going to give him the satisfaction.

"Date of birth? Place of work? Home address? Telephone number?" David listed in quick succession.

Amy looked at him for a few more seconds before turning her attention to Raj. "So, you're not going to help me?"

Raj sat back in his chair and looked apologetic. "I'm sorry, there isn't a lot we can do. This is a busy motorway service station, people come and people go. This... Carla—"

"Cara," Amy corrected.

"Sorry, Cara, she may have moved away from the area. Got a new job, like Officer Rowe suggested. There's no evidence that there has been a crime committed. Just that someone changed their pattern, which isn't against the law, Miss Hewitt."

"This is ridiculous." Amy shook her head and stood up. She pushed the plastic chair back under the table and picked up her apron from the hook on the wall. She hooped the apron over her head and started to tie it around her.

"What's ridiculous is that we're not giving you a caution for wasting police time," David told her.

"You're banned," Amy told him sternly.

"What?" he looked baffled.

"Banned. You." Amy pointed her finger at him. She walked around the table and headed towards the door. "I'm not serving you coffee until you fix your attitude."

He stared at her. "You can't do that."

"I can. I just did. And you called my coffee swill, so presumably you'll be glad to not have to drink it anymore. Banned."

She opened the door and stormed into the corridor without a look back. She angrily strode through the staff-only areas of the motorway service station. She was thankful that she was away from the general public and able to have some small respite from the crowds. She needed some time alone to process what was happening. The police clearly didn't think it was an important matter, but it was. A woman was missing.

Amy knew that Cara would have told her if she wouldn't be coming back. She had even said that she would see her on Monday morning, as she always did on Fridays. Nothing about her last visit indicated in any way that it would be her last. Something must have happened to her. Women like her didn't just vanish into nowhere. Cara was beautiful in an exotic way that Amy had just read about in books. People like that didn't just disappear.

Amy sighed. She'd not wanted to give any indication that she had a crush on Cara. She knew that doing so would give the police something to laugh about, and ensure they didn't take her seriously. She hadn't been able to keep that particular piece of information to herself. She wondered how obvious her feelings were for David to have caught on so quickly.

Despite her crush, nothing had ever happened. Every morning she would anxiously await Cara's arrival. The tall Spanish woman would stroll into the services, hair and outfit perfect despite the early hour. She would approach Tom's Café in the corner of the services where Amy would be standing behind the counter, smiling and hoping her hair was behaving for once.

Cara would order breakfast. Everything was precise. Muesli on Mondays and Wednesdays, wholemeal toast on Tuesdays and Thursdays, and a chocolate croissant on Fridays. She always sat at the same table as she waited for Amy to bring the order. When Amy brought the food, Cara would invite her to sit down. They'd talk about nothing in particular, never anything personal. Amy couldn't be sure, but it always seemed like Cara was flirting with her. At least Amy hoped she was. She was certainly flirting with Cara. Or doing her best to.

Cara stayed for twenty minutes and then left, promising to see Amy the next day or wishing her a pleasant weekend. Amy would go weak at the knees as she watched the well-heeled woman walk out of the services. It was the highlight of her every morning.

Until one day she vanished without a trace. Monday had been a grey and miserable day, and Amy had been looking forward to seeing Cara. She'd practiced her welcoming greeting a few times. She had a witty comment all lined up and ready to go. Despite seeing the woman frequently, Amy often found herself tongue-tied in the moment she actually arrived. Which was bizarre because usually Amy could talk to anyone about anything. There was something about Cara that just prevented Amy's brain from working correctly.

As she practiced her supposedly casual greeting, she'd watched the minutes trickle by. Though Cara was a stickler for timing and details, she had been late before. But never by more than a couple of minutes. By seven o'clock Amy was ready to call the police, the army, every hospital in the area.

After checking details of all road accidents within a fifty-mile radius and finding nothing that matched Cara's description, Amy told herself that maybe she was sick. After ten months of the same schedule, it had to happen eventually. The rest of her Monday shift had gone by slowly and painfully. The only bright spot was that she had convinced herself that Cara would be back on Tuesday.

Except she wasn't.

Nor on Wednesday.

At nine o'clock on Wednesday, Amy called the local police and informed them that she wanted to declare a person missing. By midday the two clowns had arrived and the ten-minute meeting had been the least productive of her life. She vowed to never bother calling the police for anything ever again.

While Raj had attempted to be polite, his main aim of simply appeasing her was thick in the air. He clearly didn't believe Cara was genuinely missing. If Amy hadn't corrected him, he'd be out looking for someone called Carla. If he even bothered to look for anyone at all.

At least Raj pretended to be interested. David hadn't even bothered, boredom coming from him in waves. And he'd insulted her coffee. Amy made a mental note to find his photograph on the local police website and print it out and stick it on the wall to inform her colleagues that he was banned.

She rounded the last corner and stopped in front of the swinging double doors that separated the staff area and the busy motorway service station. She looked through the round glass window and watched the crowds of people. Every kind of person could be found at the services, and Amy watched as they all came together in one large crowd. Nothing connecting them except the desire to rest following a long journey.

Despite the sight of over a hundred people, Amy couldn't help but think that one essential person was missing.

"Screw the police," she mumbled to herself. "I'll solve the damn case myself."

CHAPTER TWO
QUESTIONS

AMY SLAMMED the front door closed, and the house shook in response.

"Amy? Is that you?"

"Of course it's me, Mum, who else lives here?" Amy walked into the living room. She stood in front of the sofa and shook her shoulders until her rucksack fell from them onto the cushions below.

"How was work?"

Amy didn't know why she asked; it was always the same answer. It was clear from her tone that she was itching to say something about Amy's job. Ever since the discussion three months ago, the day after her twenty-fifth birthday, there had been an atmosphere. Julie Hewitt worked part time as the financial director to a small local company. She'd found her niche and she'd settled into it, and was anxious for Amy to do the same.

Not that Amy could blame her. Amy knew that her mum wanted the best for her. She worried, maybe a little more than the average mum did. Maybe because Amy gave her good reason to with her lack of drive and ambition.

"Work was horrid." Amy flopped down on the sofa next to her overstuffed rucksack. "The police are useless."

Her mum looked at her in surprise. "The police? Why were the police there?"

Amy blew out a sigh. She didn't want to get into it. Not now when everything was so raw. "I told you, Mum. Cara, remember?"

"Oh. So, you called the police?" The tone said it all. She didn't approve.

It was just the two of them living in the house, and neither liked conflict. Most of the time everything was rosy in the Hewitt household. They often got on well, Amy choosing to spend more time with her mum than her friends. But occasionally they had their differences. They avoided outright disagreements, neither wanting to shake the boat and ruin the close friendship they had. Instead of coming out and saying something, tones were frequently used to express points of view.

"Yeah, shouldn't have bothered though." Amy closed her eyes and leaned her head back on the sofa. She didn't have the energy for another discussion about her prospects, about when she was going to leave her job at Tom's Café. It had only been two years since Amy had graduated. Top of her class with a First-Class Honours degree in Sociology. It had been amazing. Until she had to figure out exactly what she wanted to do with her shiny certificate and her thirty-thousand pounds' worth of debt.

While generally supportive, her mum had made no secret of her disappointment that Amy continued to work the supposedly temporary job she'd had to pay her way through uni. Comments were often dropped about her school friends, who had almost all moved away from home. Most had got high-flying jobs in big cities around the UK, and some even overseas. But Amy had stayed home. Right at home. In the house she had grown up in.

Part-time waitressing at Tom's Café in the local motorway service station had turned into a full-time job. It had become normal for Amy to wake up at four in the morning to work the early shift. She'd return in the early afternoon and was often in bed by eight. While that should have put a dampener on her social life, she had never been much of a party girl.

Amy felt satisfied. Not happy, but secure and safe in her life. She knew that her mum was worried. Little comments would be dropped and certain tones would be used, but, for the most part, they were avoiding the conversation that hung over them like a dark cloud. It would have to happen one day, but for now they were both happy to be putting it off.

"What did the police say?" Julie asked, fishing for Amy to elaborate.

"Nothing much." Amy opened her eyes and looked over to her. "Just that they can't do anything. As I said, useless. One called my coffee swill."

"It's better than that stuff from the American chain," Julie reassured. The actual name of the outlet was banned in front of Amy.

"I know." Amy nodded. "I banned him."

"You banned the police?"

"Yep."

Julie laughed. "That's typical you."

"He was being uppity."

"He's a police officer."

Amy shrugged her shoulders. "He was being an arse."

"You won't get very far in life if you have trouble with people in authority."

Amy bristled. "I don't have problems with people in authority. I just don't *see* authority. I think people should be equal. Trust and respect should be handed out freely, and expected back in return. Not all this respect where it's due crap."

"Sadly, the world is different; we don't live in that Utopia you have in your brain."

"I know, Mum. Trust me, I know. It doesn't matter. I'm going to investigate it myself."

Julie raised a questioning eyebrow. "What do you mean?"

"If the police won't look for her, I'll do it myself." Amy unzipped her rucksack and pulled out a notebook. She flipped through used pages and opened where a till receipt served as a bookmark. "How hard can it be? Follow the clues. If that dog on the television can do it..."

"The dog on the television is a cartoon," Julie pointed out.

"Same principle applies. Minus the ridiculously large magnifying glass." Amy started to write some notes down, adding to the basic outline that she had scribbled earlier.

"I don't think the dog has a magnifying glass, I think that's the other one."

"Let's not get bogged down in what cartoon character has a magnifying glass," Amy said. She tapped her pen on the pad. "We need to focus on what's relevant."

"Maybe she moved away?" Julie suggested.

Amy looked up. "You too?" She didn't understand how people could just assume that Cara would leave without telling her.

"I'm just being realistic. You said yourself, you don't know that much about her."

Amy regarded her for a few silent moments before she shook her head and turned her attention back to her notebook. Her pen flew across the page. She was making notes of everything they had talked about, no matter how irrelevant it might seem.

Her mum had known nothing about Cara right up until a couple of days ago. Amy hadn't wanted advice, or worse, confirmation of her assumption that Cara was well out of her league. While supportive of Amy's sexuality, Julie wasn't her first go-to for romantic advice. The thought alone made Amy shiver.

But Amy hadn't been able to keep a lid on her frustration at Cara's disappearance, and so it all came spilling out on Monday afternoon. Amy had paced the kitchen floor while she attempted to summarise ten months of conversations and feelings into the space of ten minutes. Seeking to balance the feeling of loss and concern, while maintaining an aloofness that said she wasn't head over heels for the woman. She wasn't sure she succeeded, judging by the look on her mum's face when she was finished. Especially when her theorising suggested that Cara might have been the victim of a murder or kidnap plot.

"Is Kerry coming over this evening?" Julie asked, clearly trying to change the subject to something lighter.

"Yep," Amy replied without looking up from her notes.

"I washed your sleeping bag for you."

Amy looked up. She felt the crinkle of skin between her eyebrows as she tried to think why that was relevant.

Julie chuckled. "You're going camping tomorrow, remember?"

"Oh!" Amy suddenly remembered. "Is that tomorrow? Thursday? Yes. I completely forgot. I need to get packing."

Amy stuffed her notebook back into her bag and quickly left the room to go upstairs.

"You're only going for one night," Julie called after her. "Don't over pack!"

～

Amy tapped her pen on the notebook at a fast pace. "Good, good. What else?"

Kerry spun around on the office chair and looked up at the ceiling. "Um. Alien abduction?"

Amy pointed the pen at Kerry accusingly. "You're not taking this seriously."

Kerry stopped spinning around and looked at her best friend with a tired expression. "Amy, we've been theorising for an hour, and I still maintain that it's one of three things." She lifted up her hand and counted down on three fingers. "She's moved, her schedule has changed, or she's dead."

"Kerry! That is not helping." Amy rolled over on the bed and stared up at the ceiling. "She would have said something."

"Not if she's dead," Kerry pointed out. "That kinda thing can creep up on you."

Amy heard her get out of the office chair and slowly walk over to the bed. "Oh, hi Amy," Kerry said in a strong Spanish accent. "I won't be around next week because I'm slipping on a banana skin this weekend."

Amy looked up at her and chuckled despite the grim situation. "She did *not* sound like that."

Kerry furrowed her brow in concentration before kneeling beside the bed, her mouth to Amy's ear. "Oh no? Was it like this?" she asked in a deep, gruff voice straight from a horror movie.

Amy quickly reached out and pushed her so she lost her balance and fell on the floor. "No, not like that either. But you should keep it for yourself, you might finally get yourself a boyfriend."

Kerry laughed and pulled herself up onto the bed. She crossed her legs and looked over at Amy. "What was she like? You hardly spoke about her."

"Amazing," Amy said dreamily.

"Descriptive." Kerry rolled her eyes.

"I dunno." Amy shrugged her shoulders. "She was just... different. You know? I knew so little about her, but I felt like I'd known her for years. She had a slight accent, she wore amazing designer clothes, she smiled a lot. And I swear she was flirting with me, Kez."

"Maybe she was," Kerry said.

Amy blew out a deep breath. "Then, why did she just vanish like that?"

"Banana skin."

"Shut up." Amy laughed as she sat up.

"Look, we all know that you're not going to be satisfied until you have fully investigated this matter, Officer Hewitt," Kerry joked.

"That's true, Holmes." Amy slid from the bed and walked over to her desk. "The lady has vanished, and I think the game is afoot."

"Why did he say that?" Kerry asked. "What the hell is 'afoot'?"

"No idea, bloke was a lunatic and high most of the time. Not to mention fictional." Amy shrugged. She sat at the desk and turned on her laptop. "I just need my first clue, and then I can go from there."

"I remember when you first told me about her," Kerry reminisced. "The text came in about eight in the morning, and you were all happy about the sexy woman who had made eyes at you."

"She'd left an hour before, and I couldn't get her out of my head," Amy remembered.

"And then she came back," Kerry added.

"And I was in heaven." Amy smiled at the memory.

"And I had to hear about how amazing she was every day for a week," Kerry said.

"And you teased me."

"And you joked about my non-existent love life."

Amy turned and looked at her with a wry smile. "Yeah, fun times."

Kerry poked her tongue out, and Amy chuckled. She turned back to look at her laptop. It wasn't the most elegant solution, but surely a Google search on missing people would give her some indication on where to start.

"You haven't forgotten about tomorrow, have you?"

"Tomorrow?" Amy asked. She turned and looked at Kerry in confusion.

Kerry rolled her eyes. "Tomorrow. Camping! Focus, Amy." She snapped her fingers in her friend's direction to wake her up.

"Kidding!" Amy skipped over to her wardrobe and opened the door to reveal her fully-packed rucksack. She may have gone a little overboard, judging by Kerry's shocked expression. Kerry walked over to the wardrobe. She looked at the bag and then at Amy. Then back at the bag.

"Amy?"

"Yeah?"

"We're going for one night. In my dad's garden," Kerry reminded her.

Amy folded her arms and looked at Kerry seriously. "Remind me. Why are we going camping, again?"

"To check we're able to look after fifteen kids from my mum's Guides group. So, we can say with honesty that we've been camping before. Even if it is in Dad's garden."

"Exactly," Amy told her. She pointed to the rucksack, which was bursting at the seams. "And I have in here everything we could possibly need for two nights in the woods with fifteen under-10s. What's the point in doing a trial run if you're just going to pop into your dad's house every time you need a glass of water? If we're doing this, let's do it properly!"

Kerry pinched the bridge of her nose. "Yeah, that does make sense."

"Which is why you asked me to go with you, because you know that my organisational skills are second to none."

"Well, they're better than mine," Kerry said. She reached into the wardrobe and tentatively lifted the rucksack. "Wow. What have you got in here? Bricks?"

Amy picked up her packing list from the desk and handed it to Kerry. "This is my packing list. Thought you might like a copy so you know what you should pack, too."

Kerry dropped the heavy bag to the floor. She took the list, scanning through the items. "Shampoo, conditioner, lotion, cotton pads, torch, ear plugs, duct tape... Amy, we're camping for two nights. What do you need all this stuff for?"

"You never know," Amy told her. "Besides, when that dry spot on your forehead flares up and you want some lotion, don't come running to me."

"If I have all this in my bag, I won't be running anywhere. I'm going to have to go to the gym before I pack all this stuff."

"You joke now, but when the kids need something... anything at all, I'll have it."

Kerry nodded. She folded the list in half and put it into her pocket. "Very true, thank you for doing that."

"You're welcome. But, I'm helping you with your thing, so now you can help me with mine," Amy said.

Kerry sighed. "Fine, fine. You need to get it out of your system, I get that."

"I need to know that we've exhausted all lines of investigation," Amy explained.

"Considering we don't know anything about her, this won't take long," Kerry said. Amy pouted at her, stormed back to her desk, and sat down.

"Bottom line, you need to identify her. Woman in coffee shop isn't going to get you far," Kerry continued. "Did she ever pay by card?"

Amy shook her head. "No, always cash. Trust me, I would have checked for her surname long ago if she ever paid by card."

"Stalker," Kerry whispered.

"Guilty."

"Okay, so no surname." Kerry paced the room. Amy picked up her pen and tried to recall previous conversations with Cara, anything that might be a clue.

Kerry snapped her fingers. "Got it. What does everyone at the services have in common?"

"They desperately need a wee?" Amy guessed flippantly.

"Well, yes, and?"

Amy shrugged her shoulders.

Kerry rolled her eyes. "And you're supposed to be the clever one... They have all driven there," she explained.

Amy's eyes snapped up. "She drove there!" The excitement started to build within. Suddenly she had something concrete to start with.

"Yep, and doesn't the car park have CCTV or something?" Kerry continued.

"Number plate!" Amy screeched happily as she ran towards Kerry and hugged her tightly. She'd show the police how it was done.

CHAPTER THREE
INVESTIGATION

AMY PEERED in through the window to the security office. The lone occupant of the room looked back at her and rolled his eyes. Amy smiled and waved animatedly. He turned away, ignoring her.

"Rude," Amy mumbled to herself. She opened the door loudly and walked into the room.

"Hey, this is a restricted area."

"Shut up, Kevin." Amy closed the door behind her and folded her arms. "I need to look at your camera things."

"No way." Kevin shook his head. "And they are not camera things, this here is state-of-the-art monitoring and recording equipment. Worth more than both of our yearly salaries put together. So, no, I'm not going to let you look at the camera things."

"Come on, Kev." Amy nudged him with her elbow. "Go on, you know you want to."

"Pretty sure I don't."

"Pretty sure you do." Amy smiled sweetly. "If you don't want me to tell your boss about that time you and that blonde—"

"Hey, you said you'd not tell anyone!"

"Yeah, but that was before I needed something. Now, I need something. So, I'm throwing you under the bus." Amy grinned. She sat down on one of the operator chairs in front of the CCTV cameras. "Go on. Just show me which buttons to push, and then go for a walk. I'll do the rest."

Kevin looked at her. He shook his head in disgust. "You know that's blackmail, right?"

"Such a nasty word!" Amy exclaimed with her hand on her chest. "But yeah, don't make me mention last December, when you clocked in here and then went Christmas shopping with your mum—"

"Okay, fine, fine." Kevin sat forward in his chair and picked up the CCTV remote console.

"Thanks, Kev. You're a pal. Did I ever tell you that?" Amy leaned forward and watched as he accessed the recordings.

"Yeah, whatever." He pushed some buttons on the console. "Here's the camera numbers. You change them with this dial. Then you go back and forward by days with this dial and then you rewind or fast forward here."

"Ooh, gimme." Amy snatched the console from his hands and started to play.

"I'll be back in fifteen minutes. You better be gone by then. And if anyone catches you in here, I'll throw you under the bus," Kevin told her. He pushed his chair back and stood up.

"Love you, too, Kev." She waved goodbye.

Kevin left the room, and Amy let out a deep sigh. She started to focus on the screens in front of her. She quickly mastered the controls and looked for the familiar face in the crowd. She blitzed through hours of footage in seconds and saw thousands and thousands of people speed-walking through the motorway services.

Even early in the morning, the services were busy. First were the office types and sales people in their suits, who were blurring into one long stream of dull colour. They entered the building, went to the bathroom, and left again. At high speed it looked like a nature documentary's most boring migration.

The elderly contingent, who were solely responsible for the shops starting to sell wooden giraffes, sleeping pillows, and tartan blankets, appeared to move at a normal speed when the playback was doubled. Amy smothered a laugh with her hand as she watched a group of old people hurriedly zigzag the entire footprint of the huge services building. Buying crap and getting in everyone's way as they went.

Then she saw her. Cara. Stuck behind a woman who was surely approaching her centenary. Amy let go of the switch, and the playback automatically snapped back to standard speed. She leaned forward and watched as Cara gracefully made her way around the older lady. She strode across the services like she was floating on air, heading straight past the generic coffee shop and towards Amy. Cara moved out of the shot. Amy hurriedly looked at the remote console for how to access the next camera.

In quick succession, she followed Cara across the services and towards the coffee shop. She winced as she saw herself on camera. She sighed at the recorded image of her awkward-looking self.

"Smooth!" She mimicked the ridiculous smile she had thrown Cara's way and smacked herself on the side of the head. "So stupid."

Seeing herself on camera, so clearly enamoured with the woman, was painful. She turned the knob to find the end of Cara's visit. She used various cameras to follow her out of the services. In the car park, she flipped between cameras until she found where Cara had parked. She sighed. The car was obscured by an overgrown tree. She couldn't even tell the colour of the vehicle.

She spun the knob and hurried backwards in time a few

days at random. She soon realised that Cara's car always appeared in the same spot. Leaving and arriving by a blind spot in the camera. She sat back in the seat and furrowed her brow.

Must be a coincidence, she told herself. *She's a creature of habit. Same breakfast place, same food on the same day. It makes sense that she parks in the same space. It just happens to be obscured.*

Sitting forward, she returned to the camera in the coffee shop, found a random day, and watched Cara's arrival. She winced again at her overly keen behaviour towards the mysterious woman. She didn't realise how obvious she had been until she had seen it repeated back to her.

She watched as Cara sat at her usual table. Always the same table. Amy had come to think of it as Cara's table.

She really is a creature of habit, Amy mused to herself.

Her expression softened as she watched Cara talking to her. Seeing the interaction on the screen was such a different experience to living through it. In real time, Amy was always nervous and terrified of saying the wrong thing. When Cara left, she often found herself struggling to remember the exact details. But the recording was unemotional, factual. The clarity it offered proved something that Amy had always wondered about.

"She *is* flirting with me," she whispered.

She tried in vain to remember the exact details of the conversation as she watched Cara invite her to sit at her table. Cara was speaking in hushed tones, making Amy giggle and blush. Amy looked at her recorded self and smiled. She looked so happy. Cara looked like she was sharing a secret with her, leaning in close and whispering something. Amy felt her cheeks burn at the memory. She watched on, even as her recorded self turned away to avoid Cara's intensely warm look.

"What was that?"

She hit the pause button.

She stared at the screen, shocked.

Slowly, she started to move the recording, frame by frame. Wondering if she had seen what she thought. She leaned forward, feeling the heat of the screen against her face as she carefully watched. Frame by frame she stared. Waiting for the moment.

She hit the pause button.

She sat back and swallowed nervously. The paused screen showed it clearly. It all became so obvious. Cara wasn't flirting with the awkward, bumbling coffee shop worker with no prospects. She was distracting her. Waiting for the second that Amy turned away so she could attach something to the underside of the table.

Amy swallowed again, trying to get some moisture back into her mouth which was suddenly bone dry. Tears were starting to form in her eyes. She quickly blinked, wiping the stray moisture away with her sleeve.

She focused on the screen again and grabbed the speed switch with a shaky hand. She sped up the recording, flying through the day. She watched as blurs came and went. Happy to see the traitorous Cara gone. Happy to see Cara's precious table being occupied by others. The shift change came in the afternoon. She watched as she left the services, waving to her colleague Daniel as she left.

She sped up the recording even more. The evening crowd came in, and the place was busy with commuters on their way home. As quickly as the hundreds of customers arrived, they left. She watched Daniel work the lonely night shift, cleaning the tables and shutting down some of the machines in the shop.

Something caught her attention, and she released the switch, resetting the playback to normal speed before quickly rewinding and watching the last customer again.

A man entered just before the coffee shop closed. He

placed an order for takeaway and gestured his cup in farewell to Daniel. Daniel said goodbye and then returned to the back room. The moment he did, the customer slipped his hand under a table, Cara's table, before leaving. It was so smooth. So slick. As if he did it every day.

She rushed through more recordings. Every morning, Cara arrived and waited for Amy to be distracted before placing something under the table. Every evening the man arrived and removed it. The man was tall with black spiky hair, but was always shielding his face from the cameras. He seemed to know exactly where each one was. He skilfully looked in other directions as he passed each lens.

She blew out a long breath.

"Fuck."

Amy didn't know what she was looking at, but whatever it was, it wasn't good.

"What were you up to, Cara?"

She turned around to check that she wasn't being watched before nervously dragging her fingers through her long hair. Looking back to the screens, she accessed the last day that she saw Cara. She watched as the now-usual occurrence happened. In the split second that Amy looked away, Cara placed something under the table. Amy sped time up and landed on the evening when the man came and removed the item.

Leaning close to the screen, she blitzed through to the Monday morning Cara never showed. She played through the day at a faster speed, her eyes straining with the effort of tracking the fast-moving blurs. She slammed the pause button upon seeing one particular blur. A blur she would recognise anywhere. Cara.

She looked at the time index and realised that Cara had come in on Monday after all. She'd just come in the afternoon, when Daniel was on shift.

"Daniel. Shit, I didn't think to ask Daniel. Stupid."

Cara looked different. She was hurrying. Gone was her usual grace as she stormed across the café, looking over her shoulder as she went. Amy found herself mesmerised by the image. Cara always looked so put together. Calm and impressive. But now she was a mess. She was frightened. She approached her usual table in the empty coffee shop and hesitated a moment. Amy leaned closer to the screen, she watched Cara look around. It was almost as if she thought she was being watched. A moment later she turned to leave, pausing to place something under a different table before she left.

Amy felt her eyebrows rise at the change in procedure. Her hand went to the speed dial, and she watched the coffee shop carefully as she sped up proceedings. The evening came, Daniel cleaned as he always did. The man entered the coffee shop and placed his takeaway order. He didn't look any different. Unlike Cara, he wasn't stressed or scared, he waited patiently for his drink before gesturing goodbye to Daniel as usual.

His calm demeanour left him when he looked under the usual table and found it empty.

"Hah!" Amy laughed, feeling vindicated.

Panic seemed to grow in the unidentified man as he frantically searched a couple of nearby tables.

"Ooh!" Amy whistled low. "Warmer, warmer... nah, cold, cold... freezing, mate. Stone bloody cold."

He gave up and rushed away from the coffee shop without looking back. Amy slammed her hand on the pause button. She leaned back in the chair and thought about what she had seen. She feared that she didn't want to delve too deeply into what had just played out before her. She'd uncovered something that probably should have stayed secret. But now she was too involved, and she knew she wouldn't be able to let it go.

She reset the cameras and screens to the way she found them and left the security office.

Her mind was swimming with questions, but on top of them all she had one goal. That goal caused her to walk faster down the corridor. She sped along, bursting through the double doors and into the public area of the services. Ignoring the people who dawdled in front of her, sidestepping the wooden giraffe purchasing octogenarian, she entered the coffee shop. Ignoring the line of people hovering grumpily around the *"Be right back"* sign, she marched to the table at the edge of the shop.

Blowing out a deep breath, she bent down and looked at the underside of the table. She gasped when she saw it. With a shaky hand, she reached up and unfastened the black object. She turned it around in her hand and swallowed. It was a USB stick, fastened with black tape. Discreet enough to be overlooked from a distance, hidden in the groove of the table.

"Excuse me, are you serving?"

Amy looked up at a man in his sixties. He looked down, completely ignoring the fact that she was grovelling on the floor and picking strange objects from the underside of tables. It was one of the fascinating social elements of the services. The services were a place out of step with the rest of the world. To its visitors, it wasn't a place of importance, it was just a random building that people visited for urgent supplies.

To this man, she was just a worker. Someone who pushed the complicated buttons on the machines that provided him with a hot drink.

It was the anonymity of the services that attracted Amy. She was just a worker in a building that people didn't understand. The building was an oasis in a desert, somehow not real. The people who stopped at that building were vulnerable and honest. They were tired, hungry, and thirsty. They were people out of time, existing in a place that didn't seem real. Everything between stopping their car and restarting their journey was disposable, wasted time.

Amy stood up and smiled at him. "Of course, what can I get for you?"

CHAPTER FOUR
GO, GO, GO!

THE MORNING HAD RACED by in a sea of bewildered and tired faces mixed with complicated orders. Despite this, Amy loved serving members of the public. She had always enjoyed dealing with people. Even at a young age she had set up a shop in her front garden and sold all her toys to the neighbourhood children. Of course, her mum had been furious when she found out. Especially as Amy's grasp of finance was nowhere near as good as her customer service skills.

No two days at the services were ever the same. Some familiar faces appeared, but the vast majority were just passing through. Amy loved to watch the throngs of people and wonder what everyone's stories were. Motorway service stations were magical places, places where people came together no matter their differences. During a long journey, it didn't matter who you were, everyone needed to pee.

Obviously, it wasn't all fun. Amy was reminded of that as she cleaned the coffee filter, watching in disgust as large lumps of used coffee grounds fell into the bin.

"Excuse me?"

"One second, my love," Amy called out over her shoulder.

The other joy of the services was that it was her own little bubble. Her home away from home. She could be herself without fear of judgement. And if she was judged, well, who cared? She'd never see that person again anyway. If she wanted to use old-fashioned terms of endearment to strangers, she could. No one ever complained. It was an unwritten rule of the services. You could do whatever you liked when you were an oasis in the middle of long stretches of tarmac.

She turned around, wiping her hand on her apron before looking up and smiling at her next customer. Recognition hit her and she faltered for a moment, struggling to keep the smile on her face.

Luckily, he was looking around the café and not at her. Hopefully he hadn't noticed her initial shocked expression.

"Hi," she said, attracting his attention.

"You seen a USB stick?"

Amy swallowed. It was definitely him. Tall with black, spiky hair. The man who took the USB stick from under the table every evening. She licked her lips as her brain struggled to give her any information to work with.

She wondered if she should ask him where Cara was. Would he know? Maybe he was the reason she went missing? But surely, Amy pondered, he was a colleague in whatever Cara was doing. Her desire to find, and potentially save, Cara was warring loudly with her desire to get the intimidating man in front of her to leave.

"Nope." She popped the P loudly. She shook her head and pretended to look around the counter. "Nope, no USB stick. I mean, USB stick? Like a flash drive?"

He looked at her and let out a sigh. "Yeah. Flash drive, memory stick, USB stick. Little black thing that plugs into a computer and saves files? I lost mine in here a couple of days ago. I really need to find it. It must be here."

She leaned one arm on the counter, trying to appear casual

as she looked up at him. "Wow, that's bad luck, um, no. Not seen one."

He looked at her, and Amy felt for sure he was reading her mind. Somehow, he picked up on her lies and knew that the USB stick he sought was in her backpack in her staff locker in the break room. The more she thought about it, the more she was sure that he was able to peer into her mind.

He reached into his pocket, and Amy held her breath for a second. He pulled out a business card with just a phone number on it.

"If you find it, call me. There's ten quid in it for you." He placed the card on the counter and turned and left.

"Ten whole pounds?" Amy muttered under her breath when she was sure he was out of hearing range. "Whatever would I do with such riches?"

She picked up his card and turned it over and back again. She looked at it thoughtfully. Despite the pathetic finder's fee, he was clearly desperate for the USB stick. She wondered what was on it and why Cara was exchanging it with him.

What do you put on a USB stick? She leaned on the counter and stared at the business card. *I put holiday photos from Malaga on mine.*

She smiled to herself as she wondered if there were pictures of Cara on the USB stick. She shook her head. She was being silly again; this was a time to be serious. Cara was missing. Probably tied up in a basement somewhere, and Amy was the only person who could rescue her. The only person who cared that she was missing.

Maybe the USB stick had information on where she was being held? Maybe she left it elsewhere for Amy to find. She had once complimented Amy on the thoroughness of her cleaning. Presumably she thought Amy would find the USB stick and launch an immediate rescue.

Sadly, Cara didn't know that Amy rarely cleaned the café.

Most of that was left to Daniel on the nightshift. In fact, the only reason Amy got up at four o'clock in the morning was so that she didn't have to clean. Working the morning and early afternoon shift meant that she was busy. And even when she wasn't busy, she was still too busy to clean.

~

It was two o'clock, and her last break of the day finally came. She hung up the sign on the till and hurried into the staff area. She pulled her keys out and unlocked the Hello Kitty padlock on her locker. It wasn't strictly necessary to unlock the flimsy device; one good tug and it would fall open. Her theory was that the better the padlock, the higher the quality of the goods inside. Who would bother to break into a locker with a Hello Kitty padlock? Surely, most people would pity the adult who was poor enough to use the miniature padlock from the pink and glitter-coated diary they got for Christmas ten years ago?

She heaved out the large backpack, cursing Kerry for picking today of all days to do a trial run for camping. With a struggle, she lifted the backpack to the table. She opened the top clasp and pushed aside clothing and supplies to look for her laptop.

Of course, she knew she'd gone a little overboard with the packing. The last time she went camping she forgot her knickers, and she was damned if she was ever going to be caught out again. This time, some fifteen years later, she was prepared for any eventuality. Even if they were camping in Kerry's dad's back garden. Kerry's dad was minted, so his back garden was similar to sleeping in Richmond Park. There was a high probability of animals. Probably only moles and the occasional badger, but Amy would be prepared nonetheless.

Returning her attention to the task, Amy booted up her laptop. She looked around to check she was alone before pulling her Pez dispenser out of a small compartment within her bag. She opened the Pez dispenser and removed the USB stick. Her stomach still regretted the decision to eat all the sweets in the container to make room to hide the device. Still, sacrifices had to be made.

She put the USB stick into the laptop and watched as it automatically opened. The folders and files had long, complicated names that made no sense to her. She cocked her head to one side as she looked at the data.

"Is this code? Is Cara a programmer?"

She moved her finger over the trackpad as she looked at the folders. She eventually decided on a random one and clicked to open it. Inside were more files comprised of more confusing file names.

Amy scrunched up her face and navigated back to the root directory. She chose another folder and was confronted with the same complex file names that made no sense.

"Hand it over!"

Amy jumped at the intrusion. She shook her head and let out a sigh. She couldn't believe that the freak from the coffee shop had followed her.

"Look, Spiky, this isn't even yours, okay? And this is a restricted area, so you need to leave."

"Hand it over, now." He took a menacing step towards her.

"Um, how about no?" Amy replied cockily.

He reached into his jacket and pulled out a knife.

"Whoa, what the hell?" Amy yanked the USB stick from the laptop and took a step back. She picked up her overstuffed rucksack and held it in front of her like a shield. If he wanted to stab her he'd have to go through half a metre of pointless packing.

He laughed bitterly as he stepped forward. "You have no idea what you are getting yourself into."

She took a step backwards, and they slowly circled the

cluster of tables in the middle of the room. She held the bag up protectively and gripped the USB stick tightly in her hand. Part of her brain was saying she should hand it over. The other part warned that he may kill her once he had it.

"The second you plugged that USB stick into your laptop, it connected to the Wi-Fi and activated a signal. People are listening for that signal. You have no idea who is coming. You are mixed up in things you don't understand."

"I've got a degree, a First, you could explain it to me."

"I'm not kidding around."

"Neither am I, don't let the apron fool you. I'm a member of Mensa. Well, I was until I washed the membership card. Paper? Really? They couldn't spring for plastic? Technically, I'm still a member. I just couldn't prove it to you with the card. Not that I wanted to be a member of Mensa, I think it's a bit pretentious. But, my mum, you know—"

"Shut up! God, do you ever stop talking?"

Amy opened her mouth to reply and point out that she often spoke to herself and even spoke in her sleep. But something told her that now was not the moment to volunteer that information.

"Stop edging towards the door," he ordered her.

"Nuh-uh. Dude, no offence, but you have a knife, so I'm not listening to you. You're probably a murderer."

"You want to test that theory?" he asked her.

Amy quickly lifted her leg up and kicked the table in front of her, causing the rest of the flimsy tables to disperse around the room. One hit Spiky, the others momentarily blocking his path and giving Amy the opportunity to run. She hurried out of the break room, throwing her backpack on. She exited the first set of double doors and spilled into the public area.

"Fucking great." She looked around at her would-be rescuers. A busload of pensioners all shuffling towards the toilets like penguins on the ice. In the distance was a group of

French schoolchildren. "Perfect, just bloody perfect," she mumbled.

"Amy!"

She spun around and saw Kerry walking towards her. She suddenly remembered that Kerry had offered to pick her up after work.

"Are you practicing carrying your backpack, you weirdo?" Kerry asked in confusion.

The doors to the staff area smashed open, and Spiky came out. He took a quick step back as he looked up at the ceiling.

Amy looked up, too, seeing the CCTV cameras and realising that he didn't want to be seen.

"They are coming," he told Amy seriously. "You don't have much time."

"Who's coming?" Kerry asked. She looked at Spiky. "Aliens? Right? I always knew we are not alone."

"Kerry, don't, he has a knife," Amy warned her friend, quietly to not cause a panic.

Kerry took a few steps back, her hand on Amy's arm to pull her back with her. As they stepped further into the middle of the concourse, Spiky walked around the edge of the wall, circling them but not daring to enter the main area.

"Just hand over the USB," he said to Amy. "The government are on the way here right now, and they are going to have more than just a knife. If they catch you with that USB, they will brand you a spy and throw you in a hole to rot."

"Is that what happened to Cara?" Amy asked.

"Amy's not a spy," Kerry added. "She'll tell them, she's not a spy. Or they'll take one look at her and deduce that for themselves. I mean, look at her."

"Thanks, honey," Amy quipped.

"You're welcome, babe."

"You think they'll listen? To you? When I'm done with your records, you'll read like a couple of Jihadi Janes," Spiky told them. "Your name will be mud. Both of you. But, if you hand it over now, I can make sure that all of this goes away."

Amy swallowed. She had no idea if he was capable of what he was saying. And if he was, did she really want to give him a USB packed full of God knows what?

"No." Amy shook her head. "No, I'm not giving this to you and that hair."

"How much gel do you use, anyway? It doesn't even move." Kerry vaguely pointed at his head.

"I know, right?" Amy said.

"Shut up!" Spiky shouted in exasperation. He looked up at the large glass frontage to the building and smirked. "They're here."

Amy followed his gaze and saw three black SUVs and two black vans screeching to a halt in the car park. The backdoors of one of the vehicles opened and a stream of armed police in black ops outfits poured out.

Pensioners in the car park were starting to point and stare at the sudden arrival. Luckily, most of them were also in the way and slowing down the progress of the officers.

"Give me the USB stick now," Spiky told Amy, "and I'll make sure that you are left out of this. Don't give it to me, and I will tell them that you are armed and carrying a bomb. Do you think your First and your Mensa membership can talk you out of that? You seem to like talking so much."

"Oh, you are so mean!" Amy told him.

"Babe," Kerry whispered. "I think we need to get out of here, regroup."

"Agreed," Amy murmured in reply.

In a move they had used many times over the years, both turned around and ran towards the ladies' toilets, the obvious refuge for any given situation. The ladies' toilets were the perfect place to escape anything. Except Amy's mum. But Amy was pretty sure that she wasn't about to be rescued by her mum.

"Shit, shit, shit, shit," Kerry repeated under her breath as they entered the ladies' toilet. She weaved around old women dithering in the cramped space.

"What do we do?" Amy asked, fiddling with the backpack straps and seriously wishing she hadn't packed Pocket Scrabble. The pack was damn heavy, and she hadn't thought about the fact she would have to carry it at some point.

"What is he talking about? What USB stick?" Kerry asked.

"Short version." Amy took a deep breath. "I looked at the CCTV, couldn't find Cara's car. *Could* see Cara. Every morning she tapes a USB stick underneath a table in the café. Like, some kind of stealthy shit."

Kerry gasped.

"Every evening, Spiky out there comes in and gets it. Every day this happens. Until Monday. Cara didn't come in in the morning. She came in the afternoon and put the USB under a different table. Spiky came in later and couldn't find it." She held it up. "And now I have it."

Taking another deep breath, she continued, "I plugged it in. I think it's in code or something. The second I plugged it in, he came into the break room all *whoosh whoosh* with a knife. He said it had activated some kind of alarm. Said I had no idea who was coming. Now some government black ops shit is outside. With guns." Amy pocketed the USB.

"We don't know they are the government," Kerry pointed out. "I don't think we can trust anything Spiky has to say."

"Whoever they are, they have guns. Like, a lot of guns." Amy watched as an elderly lady waved her hands under the tap for the twentieth time to no avail. She leaned forward and pushed the button on the top of the tap. "We're not that advanced here, still got buttons," Amy told her kindly.

"Oh, thank you, dear!"

"You're welcome," Amy replied. She grabbed hold of Kerry and walked to the end of the toilets. "What do we do?"

"Regroup," Kerry replied.

Amy indicated their location. "I thought this *was* us regrouping?"

"I don't know about you, but there is only so much regrouping I can do in the ladies' toilets with, like, twenty men with guns about to burst in."

"Right, you're right. We need more time. We need space."

Kerry looked at the fire exit thoughtfully. "I'm parked near this exit." She looked at Amy. It was obvious what she was suggesting. It was crazy. Running away. From armed men. But then Amy didn't know what else to do. She didn't know who to trust and who to believe. And she sure as hell didn't want to be shot. She had a two-part *Casualty* special recorded and she wanted to know what happened. Dying today was out of the question.

"Okay. We open this door. We run to your car and we... we just go," Amy said. "Right?"

Kerry swallowed hard. Probably also considering the gravity of what they were about to do.

"Because, I don't know if I trust this..." Amy used her finger to draw a circle around her face, "... to be able to explain without getting us killed. I need some time to process this. To think about the best thing to do. The best thing to say."

Kerry slowly nodded her head. "We open this door and run to the car... and go. Go where?"

"Out of here. Fast."

They looked at each other for a few seconds before nodding agreement.

"One..." they counted together, "two... three!"

They burst through the door and started screaming loudly as they ran towards the car park. Amy looked around as she ran.

Amy paused her screaming to shout, "Where's the car?"

"Shit," Kerry shouted back. "It was the other door!"

"What?" Amy stared at her, still running but now apparently not towards the car.

"Other door!" Kerry pointed to another fire exit in the distance.

"Shit!" Amy shouted.

They both turned and jumped over a flower bed before starting to scream again. They ran across the car park, around the building, and towards the back of the services. They weaved in and out of parked cars, panting in exhaustion as neither of them had run anywhere in about ten years.

"You said you parked here," Amy complained loudly.

"How am I supposed to know every fucking fire exit?" Kerry returned over her shoulder. "Anyway, there it is!"

Without the added weight of the backpack, Kerry arrived at the two-door car first. She unlocked the driver's door and threw herself into the seat.

"Hurry!" Kerry called out of the open door.

Amy opened the passenger door and saw Kerry's own enormous backpack taking up the seat. She pulled on the catch to lift the seat forward so that she could climb into the back. The seat moved halfway, stopped due to the bulk of the bag. Amy attempted to throw herself into the back but was stopped by the size of her own rucksack. She tried again to squeeze in, but it was wedged in the doorway. She knew she shouldn't have brought the painting by numbers kit.

"Shit." She climbed out and slammed the door shut again. She rushed to the back of the car, opened the boot, and started to fiddle with the straps of her bag. Attaching it firmly to herself had made running with it easier, but she was now wondering if she would ever be able to get out of it.

"Come on!" Kerry shouted as she revved the engine.

"You try hurrying with all these fucking straps!" Amy yelled back.

Eventually, she managed to unhook one strap, but the other clasp blew around in the breeze. She completed two full circles on the spot just trying to catch it.

"Fuck it," she muttered. She threw the backpack, still attached to her body, into the boot of the car. Her legs and arms were still outside, but she was weighed down by the backpack. She realised that she was as in the cramped space as she was going to get, and slammed her hand against the boot to get Kerry's attention.

"Go, go, go!"

ANDREW BARR LOOKED around the briefing room at the assembled group. Seventeen people. Supposedly the best of the best. Not that anyone would have been able to tell by their performance to date. A fact that weighed heavily on his shoulders.

He tilted his neck from one side to the other to release the pressure that had been building over the last six months and now threatened to turn him to stone. He looked down at the documents in front of him. The crisp foil seal of MI5 intelligence glittered in the dim light of the room. The importance of the black and white imprint of the royal coat of arms surrounded by a ring of the words 'Her Majesty's Secret Service' weighed as heavily today as they had when he joined the service thirty-three years ago.

He rubbed his eyes. Logically, he knew why the MI5 briefing rooms were in the middle of the building and, therefore, without access to natural light. What he didn't know was why the damn lighting always had to resemble the rig used to film *The X-Files*. Surely, they could find bulbs that actually gave out light, rather than the pathetic glow he was now bathed in.

He looked around the assembled company and wondered if they struggled as much as he did. Or if it was simply his age. Not that fifty-eight was that old, he reminded himself. But more and more, it felt old. As the bad guys got faster, he felt himself getting slower. The intelligence service was becoming a young person's game. But, looking around at some of the youngsters gathered, he didn't fancy putting national security into their hands just yet.

The final attendee entered the room, apologised, and closed the door behind her before hurriedly taking her seat.

Andrew stood up. "Thank you all for coming. Most of you know why we are here, but you'll forgive me for repeating the pertinent facts for those who are new to this particular investigation."

He picked up the projector remote control and pressed a button. Two large screens at the head of the table sprung to life. Copies of the briefing documents were displayed on the screens for all to see.

"As you probably know, our senior analysts have reported significant chatter regarding confidential government information being stolen." He pressed a button, and the screen changed to display screenshots of online forums with coded messages being sent back and forth.

"Over the last several months, the information being stolen and sold on the dark web has increased in both frequency and in security level. It remains unclear exactly what this data is. The code the seller uses changes on a frequent basis, and we have yet to identify a cipher."

"Have we attempted to purchase this data from the dark web ourselves?"

Andrew looked up into the darkened room for the location of the question. Miranda Haynes. *Of course*, he thought.

Miranda was the lead analyst responsible for gathering information leading to the capture of the 7/7 bombers. Miranda was known to be argumentative and strong-willed, which was presumably why the higher-ups had brought her into the investigation.

"We have. Our attempts to establish communication with the seller have been unsuccessful," he replied. He hit the button on the remote again. He gestured to the screen with a tilt of his head.

The screen changed to display a series of conversations aimed at the seller with no replies.

"So, they are probably sophisticated enough to crack through our encryption protocols, and presumably know it's us," Miranda surmised. "I have said again and again that we need to tighten up those protocols if we are to win this so-called war on terror."

"That may be so," Andrew soothed. He was in no mood to get into a technical debate with the woman. He knew his knowledge in the area was limited, and he had no desire to make himself look a fool. "However, following the lack of response with the seller, we turned our attention back to identifying the source of the leak."

He looked towards Miranda, pleased that she seemed happy to remain silent. For the time being at least.

"Following an interdepartmental briefing yesterday evening, it is believed that this initially minor data breach may now be tied to a suspected upcoming attack planned by a terrorist agency or agencies. Similarities in the language and codes being used are consistent with a group calling themselves Green Falcon, who have been very active recently."

He clicked the remote control and comparison documents filled the screen. He gave the agents time to read the information.

"If these two are working together, I don't need to tell you how potentially dangerous that could be."

"I've worked cases with Green Falcon," Miranda spoke up. "They are indeed very dangerous and extremely slick. We know of them, but we've yet to see them make a mistake. How can we be sure that they are working with the individual selling the stolen government data?"

Andrew stood up straight and grasped his wrists behind his back. "It is our belief that the sale of the information on the dark web is simply a mistake. Probably made by someone lower down in the chain of command. Or by the person obtaining the data themselves. As you say, it seems unlikely that anyone within Green Falcon would be stupid enough to flag up their access to this information."

"I'm constantly amazed how lucky we are by terrorists' stupidity," Miranda quipped. "God help us when someone who knows what they are doing steps up."

"The IT boffins have made a network-wide change to a number of government facilities which we believe may be the source of the breach," Andrew changed the subject. "They have added a sophisticated virus which will be attached to all pieces of data leaving the system via any means."

"So, we know where this breach is?" Miranda asked.

"Not exactly. We have narrowed it down to one of six government offices based upon the type of data we believe is being sold."

"Wait a minute, let me get this right," Miranda said with a chuckle. "We think information is being stolen from a government office. But we don't know which one. And we don't know what data is being stolen. We've narrowed it down to one of six data centres, but I believe we only have nine, so we've only managed to rule out three."

Andrew coughed discreetly. He pressed the remote control button to change the slide.

"The virus will signal back to us when any file is accessed either outside of government offices or on a non-government piece of equipment. I don't need to tell you that when that happens, we must strike quickly," he explained.

"Wouldn't the public be horrified to know that this fumbling in the dark is how we keep them safe?" Miranda spoke up again. "We're hoping that someone doesn't know how to disable this virus, I presume? Hoping that they will steal information and then access it on... what? A networked machine I suppose? Which isn't exactly in the terrorist handbook, for a start."

Andrew let out a sigh. Miranda wasn't going to be silenced easily. To be honest, he didn't blame her. He knew as well as she did how incompetent the agency could be. But it was his job to defend it.

"That's not entirely fair, Miranda. This is a particularly sophisticated breach of our systems. The information being stolen is not that sensitive in nature and so it was not identified immediately. I would like to stress that highly confidential information has not been obtained." He looked around the room, ensuring that the message sunk in to each person on this new task force.

"It is through working with other departments that we have identified a potential connection between this data breach and Green Falcon. This case has been investigated by several departments, and we do have a lot of information. Just nothing actionable yet. As I say, they are very advanced."

"How advanced do they need to get before we become advanced, too?" Miranda asked. "By the time we find out who they are, they'll have gone to ground."

Andrew had known that point would be made. MI5 had a long and painful history of arriving too late to the party. By the time they had the information they needed, the perpetrators had vanished into thin air. The secret service was so tied up with red tape, everything took an age. And it was destroying morale. But Andrew had a solution, and, for once, he was glad that Miranda had brought up the subject so he could play his ace.

"This one's important. So important that I think it's time we bent the rules just a little," Andrew said.

He felt the atmosphere in the room change. Agents shifted in their seats. Officers looked intrigued to know more.

"I have authority to bring in additional help. Some call her the best hunter in the business. She's willing to work with us, she's just waiting for us to give her a name."

"McAllister?" Miranda sounded almost impressed.

"Of course," Andrew replied smugly.

"She's out of the agency. How did you convince her to come back?" Miranda asked.

Claudia McAllister was famous within the secret service. It was common knowledge that she had left the previous year, citing red tape was preventing her from doing her job. She'd taken her senior analyst with her and set up her own private detective agency in central London.

McAllister was legendary in her ability to find and bring in anyone in record quick time. She was also known to be a rule breaker. The agency higher-ups went through a continuous circle of giving her a dressing down followed by giving her more work.

Her departure was felt keenly throughout the service. Of course, MI5 had tried to tempt her back several times to no avail. But Andrew had a tenuous personal connection to Claudia and he intended to leverage that fully.

"She's not coming back," Andrew said, "not permanently."

After the debriefing the previous evening, Andrew had realised that this case had the potential to spiral out of control. He was two years from retirement, and he wasn't about to have his service record blighted by a major attack just before he left.

He knew that the hunters within the service were some of the best in the country, in the world even. He also knew that most of them had been trained by Claudia. And they were all bogged down by the same red tape and procedural policies that had caused Claudia to walk out.

"I see." Miranda nodded her understanding. "Well, I'll be glad to have her assistance. She was the only one around here willing to do what needed to be done."

"I thought you'd see it that way." Andrew smiled, hoping it didn't look as smug as it felt.

"So, now we wait for the data to be accessed, I presume? Then we can pinpoint a location, pick up an asset, and go from there. As always, my department is willing to help. I'll get our best people on this immediately."

"Fantastic. I know working together isn't always the agency's strong suit, but in this case, we must band together and share information and sources." Andrew turned back towards the display screen. He clicked the remote control and moved on to the next slide.

"WE HAVE to work on our getaway," Amy complained.

"You said go go go, so I went went went," Kerry argued.

Amy pointed to the rearview mirror. "Do you know what this is? What it does? Do you use it? Well, obviously not, because if you had used it, then you would have seen that I was laying in the boot of the car with my flipping legs and arms hanging out the back."

"I apologised."

"Speed bumps, Kez. Speed bumps."

Kerry sighed. "We were evading armed men; I didn't think slowing down for speed bumps was going to help us get out of there."

"My back will never be the same again," Amy grumbled. "And I was nearly sick! Do you know how many Pez I ate this morning?"

Kerry threw the paper map into the back seat. "Look, I apologised, okay? I'm sorry. I stopped when you fell out."

"I heard you laughing," Amy muttered.

"Well, I'm sorry, but it was fucking funny," Kerry admitted. Amy pouted and Kerry blew out another sigh. "Now, come on.

Snap out of it. We need to think of a plan of action. Who are we going to call? What are we going to say? Sitting here complaining about stuff that we can't change isn't helping anyone."

The car was parked out of the way on a dirt track, in between two high hedges separating fields. Kerry wasn't sure how they managed to get away, but somehow, they had. Admittedly it must have looked like something out of a black-and-white slapstick comedy.

But once Amy was firmly in the car and Kerry could hit the gas, they were away. Kerry had driven more aggressively than she'd ever done before. She'd quickly hit the village lanes once they were off the motorway. When it was clear that they weren't being followed, she'd driven down a couple of narrow roads that led to hardly used dirt tracks.

"We should probably call the police," Amy suggested. "Tell them what happened from the start and then give ourselves up."

"Agreed. Hiding out here is just going to make matters worse. We tell them what happened. Give them the USB stick and then we go to the pub," Kerry said with a smirk.

"Ooh, pub." Amy smiled.

That was more like how Kerry had seen her afternoon off work going. Running away was probably a stupid idea, but they would call the police, explain what had happened, and flutter their eyelashes a little bit. They'd apologise and then have a quick glass of wine in the pub before heading to her dad's.

"Right, call them. Then we can go to the pub and get this camping out of the way. Did you bring Pocket Scrabble, by the way?"

"Of course I did," Amy told her. "I need to prove myself after the last match."

Amy reached into the back seat and got her mobile phone out of her bag.

"It was pretty exciting, though, wasn't it?" Kerry said. "I mean, we just did a proper getaway from the police. Like, I think I nearly wheel spun. I didn't know I could do that. A bit less screaming and a bit more knowing where the car was and that would have been epic."

"Kerry..."

"Yeah, yeah, maybe making sure we were both in the car before setting off, I know." Kerry rolled her eyes.

"No, Kerry, look..." Amy held up her phone for her to see.

BREAKING NEWS ALERT:

POLICE CONDUCTING URGENT MANHUNT FOR AMY HEWITT AND KERRY WYATT, CONSIDERED ARMED AND DANGEROUS.

Kerry felt her heart sink. There was her name. Her actual name, on the news. Alongside words like "police" and "armed". A cold shiver ran through her body as the reality of what was happening started to kick in. It wasn't supposed to go like this.

"What the hell? Armed with what?" she demanded of the screen.

Amy took the phone back and started to read the news story aloud. "'Stoneshire Police have issued arrest warrants for Amy Hewitt and Kerry Wyatt, who are suspected to have sold confidential information to terrorists. Members of the public are urged to report any sightings...' Oh fuck..."

Kerry's heartbeat quickened at the horrified expression on Amy's face. "What?"

Amy quickly turned the phone screen towards her. Kerry

squinted as she looked at the two grainy CCTV pictures of them.

"What the—?" Kerry snatched the phone. "That is the worst possible picture they could have found of me. Well, I'm safe. No one looking for that Elephant Woman is ever going to find me." She paused and looked at her friend who had yet to issue a denial. "Are they? I knew I should have washed my hair this morning. I thought dry shampoo would be enough, but clearly—"

"Kerry, focus," Amy told her calmly. "The police are after us. They think we're working with terrorists."

Kerry swallowed nervously and handed the phone back into Amy's waiting palm. Leaving the services to regroup wasn't supposed to end like this. She just saw the men with the guns and panicked. While she'd suggested they run away, she hadn't meant to go on the run. It was quickly sinking in that was exactly what they had done. For the police to issue a news alert and get their pictures from the CCTV cameras so quickly showed a level of urgency that Kerry didn't want to be tied up in.

"We can't hand ourselves in," Amy announced coolly.

"Why not?" Kerry asked.

"What if they don't believe us? Prison isn't like TV."

"Prison?" Kerry asked, the weight of the situation settling heavily on her shoulders.

"Well, they're not going to send two suspected terrorists to Disney, are they?"

Kerry slowly turned her head away and looked at the narrow road in front of her. She started to wonder how this had even happened. When she had applied for an afternoon off from work, she hadn't assumed that would be the day she would be labelled a suspected terrorist. All she had done was visit her best friend, and suddenly she was—

Amy's phone rang and she let out a yelp. She threw the

phone into the foot well, gathering her feet up onto the passenger seat to get away from the noisy device.

"Who is it?" Kerry demanded, finding her strength at the moment Amy lost hers.

"I don't know. It says no number!"

"It's them," Kerry surmised.

"Them who?" Amy looked at her, fear obvious in her eyes.

"Them! You know, them! The people who have been sent to find us." Kerry nodded. That was their dynamic now, us and them. Everyone else was a them.

"What do I do?"

"I don't know," Kerry admitted. The events of the day all seemed to be happening too quickly. She wanted things to slow down so she could take stock and make sensible decisions. So far, they'd made the wrong decisions and that had got them into a situation where they were labelled terrorists.

Amy reached into the foot well and picked up her phone.

"Amy, no!" Kerry surged forward to stop her from answering the call.

Amy pushed Kerry back. She held up her hand before answering the phone and putting the call on speaker. "What?"

"That was very stupid." The familiar male voice echoed through the car.

"What do you want, Spiky?" Amy demanded, fear giving way to anger once she recognised the voice.

"The USB. Give it to me and all of this will go away."

"No way," Kerry shouted. "Like we'd trust you!"

"Fine." He sounded unbearably smug. "Then let me tell you what's about to happen. If you go to the police, they will arrest you for suspected terrorism offences. Terrorism is a very unique charge in the United Kingdom, it prevents you from having many of your normal rights. They can hold you for longer, prevent you from speaking to others. And when they find you guilty, and I'll make sure they do, your lives will be over. Trust me when I say that I'll make sure the police find evidence linking you to certain plans."

"Do your worst!" Amy taunted.

Kerry stared at her in shock. For a genius, Amy could be an idiot sometimes. "Amy," Kerry whispered, shaking her head.

"What?" Amy mouthed.

Kerry returned her attention to the phone and Spiky. "We're not giving you the USB stick."

"Then you better be really good at running and hiding. Because they are coming for you. And I don't mean the local cops. I mean the specialists. The hunters. They will freeze your bank accounts, they will speak to everyone you know, take your personal belongings, track your car number plate, and if you ditch your car, then they will follow you on CCTV. Don't think you can call anyone for help, they'll pinpoint your mobile telephone. Trust me, you won't last a day."

"We'll go off the grid," Amy announced.

Kerry smacked her in the shoulder to shut her up. The last thing they needed was Amy giving away their plans to the enemy.

"Off the grid?" Spiky laughed. "There is no 'off the grid' in the modern world. You can't hide. Everything we do is being monitored. It is just a matter of time before they find you. Being on the run isn't a nice life. You can't trust anyone. You'll miss your home comforts very quickly. Just meet me and hand over the USB, and I'll make it all go away."

Amy hung up the call. "Okay, we have to get rid of our phones."

"I'm sorry, what?" Kerry put her hand to her forehead and massaged at the headache that was starting to take hold.

Amy waved her phone around in Kerry's face. "Weren't you listening? He just said they can track our phones. We have to ditch them."

"Are you serious?"

"Serious about not wanting to be arrested on terrorism charges? Um, yes!"

Kerry reached into her coat pocket and looked at the screen of her own phone.

Six Missed Calls

With a sigh, she showed the screen to Amy.

"See? It's started. Quick, turn it off!" Amy ordered as she turned her own phone off.

Kerry powered down her phone. She watched the operating system logo flash up before disappearing. The screen faded to black.

She looked at Amy. "What now?"

"We have to ditch the car," Amy said. She reached into the back seat and picked up the paper map that Kerry kept in case of emergencies.

"Ditch the car? I'm not ditching my car!" Kerry told her. She held onto the handbrake lever. "I love my car."

Amy didn't look up as she turned the map in multiple directions and followed roads with her finger. "They can track the number plate, they are probably on the way here now, we need to get out of here. On foot."

"Amy, you need to slow down and think about this. You're talking about going on the run," Kerry told her. "This isn't a joke anymore."

Amy put the map down and turned to look at Kerry. "Do you remember when we were kids, and we used to hang out in the school playground together? We'd look at the fence and talk about climbing over it and running away? Going on big adventures and seeing what was out there?"

"We were seven," Kerry reminded her.

"But we knew we could do it because we had each other," Amy told her seriously. "I've always thought about those chats, the plans of what we would do. How we would get around Mrs Simms, how we'd run across the park and then get on the first bus we saw. We had it all figured out. We knew exactly what we would do, no matter what happened. We were unstoppable."

Kerry had to chuckle. "Yeah, we were. We had an answer for everything."

"Kez, I honestly think we need to run. We need to clear our names and we can't do that if some terrorist with connections is planting evidence against us. Think about it. We don't know who he is but he is clearly not going to win a philanthropy award any time soon. He threatened me with a knife. He is setting us up, and we can't let him."

Kerry knew she had to be the voice of reason when Amy got like this. "We only have his word that he is doing that."

Amy shrugged her shoulders. "Oh, okay, fine, yeah, we'll take the risk. Because Spiky might be lying and it might all be fine. Or he might be telling the truth and that butt-ugly CCTV picture of your face will be across every newspaper in Britain and you'll be labelled a terrorist forever."

Kerry scowled at the mention of the CCTV image. "And how is running going to help?"

"It will give us a chance to clear our names. We'll get away from here, from where they are looking for us. We can regroup. But properly, not like this. And then, then we'll find someone who can look at the USB, someone who can help us," Amy said hurriedly as the plan came to her.

"There's... there's always Jason?" Kerry suggested.

Amy frowned. "Who?"

"You remember Jason Lawrence, I met him at university? He started the year I finished."

"Oh, the one that was always following you around?"

"Yeah, he is an IT genius. Said there was nothing he couldn't crack, he'd won some awards and stuff as well."

"Do you know him well?" Amy asked.

Kerry shrugged. "I didn't keep in touch with him, so I don't see how the police would think to connect us. And he transferred to Aberdeen University the year after I left, so it's not like it's even going back to my own university. If we could get there, he could help us see what's on the USB. He can probably help us document that we have nothing to do with the information that's on the USB. Some kind of data trail. Doesn't everything you do on a computer leave a footprint?"

Amy nodded. "I think so." She turned the map over. "Aberdeen. Jesus, that's a long way."

"I don't know anyone else who could help us with this." Kerry shook her head and took a deep breath. Running from the police seemed insane. But she had no idea if Spiky was telling the truth. Maybe he had constructed evidence that would have her thrown into a black hole forever. If she was labelled a terrorist, that was the end of her life.

She turned and looked at her rucksack. She mentally calculated what she had in her bag and how she would be able to use it. She had a tent, sleeping bag, a few spare clothes, but mainly because she was dropping stuff off at her dad's. Amy had obviously packed enough for a month.

Even so, neither of them had ever had a successful camping trip, never mind running away from the police.

"He said it wouldn't be the police looking for us," Kerry remembered.

"Yeah, he called them hunters."

"Hunters?" Kerry bristled. "That sounds awful. The people coming after us are hunters, Amy."

"The people coming after us have no idea where we are or where we'll head. I meant what I said, we'll go off the grid. They can't track our car or use CCTV if we're off the grid."

"So, we're doing this?" Kerry asked. Whatever they found themselves wrapped up in, it was obviously bad. Bad enough for someone to threaten them with a knife. Bad enough for the armed police to show up within minutes.

She watched as Amy grabbed her notebook and started to take notes. Amy was crazy sometimes, but she was also the smartest person Kerry knew. She would trust Amy with her life.

With a cold shudder, she realised she might be doing just that. Going on the run was deadly serious. She just hoped that Amy knew that, too. As smart as she was, she could also be extraordinarily stupid.

She sighed. She wanted to call her mum. Wanted to tell her that she was okay and that she had nothing to do with whatever the news was saying she did. With a sinking feeling she thought about her nan, who religiously watched the news broadcasts on the BBC every morning, afternoon, and evening. Her life revolved around watching the news, and now her darling granddaughter was going to be on it. Branded a terrorist.

Amy finished scribbling in her notebook. "Okay. We need to drive to a cash point and take out as much money as we can. We need cold, hard cash. That's if they haven't already frozen our bank accounts. I don't think they would have. They don't know we're on the run yet, as we only just decided to do it. In fact, they will probably allow us access in the hope we'll use an ATM so they can track us."

Kerry swallowed, her throat suddenly dry. "Agreed. We need cash, and then we need to lose the car." She looked around at her car, her pride and joy. She'd been so happy when she'd bought it with the money she had saved from her first job.

Amy nodded. "Okay, we'll drive to a cash point, both take as much as we can, and then drive away. I think we should ditch it in Sommerfeld Street, then we can take the cut-through to the park and then over the fence to Walton. Then we get the local trains to London and then the first fast train up north."

"Whoa, you want to go into central London? Isn't that the exact opposite of being off the grid?"

"We have to. If we want to get off the grid, then we have to get away from the area. Unless you want to walk for ten days straight to get to Aberdeen, we need to get a train. The thing is, how many trains leave London every day? Thousands. And they don't know what we're planning. So, they would have to look through countless cameras in some of the busiest stations in the country. That's gotta be a needle in a haystack, right?"

Kerry felt herself frown as she considered the risk they might take.

"Once we're in London, we'll get the oldest train we can up to Scotland, anywhere in Scotland will do. It's bound to not have CCTV on it if the train is old enough. We'll try to avoid the station cameras. Even if they see us at the station, they won't be able to track us beyond that."

Kerry felt uncertainty in her stomach like a brick.

"I know it's a risk, but I think it's a calculated one," Amy concluded. "We have the element of surprise. Look, let me show you what I'm thinking."

Amy angled the paper map towards Kerry. She followed the route that Amy had pointed out. She nodded her head. It was as good a plan as any.

CLAUDIA MCALLISTER WALKED into the debriefing room and looked around at her former colleagues with barely disguised amusement. It had been nearly a year since she had last been in the darkened meeting room. That meeting had been very similar to this. The large boardroom table still had the same boring faces who wore the same sour expressions. The windowless room was still lit by the same dim artificial lighting and the sound of the air conditioning units rumbled familiarly in the background.

The main difference was that meeting had been the one where she had walked out of the service. A terrorist mastermind had gone to ground, and it had been the final straw for her. She would have caught him if she had simply been allowed to break a couple of laws. Nothing major. She wasn't asking to kill anyone. Just to not have to wait for a 651-C form to be signed off by three different department heads. While uninformed suits in their offices read through pages of intelligence reports in order to make decisions on subjects they couldn't possibly understand, the window of opportunity had slammed shut.

MI5, like any other branch of government, was annoyingly full of red tape. So much so that operations often ground to a halt.

Claudia had been tracking the suspect for six months. She'd seen his plans with her own eyes. Most importantly, she knew the man. Knew he had killed before and planned to do so again. He'd taunted her, left messages for her to find every step along the way. He'd known that she was unable to act, known that her hands were tied by bureaucracy.

So she had left the intelligence service. In a blaze of language not suiting her position or temperament, she walked out that day and never looked back. Plenty of other hunters left MI5 and went on to have wildly successful careers. Some worked for other governments around the world, some went freelance. Some even worked for the terrorists. Hunting people was a skill, a job just like any other.

Claudia had set up her own firm in London. At first, there was the thrill of being her own boss, she only took on the cases she wanted to investigate. The pay was good. The red tape non-existent. She operated within the law, of course. But sometimes the law was a little grey, and she took full advantage of those murky shadows.

When Andrew had called her the previous week, she'd hung up the phone. Partially because it felt oh so good to hang up on her former boss, and partially because she knew he would only be calling to say that he needed her. Hanging up the phone delayed the inevitable.

He didn't call back, and she wasn't surprised to see him in the waiting room to her office the following morning. He looked like he'd aged five years in the last twelve months.

He looked like he'd aged another five years since that meeting just last week. She took the only available seat at the table and looked towards her former boss.

"Thank you for joining us, Claudia," Andrew said pleasantly.

Claudia nodded in reply and placed her interlaced fingers on the desk as she waited for him to begin. Andrew hadn't given her many details in her office. Red tape, of course, dictated that he couldn't speak to her in an unsecured environment. But she knew it was important. He had promised that she would remain a contractor, not working for the government. She would be allowed to operate the investigation in her own way with no limitations. That alone indicated to Claudia that they had slipped up. Big time. And they needed her to help them fix it.

Andrew picked up a remote control from the table and pressed a button, causing the dull lights in the room to dim even further. A moment later the projector screen came to life.

"Amy Philippa Hewitt." Andrew pointed to the photograph on the screen. "Twenty-five years old. She's been on the run for six hours, and her capture is of national importance."

Claudia leaned forward and examined the photograph of the smiling young woman, presumably taken from a social media site. Long blonde hair was tied loosely back, sparkling green eyes shone in the summer sun, and a crooked, though genuine, smile filled the frame. She couldn't see a single hint of malice in the picture. But she knew that even the most innocent-looking person could turn out to be guilty of the most terrible crimes.

"Kerry Wyatt, also twenty-five years old, is with her." Andrew pressed a button and the photograph of Amy was replaced with one of a new, equally friendly smiling face. This time the woman was slightly larger in build but with the same carefree look. Short brown hair, blue eyes, Claudia noted. Andrew pushed a button on the remote, and both pictures appeared side by side.

"Miss Hewitt and Miss Wyatt are considered to be highly

dangerous, well-organised, and have been effectively off our radar since they ran from a motorway service station six hours ago," Andrew continued. He pressed the remote control again. This time a satellite image of the local area appeared on the screen.

"Our agents have not been able to track Miss Hewitt or Miss Wyatt down through conventional methods. Due to the sensitivity and urgency of this case, we have had to bring in additional support." Andrew looked towards Claudia.

She pushed back her chair and walked around the table to get a closer look at the photographs. Her eyesight had never been great, and she refused to wear her glasses amongst her former colleagues.

"She needs to be found and brought in for questioning within the next twelve days," Andrew explained as he stood by and watched Claudia examine the photograph.

"And what happens in twelve days?" Claudia folded her arms and looked up at Andrew with interest.

Andrew bit the inside of his cheek thoughtfully, clearly weighing his options. After a moment he nodded towards Louisa Hayward, who was sat closest to the projector.

Claudia turned to look at the Information Officer and raised her eyebrow. While no one in the room particularly liked Claudia, Louisa disliked her the most. Claudia couldn't help but enjoy making the woman squirm.

Louisa let out a sigh. She folded her hands over a restricted information dossier laying on the desk in front of her. Protecting the secrets within.

"We have information that, in twelve days' time, multiple terrorist attacks will take place in multiple, as yet unknown, locations across Britain," Louisa spoke measuredly. "Amy Hewitt has a USB stick on her person. It contains stolen government information and a tracker virus which she has already accessed once. We have recovered her laptop and have discovered evidence of her involvement with known terrorist agencies. Her capture and questioning is essential to national security."

Claudia discreetly swallowed and nodded. Of course, she had known that it was serious for them to be calling her in. But the stakes were higher than she'd imagined. An operation of this magnitude was rare for MI5; it needed to be successful.

She pushed aside her personal feelings, her bitterness towards her former colleagues, and turned back to regard the photographs. The smiling faces peered back at her. She cocked her head to the side and narrowed her eyes. They didn't look like typical terrorists. But in the new terror age they lived in, anyone could be converted to extremism.

"So, who are these girls?" Claudia asked.

Following a nod from Andrew, Louisa opened the file in front of her. She shuffled the pages as she began to read off information. "Amy is twenty-five and works in a coffee shop called Tom's Café in a motorway service station close to where she lives."

"Where she ran from," Claudia guessed.

"Yes. She has a degree in Sociology and lives with her mother in the village of Wakeham. No romantic partner that we know of, but she is extremely popular socially, mainly online. Kerry Wyatt is her best friend; they grew up and went to school together. They live one mile away from each other. They attended separate universities, Kerry graduated with an accountancy degree and now works in a local accountancy firm. She recently ended a short relationship with a Martin Reed, we're looking into him now. She lives alone in a small flat in Wakeham."

"Family?" Claudia asked. She sat on the edge of the table and attempted to look at the file Louisa was reading.

Louisa slammed it closed and looked up at Andrew beseechingly.

"You know the rules, Claudia," he told her with a sigh. "You don't have security clearance to see all of the information we have gathered. Only the standard bios."

Claudia shook her head. Nothing changed. "So you call me in, you want my help, but you won't bring me in on what you already have?"

"I don't make the rules," Andrew replied.

"No, but you do blindly follow them. Even when, in your own words, national security is at risk."

"You don't work here anymore, Claudia. You saw to that," Andrew argued.

"No, I think you all saw to that," Claudia replied. "Each and every one of you knows that things need to change in this agency."

"The truth is that you aren't accountable in the same way we are," Miranda Haynes spoke up from her seat beside Louisa. "You can deliver results without having to jump through the endless hoops of bureaucracy that we have to."

"So, now that it suits you…" Claudia stood up and walked towards the projector screen. She folded her arms and looked at the photographs, soaking up every detail she could. "You want me to break the rules?"

"If you must, yes," Miranda spoke plainly. "Now that I don't have to justify your decision-making process to the board."

"Of course we can't be seen to be working with you," Andrew explained as he sat down. "You will work alone, and we will not be able to support you. You use whatever methods you feel necessary. If you find her before we do, then you can bring her in and take the reward. But this meeting never happened."

"This is pathetic," Claudia mumbled under her breath. She turned and looked at Andrew. "You clearly know that your methods aren't working. When will things change around here?"

"Change takes time. Consider how serious it must be for us to be willing to take this course of action," Andrew said. His serious expression silenced any further arguments. Now was clearly not the time.

Claudia nodded. "I'll find them. Just give me the basics, and I'll go from there."

Andrew, in turn, nodded at Louisa. She pulled a sheet of paper from her file and handed it to Claudia.

"Full name, date of birth, last known address. All you'll need to begin your own profiling," Louisa said.

"How kind of you," Claudia said sarcastically.

"Remember, they are both considered to be extremely dangerous." Andrew spoke again. "I know you think we're all incompetent, but they vanished from our hunt team immediately. They had backpacks with them, so they were clearly prepared to run. You need to consider these girls well-organised and dangerous."

~

"How was it? Has anything changed?" Mark Richards removed his glasses and methodically cleaned each lens with a disposable cloth.

Claudia snorted. "No, of course not. Same old people. Same old problems." She plugged her mobile phone into the charger, the only thing on her large and empty desk.

"We have a new case," she said simply.

"A new case?" Mark raised an eyebrow. "So, that's why you asked me to hang around?"

Claudia looked at the clock on the wall. It was now ten in the evening, which meant her suspects had an eight-hour head start. At MI5, an eight-hour head start was a disastrous prospect. But Claudia knew that she and Mark were the ultimate dream team when it came to finding anyone. Mark had been the best analyst in MI5, and now he worked exclusively for her. Part of Louisa's animosity towards her was the fact that she had managed to steal Mark from her team.

"I thought you were in trouble," Mark continued. "I thought it was about you interfering with that recovery case last month?"

"Seems they don't know anything about that." Claudia shrugged. "Just think, Mark. Our survival is in their hands. Isn't that a terrifying thought?"

"They gave you a case?" Mark questioned again.

"Don't sound so surprised."

"You left. We left."

"Well, we haven't returned, if it's any consolation to you? They just want help locating someone, they need some rules bent to do so." Claudia opened her desk drawer and pulled out a red marker pen.

"What about Mrs McEnroe and this divorce case?" Mark asked, gesturing towards a stack of papers on his desk.

Claudia walked over to the large whiteboard. "This comes first, and then we'll go back to the McEnroes and their marital woes."

She pulled the cap off the pen with her teeth and started to write the basic information that she had been given. As she wrote, she heard Mark typing the details into her computer.

"Amy Hewitt, lives in Wakeham?" Mark asked.

Claudia took the pen cap out of her mouth. "That's the one."

"May I?" Mark indicated the whiteboard, and Claudia nodded.

With a few taps of the keyboard, Mark's screen was projected onto the whiteboard. Numerous windows from multiple social media sites as well as telephone directories and search engines filled the board. Claudia looked at the info with interest.

"Neither of these women are shy about sharing their data," Mark commented.

"That's good for us," Claudia said as she took in all the information.

"Amy has a driver's licence, but no vehicle is registered to her and she doesn't hold a parking permit with the council for her home address. So I think we can assume no vehicle there. Kerry holds a driver's licence and owns a vehicle."

Claudia nodded. A car was a great start. The Automatic Number Plate Recognition System had often allowed her to track suspects in real time.

"Have MI5 requested ANPR on Kerry's car?" Claudia asked.

A new screen appeared, one that Mark probably shouldn't have had access to. Claudia wasn't about to complain.

"Yes," he replied. "But there have been no hits."

"No hits in eight hours," Claudia said. "Let's assume they have dumped the car."

"They've been missing eight hours?" Mark clarified. "And they are calling us in already?"

"They have terrorist links. They both ran from the motorway services, both wearing large rucksacks which presumably contain supplies to go on the run. They had clearly been planning this for a while. Amy has a USB stick with her which contains stolen government information that may be relevant to an attack that is being planned. They didn't say directly, but I assume it's that Green Falcon group we hear so much chatter about. Amy is the ringleader, we don't know Kerry's full story yet."

Mark blew out a low whistle. "Serious stuff then."

"Very. These two may look like nursery school teachers, but they are extremely dangerous." Claudia turned to face Mark.

"Call your friends in. We'll need access to CCTV, facial recognition, phone records. The works."

"I say this every time, but—"

"It's not exactly legal, I know, I know." Claudia cut him off with a wave of her hand. "This one's important. We have nowhere to start, and we need to get these girls before they completely go to ground. We need data, and we need it now."

"MUM?"

"Amy?" She sounded panicked. Amy's heart clenched.

"Mum," Amy let out a sob. This was the last call she was going to make before she ditched her phone. "I just wanted to tell you that... that I'm okay and that I didn't do it."

"Oh, Amy, the police have been here. They are saying that you have links to terrorism!"

"It's not true. I... I just got mixed up in something. I haven't done anything wrong, I—"

"Then come home."

Amy rubbed at her forehead. "I can't, they won't believe me. I'm going to prove I'm innocent, and then I'll come home, I promise. But I... I can't contact you again. I have to get rid of this phone."

"Amy, please..." The sobs were coming thick and fast now. Amy couldn't stand to hear her mum cry.

"Mum, please, I'm okay. I promise that I'm okay. Just... just don't worry."

Muffled sobs came down the line, and Amy took a deep breath. "I love you, Mum, so much. I love you, okay?"

She hung up and hurriedly turned the device off. The train jolted, and she nearly fell from the toilet seat she had been perched on to make her call. She stood up and looked at her reflection in the mirror. She ripped off a few sheets of toilet paper and tried to wipe away the tears and tidy herself up a bit. Calling home had been a stupid idea, but she just had to do it.

"Kerry's going to kill me," she mumbled to her reflection.

She made her way along the carriages back to her seat. The train thundered along the tracks towards a destination. Amy couldn't even remember where it was headed. Every now and then the train would sway from side to side, and Amy would pause in the centre aisle and hold on to the seats on either side. Sometimes she wondered if it was the train swaying or if it was her. The people who passed her didn't seem to have the same problem.

Eventually she arrived back at her seat and fell into it. She had high-fived Kerry when they managed to snag a table seat upon boarding the train. Now she stared across the table at Kerry and swallowed with nerves. How things changed over the course of two hours.

"I thought you'd fallen in," Kerry joked.

"I called my mum," Amy admitted.

Kerry stared at her in horror. "Tell me you're kidding," Kerry pleaded.

"I'm not kidding," she whispered softly. "I had to tell her. It was eating away at me. You know we never go more than a few hours without contacting each other."

Kerry grabbed her belongings from the table top and shoved them into her bag. She stood and pulled her coat down from the luggage rack.

"I can't believe you, Amy. I can't believe you did that without telling me." Kerry struggled into her coat. Her rage made it difficult for her to find the arm holes.

"I had to speak to her," Amy defended herself as she also packed her things away.

Kerry stared at her hard. "You think I don't want to call my mum? You think this is easy for me? Is it somehow harder for you than it is for me?"

"I know, I'm stupid. What are we going to do?" Amy asked, fearing she already knew the answer.

"We have to get off the train," Kerry told her. "The train that we specifically waited for because it would be old and wouldn't have CCTV. We made the rules together, Amy."

Amy looked at her notebook where the rules they had scribbled out stared up at her. This particular rule was underlined three times: If for any reason they felt their location had been compromised, they had to move quickly.

"I know, I know," Amy told her. "I messed up."

Kerry put her backpack on the table to balance the weight and started strapping herself into it.

"Look, if we're doing this, we have to work together, okay?" Kerry explained as she adjusted the straps. "It's us against them. But that means we have to work together. You can't go off and do things without telling me."

"I'm telling you now."

Kerry looked at her for a second before shaking her head and stalking off up the train carriage.

"Kez, wait!" Amy called out as she struggled with her own bag. She eventually heaved the backpack into place and walked up the carriage towards the doors. The doors opened, and she saw Kerry slumped on the floor, dejected and staring at the wall.

"I'm sorry, okay?" Amy told her. She held out her phone. "Here. Take this so I don't do anything stupid again."

Kerry stared at her for a moment before taking the phone. "I'm really pissed off with you, Amy."

"I know."

"Four trains. Four trains left Kings Cross, going north, while we waited for an old train. And, when we finally got on a train with no CCTV, a train that we could have curled up and had a nice sleep on, you decide to call your mum."

Amy sighed and slipped to the floor as well.

"We know they have your mobile phone number. When they see it was activated and you were moving at eighty miles an hour across countryside, it won't take long for them to figure out that we're in a train. So, not only do we have to get off the train, we have to get off the train line. And, if you'll remember from our early research, it is the only bloody train line in the area. It isn't like they have a choice of which one to search. It's this one."

Amy rubbed at her face with her hand. "I know, I'm sorry. It was just a split-second reaction. I didn't think. I'm sorry. I'll fix this, I promise."

Kerry let out a sigh and shook her head. She turned her head to avoid eye contact. "Amy, you have to tell me what you're thinking. Going off and doing something without talking to me first is not going to cut it," she said as she stared at the wall of the train. "We're in deep shit. We have to stick together. Spiky had a knife. Suddenly, we're known terrorists, armed and dangerous. This is serious."

"I know," Amy whispered. "I know contacting Mum was stupid—"

"Whatever is on that USB stick, it's something big, something important," Kerry continued. "If we weren't in a public place, I think Spiky would have killed us for it."

Amy slowly nodded. "I think so, too."

"So, on one side we have him—let's call that choice 'certain death'," Kerry said. "And on the other, we have the intelligence services. Who have been told that we are dangerous terrorists. I can't see us easily talking our way out of either situation if they catch us."

"No," Amy agreed. "If Spiky can convince them that quickly that we're terrorists and send them after us, he must have someone on the inside. Hell, maybe he's on the inside. Either way, we can't trust the authorities either."

Kerry nodded. "Agreed, and so we'll call that option 'prison'. Until we get to the bottom of what is on the USB stick and find a way to clear our names, being caught is a choice between death and prison. And you're too pretty for prison."

Amy grinned at the half-joke.

"Look, Amy, we need to have a plan. A plan for what we do in case we get split up," Kerry said.

Amy shook her head. "Don't think like that."

"No, seriously, we have to. I've been thinking about what's on that USB stick and why someone wants it so badly."

Amy rubbed her tired eyes. "It might be a recipe for sponge cake, it might be the nuclear launch codes... if such a thing even exists."

"Exactly. This is bigger than us. If there's even a one percent chance that there is something on that USB stick that might harm someone, we have to do everything we can to get it to the right people. Whoever that may be."

"That's phase two," Amy said. "Phase one is to figure out what's on it. Phase two is to decide what to do with it. If it's an awesome sponge cake recipe, then I'm sending it to *Woman Magazine* to get a hundred quid."

Kerry chuckled. "Yeah, you do that, babe." She reached into her pocket and pulled out the money they had taken from the ATM. She took half of it and gave it to Amy.

Amy took it. She raised her eyebrow in surprise. "You never trust me with money."

"I'm trusting you with the nuclear launch codes."

"Or a really awesome sponge recipe."

"If you're going to carry the USB then you should have some money, in case we do get split up."

Amy swallowed. The inference was clear: Kerry wanted her to carry on no matter what.

"I won't leave you," Amy said.

"You will. If I get caught, or something happens, I want you to take the USB and that money and carry on. I need to know that you'll finish what we started. I'll be able to deal with it all better if I know that you're okay."

But I won't be okay without you, Amy thought. She brushed her messy hair out of her face. She suddenly felt young, like they were back in high school and Kerry was telling her she could defeat the bullies alone.

"I'm going to go back to ignoring you now," Kerry announced. "Because I'm still pissed off with you for calling your mum."

Amy nodded in understanding.

"I'm so—" Amy stopped at the glare Kerry sent her way.

CLAUDIA RANG THE DOORBELL. She took a step back from the front door and looked at the house. Illuminated by the streetlamp, it was nice enough, though it could do with a lick of paint and some general upkeep. The street was the average suburban set-up, but Claudia had seen it all before, terrorism lurking behind respectability.

It may have been close to eleven at night, but Claudia knew that for the occupant of the house, time stood still.

The door opened. The elder woman looked at her wearily.

"My name is Claudia McAllister, I'm investigati—"

"Come in."

Claudia followed Amy's mother into the house, closing the door behind her. On the telephone table by the door, she noticed a business card from the Stoneshire Police Force. She knew the local constabulary would have visited, she just hoped that they hadn't completely destroyed her investigation. A lack of communication between MI5 and ground crews often meant that too much information was given to the suspect's family.

She walked into the living room.

"I'm sorry for the late hour," Claudia apologised.

"I won't sleep while my girl is out there, god knows where." Amy's mother sat in an armchair and anxiously played with the frayed arm.

"Mrs Hewitt, I'm sorry to have to go over all of this again." Claudia perched herself on the edge of a well-worn sofa.

"Call me Julie, Mrs Hewitt was my mother. And I'll tell you what I told the officers that came before you; my girl isn't a terrorist."

"I'm afraid that I've heard that many times before." Claudia pulled her phone out of her pocket. "May I record our conversation?"

Julie shrugged.

"Julie, I need your verbal permission." Claudia wasn't about to let a vital piece of information slip by because she hadn't dotted the Is.

"Yes, fine," Julie said bitterly.

Claudia activated the recording app and placed the phone on the coffee table in front of her.

"Have you heard from Amy since she ran away?"

Julie shook her head. "No."

Claudia knew a lie when she heard one. She also knew that she needed to get Julie to trust her if she was going to find out the truth.

"We have evidence which suggests that Amy is in contact with a terrorist organisation. That is a very serious charge."

"And a completely ridiculous one. My Amy is kind and honest. She doesn't have a mean bone in her body." Julie reached into her cardigan sleeve to pull out a tissue and dab at her eyes.

"In my experience—"

"Are you a mother?" Julie's eyes flashed with anger.

Claudia bit her lip and shook her head. "No, I'm not." She wanted to say that her lack of children gave her a perspective that a mother could never have. But she knew that would just antagonise the woman in front of her.

"I know Amy better than anyone. We're like best friends. If she was a terrorist, or had those kind of inclinations, I'd know about it. She's a sweetheart, and she may sympathise with people, but she would never use violence. Never."

It was obvious that a change of tactic was required. Claudia realised that she would not reach Julie by appealing to her doubting nature. The bond between mother and daughter was just too strong.

"Julie..." Claudia let out a soft sigh. "I'll be honest with you; I am not the only person looking for Amy. But I am the only unarmed person looking for her."

Julie swallowed. Her eyes bore into Claudia's with barely disguised panic.

"Our information directly links Amy with terrorist activity. We must speak to her so we can find out the truth. I want to bring this to a non-violent conclusion. In fact, I promise you that if you help me to find her, I will protect her."

"She's just a girl..." Julie's voice was weakening with building emotion.

On the table, Claudia's phone started to ring and vibrate. She glanced at the screen to see it was Mark. She picked up the device and gestured towards the hallway. "May I?"

Julie nodded. Her fingers grasped at the tissue, and Claudia hoped that a few moments to herself might encourage the woman to give up information.

She walked into the hallway and answered the call quietly.

"The car has been found abandoned," Mark said without embellishment. "I'm sending you the location."

"Okay." Claudia looked at the screen and clicked the link to the coordinates. Her map sprung to life, and she quickly analysed the location. While it was a residential street, it wasn't that far from a railway station.

She lifted the phone back to her ear. "They caught the train. It's a local station, so it wouldn't take them far. I'm guessing they are going to try to go to London."

"You think they'd take that risk?"

"Yes, they are going to want to move quickly. They abandoned the car near a railway station for a reason, to get a train. Around here the trains don't really go anywhere, other than London. See which mainline stations they could connect to from there and then use the facial recognition software on the CCTV feeds at the stations."

"Again, not entirely legal," Mark told her.

Claudia knew that every time they broke into the systems, they ran the risk of being caught. It was a risk worth taking in this case. "Without this lead, they could be anywhere," she told him. "Oh, and don't use the police photo fit that has been released. Use pictures from their social media accounts. They look nothing like those photo fits."

"No problem, I'll get onto it now, and I'll talk to you as soon as possible."

"Thanks, Mark." Claudia hung up the call. She tapped the edge of the phone to her lip as she thought. It was usual for terrorists to use their considerable networks to move around the country. Catching a train was a risky move, hopefully one that would pay off for her.

She took a closer look at a picture that hung on the wall. It was a sunny scene of Julie and Amy smiling, presumably while on holiday. It looked like it was a few years old. She cocked her head to the side and stared at Amy's face, trying to get into her mind and figure out the girl's next course of action.

She took a breath and walked back into the living room. She placed the phone back on the table and continued recording.

"Sorry about that."

"You've not found her?" Julie asked hesitantly.

Claudia shook her head. "I'd not be here if we had."

"She was meant to be camping tonight," Julie said. "If I close my eyes I can almost believe that she is there."

"Camping?" Claudia asked. Of course, the information had already been sent to her in the official pack, but there was nothing like information directly from the source.

"Yes, they were camping tonight. Only in Kerry's dad's back garden, though. They were doing a practice run for a camping trip they are organising for some younger kids. That's why they had the bags with them, they weren't planning on running away. It's all just a big coincidence." Julie chuckled and gestured to Claudia. "I suppose you don't believe in coincidences?"

"Not really, no," Claudia admitted.

"Well, it's the truth." Julie shifted in her seat and rubbed her forehead. "She's never been in trouble before. She's always been such a good girl."

"Is it just the two of you?" Claudia asked. She already knew the answer. As far as she could see, the house was littered with pictures of the two of them.

"Yes. Amy's dad died when she was little."

"I'm sorry for your loss," Claudia said.

"Don't be. He was a monster. We're all better off without him."

Claudia nodded and mentally ticked off that line of enquiry.

"I bet this has something to do with that woman." Julie shook her head angrily. "I thought she was trouble."

"Woman?" Claudia questioned, trying to keep the interest out of her tone. This certainly wasn't in the information pack.

"Cara whatshername." Julie blew out a breath. She looked at the ceiling and shook her head. Despite the situation, Claudia couldn't help but feel for her. Her entire life had been turned upside down in under twelve hours. But she also knew that stress eased the path to information, and she wasn't above using that leverage.

"Cara?" Claudia prompted.

Julie turned to her with a frown. "Cara. She was a regular at Tom's."

"The coffee shop?" Claudia clarified.

"Yes, she came in every day. Amy was very taken with her."

"Taken how?"

"She fancied her," Julie said with a casualness that made Claudia ache for that kind of acceptance from her own mother. "Although she never mentioned her to me. Not until one day when she stopped turning up. Suddenly, Amy looked like the bottom had fallen out of her world. She'd never spoken of the woman before, but once she vanished it was Cara-this and Cara-that."

Claudia itched to point out Amy's secretive behaviour could also be applied to terrorist activities but kept quiet. She needed Julie on her side, and pointing out flaws in her relationship with her beloved daughter was not the way to do it. Whomever this Cara was, she could be a link that the other hunters were unaware of.

"It was only a few days ago," Julie continued. "She'd called the police about it. But they were useless."

Claudia resisted the urge to roll her eyes. This potentially critical piece of information was still swimming around the antiquated police database. She wondered how long it would have taken to reach her if she hadn't used her initiative and come to visit Julie Hewitt herself.

"Yes, they often are," Claudia agreed. "Do you know anything else about Cara? A surname? Anything that I could use to find her?"

Julie thought for a moment but shook her head. "No, just that she was older than Amy. In her thirties. A bit exotic, I think. Maybe Spanish? Other than that, nothing. She came in every day, they spoke. One day she stopped showing up."

"I see." Claudia filed the information away. Something told her that it was relevant. "Would you mind if I ask you some other questions about Amy?"

An hour later, Claudia got back into her car. She threw her phone into the drinks holder and waited for the Bluetooth connection between her car and her phone to be established. She started to drive away from the Hewitt house, pressed a button on the steering wheel, and asked it to, "Call Mark."

The car filled with the sound of a ringing tone.

"Hi, how did it go?" Mark asked.

"She thinks her little girl is an angel who can do no wrong. I didn't learn a lot, in fact I think we already know more about Amy than she does. But I did find out one thing," Claudia told him. "I need you to look for a needle in a haystack."

"I enjoy nothing more. What is it?"

Claudia smiled. "A woman in her thirties, possible Spanish origin. Her name is Cara. She went to Tom's every day, early in the morning, before suddenly stopping a few days ago. Amy reported her missing to the local police."

"Anything else?"

Claudia chuckled. "I thought you liked a challenge?"

She could hear Mark typing. "I'll see what I can find... Hold on..."

There was the sound of a mouse clicking and more typing. He changed tacks. "I have a hit on the facial recognition. They were at Kings Cross. Tracking their exact movements now."

"Kings Cross? That means north," Claudia surmised. She accessed her satellite navigation system and plotted the nearest route to the M1, the quickest route to the north of the country.

"I... I can't follow them," Mark said. "I see them, but then they walk out of sight. Dammit, they're looking at the cameras, they are actively avoiding them."

"So, they know we are using the cameras to find them. The fact that they are avoiding them is good information in itself." Claudia turned the car around, following the route to the motorway.

"The last I see of them, they are heading down towards the platforms. There's three platforms there, I'm just going to get the train data for those platforms at that time."

"What time were they there?" Claudia asked.

"The first sign I see of them is just after six, hiding in the commuter crowds. They head towards the platforms at eight forty-two."

"They were waiting a long time," Claudia mused. "Sitting in a mainline London station for nearly three hours, you don't do that in the most surveilled state in the world. Not unless you are waiting for a very specific train."

"One platform wasn't used during that time, one was running trains to Cambridge, the other to Edinburgh."

"It's Edinburgh, has to be," Claudia concluded. She had no further evidence than her gut telling her that the girls wouldn't be going to Cambridge. Edinburgh seemed like the best bet. Far from the original scene of the crime. Most suspects seemed to feel that distance made them safer.

"Ha!" Mark exclaimed. "They're clever. Oh, this is good. The Edinburgh train was old rolling stock. These trains were withdrawn from service in 2005, but some still operate on the East Coast line. It was built between 1975 and 1988, and has no linked CCTV."

"Perfect, well done, Mark." Claudia smiled. "So, Edinburgh. What time should they arrive?" She started to set a new journey on her satnav.

She heard a few keystrokes. "Twenty past one in the morning."

"I'll be arriving between seven and eight in the morning. That gives them quite a head start. I need you to keep on the CCTV footage in Edinburgh. We need to know if they make an onward journey or if they leave the station."

"I'm requesting that data now. I'll watch it live, and I'll let you know what I see."

"I have a good feeling about this, Mark."

Mark chuckled. "I'm glad you're feeling positive. You'll need that considering the journey you have in front of you. Make sure you stop and eat something."

Claudia rolled her eyes. She ignored the mothering from a man ten years her junior.

"Did you get anywhere with the footage from the services? I'll be interested to see more details of the initial getaway."

"No," Mark sounded perplexed. "I'm finding that strangely difficult to get hold of."

"'Strangely difficult' sounds intriguing. Stay on it."

"I will," Mark agreed. "I'll call you with an update within the next couple of hours."

Claudia revved the car up as she joined the motorway. "I'll be here," she sighed.

CHAPTER TEN
FIRST NIGHT

AMY STOMPED in Kerry's footprints so she didn't get bogged down in the sticky mud. She blew strands of sweaty hair away from her forehead and let out a sigh. They had realised that the train line would be swarming with police following Amy's stupid decision to call her mum and agreed that best course of action was to get off the train and away from the entire line.

Two hours ago they had disembarked the train in Darlington. Darlington was big and loud, even at eleven o'clock on a Thursday night. They decided to start walking out of town, randomly choosing a north-easterly direction. Since then they had walked as far as possible; hoping to put distance between themselves and the railway line.

They hadn't said a word to each other during the entire hike down narrow country lanes and through parkland. Anger radiated off Kerry in waves and Amy had given up trying to get back into her good books. Amy was relieved when Kerry finally pointed to a field and mumbled something about finding a spot to set up their tents.

The silence had caused Amy's mind to drift. It wasn't long

before she started to think about Cara, and the whole reason they were in a darkened field, tired and exhausted. Not for the first time, Amy wondered where Cara was and what she was mixed up in.

Cara had seemed so nice, so innocent and kind. Amy was leaning towards the assumption that Cara was being blackmailed or coerced in some way to do something illegal. She recounted their previous conversations, searching for clues or even a subtle cry for help. Nothing immediately came to her. She cursed herself for being too swept up in her crush to see anything else.

She looked up at the sky. It was almost pitch black, only the dim glow of the full moon lit their way. Wispy clouds skittered over the moon's surface, casting spooky shadows.

Amy's legs felt like lead pipes, and she couldn't even feel her toes anymore. Her hands and feet were cold while her torso was burning up from all the layers and the pressure of the rucksack. She had to stop. She had to rest.

"Here's good," Amy shouted towards Kerry. She was convinced that Kerry would walk for another two hours if she wasn't stopped.

Kerry turned around and regarded the spot where Amy stood. She shrugged and released the straps of her rucksack.

"Are you going to speak to me ever again?"

Kerry trudged back towards her. "Maybe. When I don't feel like every other word will be a swear word."

Amy removed her own rucksack. "That's never stopped you before."

Kerry hid a burgeoning smile behind her hand as she scratched at her cheek.

"I'm sorry," Amy said. "I know I've said it already, but I want you to know that I really am sorry. I know that calling my mum was really stupid, and I should have spoken to you. We have to stick together."

Kerry glared at her. After a few seconds, she heaved a large sigh.

"Fine," she mumbled, unable to maintain her anger any longer. "But seriously, don't pull any stupid shit like that again."

Amy felt a grin form on her face. She launched herself at her best friend and wrapped her in a hug. "Thank you, thank you. I'm sorry. I'll stop being an idiot now. I promise."

Kerry put her arms around her and squeezed. "Well, let's not make promises we can't keep."

Amy laughed. They pulled apart and Kerry shrugged her rucksack off her shoulders. They stood beside each other, their bags on the muddy ground. They both looked around the field.

"So, I'm guessing you have no idea how to put a tent up either?" Kerry eventually asked.

"Pitch."

"What?"

"Pitch," Amy repeated. "You don't put a tent up. You pitch a tent."

"Well, excuse me." Kerry tucked her hands into her coat pockets. "Do you know how to pitch a tent? Because it's bloody freezing."

Amy opened her bag and dug around inside. Her hand latched onto smooth metal. She grabbed onto the torch and handed it to Kerry. "Hold this."

Kerry switched the torch on and pointed it into Amy's rucksack. Amy peered into the bag and shuffled the contents around as she looked.

"Ah, here it is. I was going to read this on my tea break at work, but we were kinda busy."

"Running away from the police, yeah, I remember."

Amy pulled out a big yellow book and waved it towards Kerry.

"*Camping for Dummies*? Really?" Kerry shivered and stomped her feet on the ground.

Amy stood up and opened the book to the first marked page. "Well, we don't know anything, so we might as well consult the experts. I'm sure it will tell us everything we need to know."

"It better," Kerry said. "Because I think our chances of survival rest on it."

"If it doesn't, it will make excellent kindling for a fire."

"Now you're talking." Kerry shone the light onto the book, and between them they started to read about the basics of camping.

They read like they had done for years, each holding a half of the book. Amy skimmed to the bottom of the page and waited for Kerry's small nod that she too had finished. Then Amy would turn the page.

"Sorry I've been a moody bitch," Kerry mumbled.

"It's okay, it's my fault we're even in this situation," Amy admitted.

"I'm glad I arrived when I did," Kerry said. "If something happened to you, or if you were doing this on your own…"

"I'd be caught within half an hour?" Amy joked.

Kerry chuckled. "Maybe. But I'm glad I'm with you. It's kind of hitting me how serious this is."

Amy licked her dry lips. The thought had occurred to her as well. The further they travelled, the more the invisible noose around her neck seemed to tighten.

"We're doing the right thing," Kerry announced, as much for her own sake as for Amy's.

"We are. I'm not giving up this USB until I know I'm handing it to the right people. Or until someone takes it from my cold, dead hand."

"Let's hope it doesn't come to that," Kerry said. "I'm not explaining that to your mum."

CHAPTER ELEVEN
FIRST CLUE

CLAUDIA BIT into the sandwich and ruffled her nose at the strong, unpleasant flavour. She put the sandwich back into its packet and threw it into the plastic bag on the passenger seat. She was hungry, but not that hungry. She swallowed down some water to get rid of the taste, wondering how a simple sandwich could go so wrong.

She'd been driving for two hours, and the roads were completely empty, allowing her to push the speed limit just enough to make good time. It wasn't her first time driving across the country in the middle of the night, and it certainly wouldn't be her last. But it was tedious, and the nagging worry that she might have made the wrong call itched at her brain. Driving to Edinburgh only to find that the suspects were actually in Cornwall would be a nightmare scenario that she couldn't cope with. Especially with the case being such an important one.

She accessed her phone directory and called Andrew at MI5. It was getting late, but she knew he'd be in the office non-stop until the case was closed.

"Claudia," he greeted.

"Andrew, what have you got?" She didn't have time for pleasantries. Her abrupt greeting was also more likely to throw him off course and cause him to give out information that perhaps he shouldn't in the heat of the moment. Andrew was stuck in his ways; he was getting a little older and a little slower. Claudia wasn't above using that to her advantage.

"A complete mess, that's what I've got," he replied gruffly.

"Nothing new then." Claudia looked at the satnav screen. She was approaching Sheffield, a little under halfway into her journey.

"We had report of a sighting, all our people converged on the location, and it wasn't them."

Claudia held back a snort of laughter as Andrew sounded like he was having a total sense of humour failure.

"And where was this location?"

"Fucking Brighton," Andrew said. "Now we have a report of a mobile phone being used in Shipton by Beningbrough. In case you're not up on your backwater villages of the United Kingdom, that's in North Yorkshire. Two hundred and seventy-five bloody miles away."

Claudia sat up a little straighter. "A mobile phone was used?"

"Yes. Amy rang home. But you didn't hear that from me."

I knew it, Claudia thought. Julie Hewitt must have just got off the phone with Amy when she'd arrived. Her anger at Julie's withholding of information was short-lived as the confirmation she was heading in the correct direction came as a relief.

"My lips are sealed." Claudia tapped her fingers on the steering wheel. "I'm actually just by Sheffield, South Yorkshire, if that makes you feel any better."

"That does make me feel a lot better." Andrew let out a breath. "Always a few steps ahead of the others, aren't you, Claudia?"

"Not always." Her voice wavered at the admission.

She heard Andrew swallow nervously. She rubbed her eyes. "Anyway," she said, changing the subject. Old wounds didn't need to be dredged up just because she was tired. The unspoken thing had permanently shaken her confidence. Not seeing something that was right in front of you could be devastating. More so when you had built a career around seeing through other people's crap.

"I never did apologise to you," Andrew blurted out.

Claudia shook her head and briefly looked heavenwards. "You never needed to."

"She's my daughter, I feel... I feel responsible."

"You're not responsible for your daughter's wandering eyes." *And hands.*

"Well, still, I'm sorry. I set you both up."

Claudia felt her throat dry and her eyes water. "It was a long time ago. Anyway, I really do need to go if I'm to bring these two in. I'll keep you updated."

She terminated the call and sucked in a deep breath, gripping the wheel a little tighter as she did. It was all water under the bridge. But that didn't stop her heart from pulsing a little harder when she thought about it. In hindsight, she didn't know whether she was more angry at the betrayal of the affair or because she hadn't been able to read the signs.

She brushed her fingers through her hair and blinked a few times to clear her vision. Now was not the time to dwell on the past or become emotional. She had a job to do.

She pressed the call button on the steering wheel to ring Mark for an update.

"Hi, I was just about to call you." He sounded muffled.

"Are you eating?"

"Yeah, a halloumi burger from the twenty-four-hour place across the street."

Claudia felt her stomach rumble with jealousy. "I think I hate you."

"I won't mention the cheesy chips then."

"You're fired."

"Does that mean I can go home, have a life, sleep in my own bed?"

Claudia grinned. "You're unfired. What have you got?"

"They didn't get off the train at Edinburgh. I checked every camera twice and nothing. I'm really sorry, but this might be a wild goose chase."

Claudia shook her head, despite knowing that Mark couldn't see her. "I just spoke with Andrew. Amy called home, they tracked it to Shipton by Bening-somewhere? In North Yorkshire. I knew Julie Hewitt had spoken to her, I could see it in her eyes."

"Shipton by Beningbrough," Mark said. "I have it on a map here, it's about five miles north of York."

Claudia narrowed her eyes as she evaluated the new information. She reached into the open bag of crisps atop the dashboard and started to eat a few.

"The train did make a stop at York. The question is, was she on the train passing through Shipton by Beningbrough or had they already left the train?" Mark pondered and Claudia heard the sound of keystrokes in the background. "This place has a population of less than a hundred people."

"What's the next station stop after York?" Claudia asked.

"Darlington," Mark replied. "You think they got off there?"

Claudia stared ahead at the road. She pieced together the information they knew so far and attributed most likely assumptions where appropriate. "You think they got on the Kings Cross to Edinburgh. A call was made in North Yorkshire. They didn't get off the train in Edinburgh, which means they got off somewhere before. What stops are between Darlington and Edinburgh?"

The familiar mouse clicks sounded. "Newcastle and then Berwick-upon-Tweed."

"There's no way to know for sure, but my gut says they got off that train at either York or Darlington."

"You're an hour and fifteen from York, around two hours from Darlington," Mark supplied.

"Okay, I'm going to head for York. Have a look at CCTV footage for both York and Darlington, and let me know what you find. At least then I'll be heading in the right direction, whichever they chose."

"Okay. I'll get back to my burger." She could visualise the smirk on his face. She shook her head and hung up the call without saying goodbye.

Getting off the train was a surprising twist. As was the phone call. *Hopefully they are starting to lose their nerve, making mistakes.* She knew that the first twenty-four hours were essential to any case. Once the trail went cold it was a matter of waiting for them to make a mistake. Claudia hated relying on her prey to slip up.

∼

It was half an hour later when Mark rang back.

"I have them," he announced. "They got off the train in Darlington at eleven. They then proceeded to walk north out of the town. I followed them to the edge of town, I'm sending the coordinates to your satnav. After that, I have no idea."

"They're either heading to a specific location, or they're heading off the grid," Claudia surmised. She watched as her satnav received the information and recalculated the distance. "I'm an hour away."

"I'll keep searching and contact you if I find anything."

CHAPTER TWELVE
MASTER CRIMINALS

AMY WHISTLED HAPPILY to herself as she walked across the field and back towards the tent. She cocked her head to one side as she looked at the structure; it was definitely leaning. She was happy that it had managed to stay up during the night. Pitching the tent in the dark, with frozen cold fingers, with only the aid of the dummies guide, had been difficult to say the least.

Kerry's head burst from tent, her eyes wide, hair a disaster.

"Where were you?" Kerry demanded.

"Getting breakfast." Amy held up the paper bag and the takeaway coffee cups.

Kerry blinked and then rubbed her eyes. She'd woken up recently. "Breakfast?"

"Yeah, I woke up when the sun came up. I'm not used to sleeping in a cloth dome. The sun was like *boom*, and then the birds were singing. So, I thought I'd get up."

"I was talking to you, and you weren't there," Kerry grumbled. She pulled on her hiking boots and coat and exited the tent. She stood up tall, stretching out her back.

"Did you say anything interesting?" Amy handed her a coffee.

"I was cursing your existence, telling you that it was cold and if I died out here I'd be blaming you." Kerry sipped the coffee. "Where the hell did you get this?"

"There's a little town just over the hill. The coffee shop is so cute, they have the best china. Anyway, I met a guy called Pete, and he said he is willing to give us a lift to Newcastle." Amy threw the coffee cup holder inside the tent and sipped her own drink. It was her second that morning, but there was no reason to tell Kerry that.

Kerry paused, the coffee cup centimetres from her lips. "Newcastle?"

"Yeah. It's north from here, which is where we are going. And there we can hitchhike," Amy explained.

Kerry furrowed her brow. "Hitchhike?"

"Yep." Amy threw her gloves into the tent. She opened the paper bag and handed a muffin to Kerry. Kerry would be a little more receptive to the idea of Amy chatting to half the village about their predicament once she'd eaten something. "I've been thinking, if we get on a train, or in a car, or use a bus... we're screwed. There are cameras everywhere, and Duncan in the coffee shop says they might have some kind of sci-fi facial recognition stuff. Like on TV."

"Who is Duncan?" Kerry asked, exasperation clearly starting to take hold.

"Just some bloke in the coffee shop," Amy said with a shrug. "Anyway, I think we need to be a bit random, do things they don't expect."

"Like speak to blokes called Duncan about facial recognition technology?" Kerry held the muffin in one hand and sipped at her coffee. "But, back to the point, the reason people don't hitchhike is because it's dangerous and they don't want to die."

"I'd rather take my chances with Pete than get on a train and be arrested at the station." Amy reached into the bag, picked up her croissant, and bit into it. Also, her second one of the morning.

Kerry nibbled on the muffin. Her forehead furrowed in deep concentration as she considered Amy's plan.

"I know self-defence," Amy reminded her.

"You took one lesson and strained a muscle in your thigh," Kerry reminded her.

"It's a lot harder than it looks," Amy defended. "But, Kez, seriously, I just have a feeling about this. I think we need to keep moving. I want to get out of here, and I don't fancy walking to Newcastle because Joan says that's going to take about half a day."

Kerry blinked. "Who's Joan?"

"She owns the coffee shop. I told her I worked in a coffee shop and we got talking."

"Don't you think that maybe you should be keeping a low profile and not chatting to the locals? Especially those who own the local coffee shop and are presumably very chatty. And random blokes called Duncan who seem to know about CCTV."

Amy shook her head. "No, Joan, Duncan, and Pete are cool."

"Amy, you can't just trust everyone you meet. The world doesn't work like that, babe."

Amy had heard it all a thousand times before. People told her that she was too trusting and that she needed to think more before she spoke. But it wasn't true, Amy knew that people were mainly good. People were like dogs, they could sense a good person. And Amy was a good person. She knew that Joan, Duncan, and Pete were also good people. She trusted them, even if she'd only just met them. It was hard to explain, but it was how Amy lived her life.

"I like to think it does," Amy said. She wasn't going to defend herself. She'd gotten up early, got breakfast, and found a way out of town that didn't involve hiking. As far as she was concerned, she'd had an excellent morning. "Anyway, get packed up. We're meeting Pete in an hour." Amy kicked off her muddy boots and stepped into the tent.

Inside the tent, she packed up her stuff. She was starting to reconsider the wisdom of carrying the Pocket Scrabble set, not to mention her bullet journal. She didn't think she'd get much time to draw an artistic spread on her latest cinema adventures while on the run.

"Amy?" Kerry called from outside.

"Yeah?"

"I feel like we're being watched," Kerry said. "Like, not right now. Just… always."

Amy stopped what she was doing. It was something she had been noticing more and more. The paranoia was starting to intensify. The feeling of being watched was now a constant. "Me too, all the time."

"Okay. I suppose that's what it's like now," Kerry said sadly.

Amy opened the tent flap and stuck her head out. "We'll get it sorted. I promise. But, until then, keep an eye out. You never know."

～

Amy pulled her long hair across her face and chewed on the ends. She peeked over the high collar on her coat and looked out of the car window. The road was busy, presumably with rush hour traffic. She hadn't made a note of the time. Time seemed so redundant now. Time was for people who took their kids on the school run, people who had jobs. On the run, time was a wasted concept.

"Where was it you said you were going?" Pete asked. His kind eyes sought out hers in the rearview mirror.

Kerry stiffened beside her.

"Glasgow." Amy tried to hide her wince as she lied. She trusted Pete, but she wasn't about to tell him where they were really headed.

"Ah. Never been."

"We're seeing a friend," Kerry added.

"We're on the run," Amy said. She could almost feel Kerry's glare. "We didn't do anything wrong." Amy knew that Kerry wanted to throttle her, but Amy felt strongly about telling the truth. Or at least some of the truth. The whole point in going on the run was to clear their names. If they were going to lie their way to Aberdeen, then they were bad people and Amy desperately didn't want to be thought of as a bad person.

Pete chuckled. "Well, well. Two hardened criminals in my Volvo. Who'd have thought it? Is there a reward?" He joked.

"Might be," Amy said. She turned to Kerry who was just shaking her head at her. Amy shrugged. Kerry had known Amy long enough to know her big mouth couldn't be controlled.

Kerry rolled her eyes and leaned forward to address Pete. "Of course, we're going to be caught in an instant because this one feels the need to tell people that we're on the run."

"Honesty is the best policy," Amy said.

"Aye, it is," Pete agreed. "Well, if they come sniffing around here then I'll tell 'em I saw you both and you were headed south. I'll send 'em to Cornwall!"

Amy laughed and smiled at Kerry. "See? Pete's helping us. You're a star, Pete."

Kerry shook her head and turned to look out of the window. She clearly didn't want any more to do with the conversation.

"It's the least I can do. We have to stick together. How long have you been on the run for?" Pete asked.

"A day. We're pretty new to it." Amy pulled her collar up a little higher. "It's actually really hard. They send out drones with facial recognition cameras and Tasers to hunt you down."

"No, you've made that up in your head and now you believe it," Kerry pointed out without facing her.

"So, what's the plan?" Pete asked.

"Stay off the radar," Amy said. "We're going to hitchhike up the country. I think we'll be there in a couple of days. When we get to Glasgow we're going to see a friend who will prove our innocence and then we'll go home. Probably be asked to be consultants to the police because they'll be so impressed by our evasion tactics. Or maybe not, but they should ask us because we're making them look pretty silly."

Kerry turned to face her. "We slept in a field for one night. I don't think we're going to be called up by the police commissioner and asked how we did it."

"If these drones with the cameras and the..." Pete started.

"Tasers," Amy supplied. She wasn't one hundred percent sure of the details of the drones, but she was pretty sure she'd seen a documentary on it. Kerry was adamant it was a movie.

"That's right, cameras and Tasers, if they are everywhere, then should I drop you outside of Newcastle? It might be dangerous in the town. One of those drones could see you and zap you!"

Kerry stared at Amy with disbelief. When Amy got home she was going to Google the documentary and prove Kerry wrong. Unless her Googling found that it was a movie. In which case, she'd drop the conversation altogether.

"You know, Pete, you're right," Amy said. "Drop us at a motorway services, there will be plenty of people there. Easy to catch another lift."

CLAUDIA STEPPED out of the coffee shop and bit into the flaky croissant. She straightened herself up and took a deep breath as she looked around the small village centre. Villages in England were supposed to be picturesque, but Claudia thought they all merged into one with their similarities. The tiny road through the middle of town, the village green, the old pub on the corner.

She stretched her neck from one side to the other. She reasoned that maybe she was just grouchy about only being able to catch a couple of hours' sleep in the car.

Arriving in Darlington in the very early morning had presented no clues at all. Mark had nothing further to go on and that meant legwork. Of course, legwork could only be done when there were people to talk to. At three in the morning in a small English village, every soul was sleeping soundly. So Claudia had allowed herself to sleep until sunrise.

The good thing about the locality was that most people were up with the sun. Before she fell asleep, she'd plotted a route to the eight villages to the northeast of Darlington, all were only a five-minute drive from each other. But that was at least an hour's walk.

It was in the fifth village that things had started to look up. A chatty coffee shop owner was probably the twentieth person Claudia had spoken to that morning, and she had provided some valuable information. Before she clammed up, that is, wondering if she had said too much. But it was enough.

Claudia tapped her earpiece twice, and the familiar ringtone soon sounded.

"Hey, everything okay?" Mark asked.

Claudia smirked. "Better than okay. They were here." She walked away from the coffee shop and crossed the road. "Just spoke to a woman who owns the local coffee shop. She saw Amy this morning. Said she stuck out like a sore thumb because she was from out of town and was wearing her pyjamas."

Mark laughed. "You're kidding."

"Nope. She checked the photo and said it was definitely her. Then she seemed to realise what she had said and stopped talking. But not before confirming that, at least, Amy was here."

"She was staying locally then?" Mark asked.

"I suspect so. There is a local pub here that has accommodation. But let's not forget that they have backpacks and camping equipment so they could have pitched up in a field. I'm going to ask some questions."

She stopped in the pub car park and looked around the sleepy village. "My suspicion is that they've moved on. They won't want to stay in one place too long."

"Agreed. There's no train station there, so they are either walking, taking a bus, or getting a lift from someone," Mark said.

Claudia nodded. "Yeah, I checked the bus timetable: one bus every other Tuesday unless it's a full moon. I'll speak to the locals. Clearly, they are sticking out like sore thumbs and not worried about who knows they are here. Presumably they think we're nowhere near them, so there is no need to be discreet. Which is great news for us."

"Well, I have some news of my own," Mark said. "Remember Cara, Amy's mystery lady from the services?"

"Yes?"

"She's turned up dead. Her body was found in a lake in Surrey."

Claudia raised her eyebrows at the unexpected news. "We need everything we can get on her, Mark."

"I know," he agreed.

"We need to know who she was, what she did. Andrew's team will be working on the assumption that she is the person who turned Amy. We need to know everything they know and more."

Mark posed the question back to her. "You don't think she is the one who turned Amy?"

She pursed her lips. "I'm not sure. It seems unlikely, especially considering that Amy took her best friend with her on the run. Childhood friendships are strong, but I can't see how Cara's influence on Amy would translate to Kerry too in such a short amount of time. There's something we're missing. Are we any further on obtaining the CCTV from the services? We need to see how all of this started."

Mark blew out a breath. "I'm trying, but I'm hitting a brick wall at every turn. MI5 claim that there was a recording failure at the services. But then I spoke to the services, and they say they've had no issues. They have given their tapes, and backups, to the police."

"Interesting," Claudia said. "Is this general MI5 incompetence or something more?"

"I don't know, but I'm investigating it."

"Good, we need that tape. And information on Cara."

"You got it. I'll get back to you." Mark hung up the call.

Claudia walked across the car park towards the pub. Wooden beams showed the age of the building. She pushed through the door and into the cramped bar space. She quickly looked around the room in case Amy or Kerry were sitting at any of the tables.

"Morning," a friendly male voice called out. "I'll be with you in a moment."

"No problem," Claudia replied. She sat on one of the bar stools and took in the ambiance. The low ceilings and dark wood gave a friendly and welcoming feel. In the next room she could hear the distinctive crackle of an open fireplace.

"What can I get you?"

Claudia turned to look at the landlord. He leaned comfortably on the bar, looking very much like he had spent his entire life there.

"Do you have anyone staying here at the moment?"

"No, we don't get that many people here, especially not during the week."

She pulled up Amy's picture on her phone. "Have you seen this woman?"

He pulled his glasses down from the top of his head and took the phone from Claudia's hand. He held it at arm's length and squinted at the screen. He shook his head and handed the device back to her. "Nope, she's not been in here. Is she in some kind of trouble?"

Claudia didn't like to divulge who she was and why she was looking for people, it was the quickest way to end a conversation. "Is there anywhere else to stay in town?"

"Just here. As I say, we don't get many people in the village."

"Are there any fields nearby where someone could pitch a tent?"

"No campsites," he replied.

"I'm not thinking a campsite exactly, just somewhere you could feasibly pitch a tent."

He pointed through the window. "Just out there you've got Dave's land. No animals and close to town. On the other side, you have the Cambridge farm, but they have plenty of animals so I can't imagine anyone would set up there."

Claudia looked towards the window and nodded her head. She pulled a business card out of her inner jacket pocket and handed it over to him. "If you see her, call me."

He took the business card and looked at the scant information. "She in trouble?" he asked again.

"She's not what she seems." She stood up.

He looked at her for a moment before slowly nodding. He placed the card on the shelf behind the bar.

~

Claudia walked along the low wall which separated the village green and the field. The old structure was built of rocks and slate, and it ran the length of the entire village. She paused and looked towards the coffee shop. She turned back and kept walking, all the while looking closely at the top of the wall.

After a short distance, she came upon a clump of mud which had snagged on one of the wall's sharper edges. She smiled to herself as she climbed over. Bingo. In the mud at the base of the wall were fresh footprints. Now to determine which way the footprints led.

"Can I help you?"

Claudia looked up. The man wore green wellington boots and a Barbour style jacket. His flat cap and walking stick made him appear the epitome of a farmer.

"Good morning," Claudia greeted. She started to walk towards him. "I'm looking for someone, they may have passed through here last night."

"The ones with the tent?" he asked.

"You saw them?"

He paused and leant on his walking stick. "No, just that someone had pitched a tent on my land. Honestly, these city folk seem to think they have the right to do whatever they like. They see a field and they think it's theirs. Like the countryside is free for anyone to use, however they like. Well, let me tell you, it isn't. It's my land."

"Yes, it is," Claudia agreed. "You say you saw where the tent was? Was there anything left there?"

He looked Claudia up and down for a moment. "No. Just some holes where the tent poles were and some damage to the grass."

"Do you have any idea where they went?"

"They were long gone when I got there."

Claudia blew out a breath and looked around the fields. "Are there any walking paths that cut through your land? Any obvious place they might have gone?"

He removed his cap and scratched at his head. "Why are you looking for them? They trouble?"

Claudia plucked a business card out of her jacket pocket and handed it to him. "If they come back, call me. I'll arrange compensation for any damage."

He looked at the business card, turning it over to look at the back. "Claudia McAllister."

"That's me."

"Doesn't say a company name," he commented.

"That's right. Just call me if they show up." Claudia turned and walked back towards the village square.

"City folk." She heard him mumble as she walked away. She rolled her eyes. *Country bumpkins, all the same.*

"WE'RE GOING to have to get a bus," Kerry said. "No one around here is going to give us a lift. There's no one around here *to* give us a lift."

Amy looked around the small village and the two parked cars. The place was truly deserted. "Yeah, I think you're right. Shit. We were doing so well."

Kerry stopped walking and turned to looked at her. Spinning around had caused her fringe to fall in front of her eyes, so she blew it away.

"Doing well? Since Pete dropped us off, we have been in six different cars but only managed to travel around thirty miles. Half of that time we were going back in the direction we had come. And I don't even want to talk about that last guy."

The last guy had been particularly bad. So bad that they had silently agreed to tell him that they had arrived at their destination rather than travel another mile with him. They may have ended up in the tiny village of Choppington, but at least they were away from him.

"Well, I have a hundred percent success rate in hitchhiking," Amy said happily.

"Yeah, you're infinitely murderable." Kerry smirked.

Amy chuckled. "No one's murdered us yet."

"No one's driven us for more than twenty minutes either."

"Maybe you should wash?" Amy suggested. She jokingly held her nose.

"I think that stink you're smelling is a lot closer to home." Kerry winked.

"Well, if we both stink, then maybe the police won't want to catch us?" Amy hoped.

"Yeah, maybe they'll stop looking when they see the state of your hair," Kerry shot back with a grin.

"Or, maybe," Amy continued, "the green vapour trail you are leaving behind you will be the reason they find us. Just follow the green smoke."

Kerry narrowed her eyes and glared at her playfully. She turned around and crossed the road to head towards the bus shelter.

Amy smiled. It was good to be bantering again. The pressure of being chased was more exhausting than she thought possible. It had only been around twenty-four hours since they went on the run, and already they were bickering with each other and quick to lose their tempers. It had been good to get to Choppington. They'd even had tea in a quaint afternoon tea shop. It had improved their mood considerably.

She looked over her shoulder so much that she could feel muscle knots developing already. The need to be on the move was so strong that it felt like an obsession. She was sure that sitting still for more than half an hour would result in several black SUVs surrounding her. It was like the mysterious *they* were always just a few steps behind.

She crossed the road and removed her heavy rucksack. Dropping it in the bus shelter, she sat on the cold metal bench while Kerry checked the bus times and locations. She reached into her trouser pocket and pulled out some spare change. She counted the coins to see if she would have enough money to buy a chocolate bar from the shop across the street.

That was when she heard a woman scream. Her head snapped up, and she saw an elderly lady running after a dog, a tiny, little piece of fluff. The dog's lead dragged on the ground behind it as it ran away from its owner. Amy saw the reason the woman was screaming: a lorry was driving down the road and straight towards the dog. From the angle, the driver would have no hope of seeing the dog.

Amy didn't even think. She distantly registered the sound of metal coins clanking to the ground as she sprinted across the road, bending down to scoop up the small dog and passing just meters in front of the cab of the lorry.

She held the dog to her chest as tightly as she dared. The sounds of the lorry honking and of Kerry's screams were all she heard. When the lorry passed her, she turned around and grinned.

"I'm okay!" she shouted to Kerry, who was white as a sheet.

"Monty! Monty, are you okay?" The elderly woman was racing across the road. "Is he okay?"

Amy looked at the dog in her arms. The smallest cocker spaniel she'd ever seen. "Yeah, I think he's okay."

She placed Monty into the woman's waiting arms, gathering up the dangling lead and handing it to her to hold onto.

"Oh, my dear, thank you, thank you so much. He's all I have. He is a silly boy, though. Aren't you? So silly. This lovely girl could have died, Monty."

"I'm fine, really," Amy promised. "I'm just happy that he's okay."

Kerry was next to her now. "Are you sure you're okay, Amy? That was a close one."

"Amy, I'm Beryl." The woman held one hand out awkwardly under Monty.

Amy shook her hand. "Lovely to meet you, this is Kerry."

Kerry offered a small wave and stroked Monty's head.

"How can I ever thank you?" Beryl asked. "It's nearly dinner time. Would you like to come over to my place? I can make you dinner."

"Dinner would be lovely," Amy said. "We haven't had a proper meal in a while."

"I saw your rucksacks, are you travelling?" Beryl asked.

"No, we're kind of on the run," Amy explained.

Kerry rolled her eyes and sauntered back to the bus shelter to collect their bags. She was fed up with Amy telling people that they were on the run, but as far as Amy was concerned, that was the quickest way to find out if you could trust a person. If the person looked shocked, then she would know she couldn't trust them. Most of the time, the person laughed and couldn't wait to be a part of their getaway story. Although, Amy did suspect that most people thought she was joking. One of the people who gave them a lift even asked if they could wheel spin away from where they had picked them up to add a little more drama.

"On the run? That sounds exciting. You must tell me all about that over dinner," Beryl said.

"I'd love to."

～

As it turned out, the farmhouse where Beryl lived was quaint, if a little rundown. Beryl led them to the back door after explaining that the front door was jammed. Kerry offered to help Beryl prepare the food for the meal.

"Do you have any tools? I could look at the front door for you, if you like," Amy offered. She'd never been particularly good at fixing things, but she wanted to say thank you somehow.

"There's a toolbox in that cupboard there." Beryl pointed to a pantry.

Amy opened the door and found the toolbox. She walked through the house and located the front door. She tried to open it but could see what Beryl meant, it was stuck fast. She tried various tools and eventually managed to pry the door open. Once the door was open she saw a nail had come loose in the frame. It had latched onto a piece of splintered wood from the door and was effectively holding it closed.

To Amy's surprise, she fixed the door within twenty minutes. She'd never been the kind of person to be handy. But then, she supposed she'd never needed to be. She put the tools back into the toolbox and turned around to go back to the kitchen. As she did she noticed a spindle on the staircase was hanging off. She grinned and put the toolbox back down. Rolling up her sleeves, she got to work.

It was an hour later when Kerry came to tell her that dinner was ready. Somehow time had flown by as she'd walked around the downstairs of the house, fixing things as she went.

"Did you manage to fix the door?" Kerry asked as they walked into the dining room.

"Yeah, and the spindle, a window frame, the handle on the cupboard under the stairs, and a bit of carpet that was sticking up." Amy was very proud of her achievements. She may not have been able to help with dinner, but she felt like she'd earned a home-cooked meal now.

Of course, she wasn't about to mention the fact that she'd broken the handle on the cupboard under the stairs herself.

"Wow, remind me, you're the person who put gum in a crack in the wall, yeah?" Kerry recalled.

"Yeah, I've progressed in my DIY skills since then." Amy chuckled.

She washed her hands while Beryl and Kerry carried plates

and dishes into the dining room. It seemed they were having a traditional roast dinner with all the trimmings.

"It's so nice to have company," Beryl said. "It's been years since my Barry died. There's no point in cooking for one. I often just have a sandwich for dinner."

They all sat down at the table and started plating up.

"You should still cook yourself a nice meal," Amy insisted. "You need to look after yourself."

"Amy's right," Kerry added. "Dinner should be a pleasure, not a chore."

Beryl seemed to think about it for a moment. "I suppose you're right," she finally admitted.

The conversation over dinner was wide and varied. Of course, they spoke about Kerry and Amy's adventures, but also about Beryl's husband. Everything was comfortable and homely, and before long Beryl was inviting them to stay the night. Despite the itch to keep moving, Amy couldn't stand the thought of sleeping in a tent again. They agreed and thanked Beryl for her kindness and hospitality. In turn, she thanked them for their company.

Amy felt sad. Beryl was a lovely lady, but she was cooped up in a farmhouse in the middle of nowhere. She hardly ever saw anyone, and she was obviously lonely. Her husband's death had been the end of her social life. Amy wanted to help, wanted to know that when they left, Beryl would be okay. Fixing some doors and gluing down some carpet was one thing. But cosmetic DIY wasn't going to mean much in the long-term.

After dinner, they moved into the living room to have tea and biscuits. Beryl insisted that Kerry read a book of short stories that she thought she would be interested in. Kerry, always happy with a book, set herself up in front of the fire with the book and a woven tartan blanket. The fire gently crackled and filled the room with a beautiful orange glow. Amy wiggled her toes, happy to finally be able to take her hiking boots off and relax. They may not have been on the run for long, but it was hard work. Harder than she had anticipated.

"Amy, would you help me with my laptop? People keep asking me for my email address, and I don't have one," Beryl asked after she brought in a new tray of tea. "I'm at a loss on how to go about getting one."

Amy knew nothing about computers but was happy to give it a go. "Sure, I can try."

Beryl put the tray down on the coffee table and wandered off in search of her laptop.

Amy let out a contented sigh. It had only been a few hours, but she already felt like meeting Beryl was fate. Somehow, they had all come together at just the right moment, when they all needed each other the most. She listened to the sound of Monty snoring and giggled. The dog may have been the smallest cocker spaniel she'd ever met, but he made up for it with volume when he slept. And, she reminded herself, Monty was the reason that they had a comfortable place to sleep for the night.

"So, it came with these," Beryl said as she returned. She placed a bulky laptop, a plastic wallet filled with CDs, and several thick paper manuals on a writing desk in the corner of the room.

Amy stood and walked over to desk. She looked through the paperwork and the CDs. "I don't think you need any of these. The software you need should already be on there." She sat on the chair that Beryl offered and switched the laptop on.

"You'll need this." Beryl handed her a mouse with a wire. Before Amy could say anything she had gone to fetch a chair for herself from the dining room.

"I never really used it. It was more Barry's than it was mine. But everyone seems to have email now, so why not me?" Beryl said when she returned.

"That's the spirit." Amy turned the laptop to face Beryl. "Do you know the password?"

"Oh, probably the same as everything, Barry forty-one."

Amy mock-gasped. "Don't say it out loud. They're listening."

Beryl chuckled. "You're paranoid. You think every camera is switched on and watching you and drones are following you everywhere."

"You heard that buzzing as well," Amy defended.

"It was a lawnmower in the distance," Kerry interjected.

"Hey, back to your reading, bookworm. No one is talking to you," Amy joked.

"B-A-R-R-Y-4-1," Beryl spelt out as she pressed each key down firmly.

Amy chuckled and took the laptop back from Beryl when she was finished. Beryl and Kerry talked about the book Kerry was reading while Amy quickly set up a free email account.

It was an hour later when Beryl, surrounded by plenty of handwritten notes, was confident in what she was doing.

"It's amazing what technology can do these days," Beryl commented.

"Yeah, terrifying, too," Amy said, thinking about the plethora of ways she was currently being traced.

Beryl seemed to sense Amy's unease and patted her forearm. "Don't you worry, a couple of clever girls like you two will have no problem getting to... where was it again?"

"Glasgow," Amy stuck to her previous lie.

"To Glasgow," Beryl said. She chewed on her lip. "You'll need to get a train to Newcastle and then go on to Glasgow from there."

Amy looked fondly at Beryl and waited a few moments.

"Oh, but you girls are scared of the train," Beryl recalled.

"Well, the cameras," Amy corrected gently.

Beryl closed the lid of the laptop and stood up. "I've got just the thing. Come with me."

Amy looked over to Kerry who offered a confused shrug before returning her attention to her book. She followed Beryl through the maze of unused rooms, all filled with boxes. She peered into one particularly cluttered room and wondered what on earth Beryl was keeping and for what purpose. It didn't feel right to leave her on her own the next day, but she knew she had to.

"Here." Beryl placed a stick with a hook on the end in Amy's hand. "Get the loft ladder down for me." She gestured to the ceiling hatch.

Amy aimed the hook for the hatch and carefully lowered it. She used the hook to get the ladder down. She had barely finished fixing it into position and ensuring the safety catches were on when Beryl was on her way up the stairs.

"Okay, speedy, be careful," Amy warned her.

"Oh, I'm fine, fine," Beryl mumbled. She stood halfway up the ladder and reached into some boxes near the hatch. "Now, I know they are here somewhere."

"What are you looking for?" Amy called up. She held the ladder still as Beryl threw stuff around in the cramped loft space.

"Got them!" Beryl declared. A moment later she retreated down with a plastic carrier bag in her hand. "This is the answer to all your problems. You're worried about high-tech, so you need to go low-tech."

Once she was firmly on the ground she thrust the bag into Amy's hand. Amy opened the bag and felt a smile tug at her lips. "Seriously?"

Beryl just grinned at her. Amy reached into the bag and pulled out a professional quality wig in an auburn bob style. Amy handed Beryl back the bag and put the wig on her head.

She walked over to a floor-length mirror and started to adjust her hair, feeding it into the tight space.

"This is amazing," Amy commented. "I look completely different." She smoothed the wig down and turned to face Beryl.

The elder woman laughed and nodded her head. "Oh yes, you look wonderful. Nothing like you, mind, but wonderful. Kerry! Come and see this."

Amy turned back to the mirror and stared at her reflection. She couldn't believe that she hadn't thought of it before. Small changes to her appearance could have a big effect. She could beat the facial recognition. It was like David versus Goliath, but now David had a secret weapon.

"Bloody hell!" Kerry exclaimed. "You look so different."

Amy did a little turn and curtsied. "Good, isn't it?"

"Amazing," Kerry said as she walked around Amy to get the full effect.

"I have one for you," Beryl said, holding out a long, blonde wig for Kerry.

Kerry took the wig and eagerly put it on. Amy helped her to straighten it out, and all three women giggled.

"These are amazing, why do you have them?" Kerry asked.

"I saw them in a charity shop, and I thought why not," Beryl explained. She reached up and tucked a stray strand of hair under the cap. "You look beautiful. Both of you do."

"Are you sure you don't mind us having these?" Amy questioned. "You've already been so generous."

Beryl waved her hand. "You fixed my front door, got me on the email, and have been the best company I've had in ages. I'm just happy someone will get some use out of them."

Amy turned to Kerry who was looking in the mirror and playing with her newly acquired long locks. She looked at her own reflection and smiled at the results.

"I don't suppose you two have any use for these?" Beryl asked.

Amy turned around. Beryl held two walkie-talkies that she had fished out of the bottom of the bag. She took one of them and looked it over.

"You said you can't use your mobile phones, but you could use these."

"These are perfect," Amy said. "We can definitely use these."

Inspiration struck her at that moment. A way to help Beryl reconnect with the outside world. "Beryl, you know you said you were into genealogy? Looking up your family tree and stuff? Have you ever thought about joining an online forum?"

Beryl looked confused. "What's one of them?"

"It's like a message board, but on the Internet. You can talk to like-minded people about things. In this case, genealogy."

"That sounds interesting, how do you find these boards?" Beryl asked.

CHAPTER FIFTEEN
A THREAD

CLAUDIA PINNED the poster onto the noticeboard, smoothing out the paper as she did. She took a step back and reviewed all the details.

"They in trouble?"

She turned around to see an elderly man looking at the poster.

"Have you seen them?" Claudia asked.

"Nope. They in trouble, though?" He repeated.

"They're not what they seem," Claudia said. It was the curiosity that got to most people. If you said they weren't in trouble, then no one cared. If you say they were in trouble, not only were you breaking the law, but no one wanted to be a snitch. Saying they weren't what they seemed gave an air of mystery, usually made people speak if they knew anything.

The man narrowed his eyes a little at the two photographs. "Kerry Wyatt and Amy Hewitt. Hm."

Claudia watched him. Like so many people in the area, she got the impression that he had seen them. But their reactions could just as easily be attributed to something new and potentially exciting happening in the village.

"There's a reward," she added.

"Cash reward?"

"Mm." She stepped away from the noticeboard and picked up her bag.

"If I were to see them, how would I claim that reward?"

She pointed at the poster. "Pick up the phone and call me."

He looked at the poster again before he grunted and walked away. She watched him go and then tapped her wireless earpiece. A moment later she was connected.

"Hey," Mark greeted.

"I can't tell if the locals have seen them, or if they are so bored they wish they had."

"You're still in Trimdon?"

"Yes, the posters are getting a lot of interest. I think you'll be getting some calls soon. Make sure you big up the cash reward." She walked out of the small supermarket and into the car park. It was Saturday morning, and most of the village seemed to be out. Claudia looked at their faces to see if there was anyone she hadn't spoken to yet.

People were always reluctant to speak to her, thinking that she was with the police. But she could tell from the look in their eyes that some of them knew something. Sometimes that was enough. The inkling of recognition was all she needed to know that she was on the correct path. She knew that word travelled fast in places like Trimdon and the surrounding villages. Word of some unusual travellers would soon spread like wildfire.

"Actually," Mark said, "I was about to call you. I picked up some social media chatter. Someone called Herby742 said he spoke to two hitchhikers who are on the run. He lives thirty minutes from your location."

Claudia smiled and picked up the pace in returning to her car. After Bishopton the trail had started to go cold. She had zigzagged the county, speaking to as many people as she could and putting up posters. While she hadn't had any positive identifications yet, she could tell she was in the right area.

"Perfect. Can you get me an address?"

She rolled her shoulders before getting into the car. Another few hours' sleep grabbed in the driver's seat of the car was definitely a younger person's game. She longed for a bed and a decent night's sleep, but she knew she wouldn't have either until this case was closed.

"Working on it now. I've tracked some of the photographs on his Twitter account that match a Facebook account. Through that I have his real name and I'm just locating his workplace on LinkedIn."

Claudia opened the car and quickly started the engine. "How long ago was this mention?"

"Around lunchtime yesterday, twenty-one hours ago. He's a delivery driver, and it was at the start of his shift. According to his Facebook account, he is working again today. Right, I have an address, I'm uploading it to your satnav now."

Claudia saw the map flash up and drove off. "Great. It's a start. But this does mean that they are hitchhiking which makes things a lot more difficult."

"I know. Sadly I don't think all of the people giving them a lift are going to be kind enough to tweet about it."

"Probably not," Claudia agreed. "Have a look, though, just in case. As I said earlier, for some unknown reason, these two aren't exactly making an effort to melt into the background. We might get lucky."

"Will do. I'll get on to some predictive mapping, see where they are likely to have gone in the time they've had. I'll call you later."

The line went dead, and Claudia glanced at the map as she navigated. Hitchhiking wasn't ideal. It took the pair off of the radar and made tracking them a lot more difficult. What she needed now was a destination. If she couldn't track how they were travelling, then maybe she could arrive first.

Tracking Amy and Kerry was proving confusing. The profiling wasn't adding up. On one hand the suspects were very adept at evading capture. MI5 had provided information that stated the terrorist cell were proficient in operating unseen. And yet, the women seemed to be making mistakes, more than she would have expected. They were clearly being seen by the local communities. They'd made no effort to disguise themselves. It just didn't seem to add up. Unless that was a part of the plan. Unless they were acting disorganised to throw off potential trails.

"Oh, these two are good," Claudia mumbled to herself. "I wonder who trained them."

～

"Carl Hendrick?"

Carl turned around. He furrowed his brow as he watched Claudia walk across the car park towards him. He clearly didn't recognise her and looked as though he was trying to place if he knew her.

"Who's asking?"

"Did you offer two hitchhikers a lift yesterday?"

Claudia saw the nervous swallow and already knew her answer.

"No. Wrong guy." He turned around to walk towards a delivery van, intent on ignoring her and avoiding the conversation.

"So, you're not Herby742?" she asked. "And you won't mind if I tell your bosses that you weren't sick last week, but in fact nursing an *epic* hangover."

He paused and slowly turned to look at her. "You don't

work for these guys then?" He jerked his thumb towards the large warehouse.

"No," Claudia answered. "I'm just interested in the hitchhikers."

"They in some kind of trouble?"

She smirked at his almost-admission. "Where did you take them?"

He bristled. "I didn't say I saw them, I'm just asking a question. It's against company policy to pick up passengers, so why would I do that?" He turned around and continued towards his van. "Tell my boss what you like."

Claudia realised she had pushed him a little too far with her smug attitude. "Mr Hendrick, if you have any information, I strongly suggest you tell me now."

He opened the driver's door and hoisted himself up into the cab. He slammed the door shut and leaned out of the open window. "I don't have anything to say. You're on private property, so you better go before I call security."

She took a step away from the van and nodded her head. "Okay, thank you for your help, Mr Hendrick."

He slammed the van into gear. She winced at the screeching sound and watched as he drove out of the yard.

∿

Claudia cropped the most recent photograph taken on her phone to just include the number plate and the make and model of the van. She attached the photograph to an email and sent it to Mark. She put the device in her cup holder and activated the Bluetooth as she drove out of the car park.

"Call Mark."

The phone only rang twice.

"Is this the delivery driver's van?" Mark asked.

"Yes, can you run it through the ANPR and see if we can

get a route? Any CCTV footage would be useful as well."

"Did he say anything?"

"No. I might have come on a bit strong," she admitted.

"Ruh-roh, didn't you use your feminine charms?"

"No, I wasn't born with them. I mildly threatened him, didn't work."

Mark laughed. "I'm in the ANPR system now, just going through the CCTV stills."

"Anything from our friends in London?"

"No, word is they are getting a bit stressed with this one."

"I know the feeling." Claudia rolled her shoulders gently.

"Well, this may help. I have positive identification of them both in the vehicle with our friend Herby742."

"Hallelujah."

"Tracking the route now."

The sound of a mouse clicking occasionally filtered through the car speakers. Claudia remained quiet, knowing not to distract Mark while he was working. She pulled the car over to the side of the road and parked up. She pulled out the large paper map she kept in the car and unfolded it.

She smothered a yawn and wearily ran her fingers through her hair. She wiggled in the seat. *I need a real bed tonight,* she mused.

"Choppington," Mark announced.

Claudia glanced at the map. "Where's that?"

"Northumberland, east of Morpeth."

She ran her finger over the map and found the name.

"I have a CCTV still of Herby leaving Choppington at four o'clock yesterday, and they are no longer in the van. I'm looking for CCTV in that location. Bear with me."

Claudia programmed the information into her satnav and headed off. "I get that they are hitchhiking," Claudia said, "but there doesn't seem to be any rhyme or reason in their direction of travel. I mean, overall, they are travelling north. But it's not distinctively north. They seem to be spending a hell of a lot of time not getting very far. Not that I'm complaining. They could be in the Outer Hebrides by now if they were trying."

"It does seem random," Mark agreed. "Even if their choices are limited by being at the mercy of people willing to offer them a ride."

"I just can't see them having connections in these random places."

"They ate at Simpson's Tea Rooms on the high street," Mark said.

Claudia shook her head. "A tea room? Seriously?"

"Do you think MI5 have this all wrong? These two are not acting like the biggest terrorist threat since 2005."

"Even MI5 can't be this incompetent, Mark." Claudia pursed her lips, deep in thought. She'd worked for MI5 for long enough to know that they could be. But it wouldn't help them to second guess the source of their information now. It was safer to assume that Amy and Kerry were deploying some highly skilled evasion tactic that they had yet to identify.

"There is one camera in Choppington, and it overlooks the tea room. They cross the road and wait at a bus stop for a while, but something happens, off camera, and they leave. They don't return. I'm sending you the footage."

"I'll look at it when I arrive. Have you got any idea what happened?"

"I'm not sure, but Amy sees something and runs off. Kerry follows a few seconds later."

Claudia considered the news for a moment. "Well, at least they caused a commotion, will make them more memorable. I'll be there in about an hour."

"Okay, I'll run mapping scenarios on how far they could have gotten from there by now, if they've left."

"Oh, I'm sure they've left. We're a way behind them." She smirked. "But we're catching up."

ANDREW LEANED HIS HEAD BACK. He winced at the sound of his neck popping. The briefing room was slowly filling up with people. He listened to the shuffling of feet as the team tried to cram themselves into the small room. He lowered his head and looked at the assembled group. They were, allegedly, the best. Experts and world-renowned leaders in their fields. Digital forensics experts, criminal profilers, the best man-hunters on the planet. And they were being evaded by two girls.

"Where are we?" He didn't bother with pleasantries.

"The trail has gone cold. We sent a ground team to Darlington following the CCTV footage that was discovered, but there was nothing there. We're now working primarily on profiling," Miranda explained. "If we can get inside their heads then we should be able to figure out their next step. Nothing is completely random, it's just a matter of figuring out their patterns."

George Carlton, a senior inspector within the team, spoke next, "They've not accessed any of their bank accounts since the first day, but we're continuing to monitor. We're also monitoring all incoming calls to their friends and family members. If they use their mobile phone, or we see any new numbers crop up, we'll triangulate to get a location."

Andrew placed his hands on the table and leaned forward. "Don't tell me that we are simply waiting for them to make a mistake."

George exchanged a nervous glance with a few of his colleagues. "Not exactly, but it would help speed the process up. They are young women, both very close to their families. It's only natural that they will be missing them by now, the urge to make a phone call will be very strong."

"We must have another line of enquiry," Andrew asked. *We bloody better have one.*

"We're still looking into the data breach," George said. "If we can figure out their network then we'll have more to work on."

He shook his head. "Are we any further with analysing the stolen data?"

"We have a theory," George said. "As we discussed in the previous meeting, the stolen data doesn't quite match up. There's no common theme. There is payroll information from various offices in various locations, staff details, again with no clear correlation. Then there is diary information." He flicked through some paperwork. "We believe that this is your typical data grab. Someone has gone in and taken different bundles of information, with seemingly nothing in common, in order to create confusion and to mask their real intentions. We're running simulations based upon the information we know was compromised and looking at various scenarios where that information could be used."

"Roughly how many scenarios are we currently looking at?" Andrew asked.

George's shoulders slumped. "Around sixty."

Andrew stared at George for a few moments before turning

his attention to Louise. "Louise, any further online chatter that could help us?"

"Nothing new. Following Amy and Kerry going to ground, everything has been very quiet. We're trying to use our operatives to sniff for more information, but it's proving very difficult and we don't want to blow their cover." Louise pulled a sheet of paper out of the stack she was holding. "The last thing we have is the date, nine days from now. We are tapping every resource we have, but until we know where to focus our efforts, we're blind."

"We need find these girls, now." Andrew stood up and paced the cramped space in front of the dark projector screen.

"How is Claudia getting on?" Miranda asked.

"She's following leads of her own," Andrew admitted.

"And she's not going to share that data with us?" Miranda raised an eyebrow.

"We're in a sensitive situation. We cannot share data with her, and she will not share data with us." Andrew leaned on the back of his chair. "We have the best minds in the world in this room. I know we suspect that these girls are highly trained, but they should not be able to beat us. I want every single piece of information we have checked and double-checked. We cannot miss anything. Let's not let Claudia beat us to the punch on this one, her gloating will never cease."

A ripple of laughter rolled through the room.

"Right." Andrew clapped his hands together. "Let's get this case closed."

CHAPTER SEVENTEEN
EDINBURGH

AMY SWAYED from side to side, cursing the bumpy movement of the train. She took some solace in the fact that, like the previous one they had caught, it was an old train with no CCTV on board. The positive that the train was not equipped with cameras was offset by the negative that they were taking ages to get anywhere.

They had been so far off the beaten track that it was taking a while to get back to civilisation. From Beryl's house, they had walked for two hours to get to the nearest train station. Planned engineering works on the line had meant they had to take a local train south before finally being able to board a fast train north to Scotland. It wasn't going all the way to Aberdeen, but it would have to do.

They'd been on the run for nearly forty-eight hours. Which was about forty-seven hours longer than Amy had thought they'd last. Between their inability to consistently travel north, and Amy's inability to not tell everyone they met that they were on the run, it was amazing that they hadn't been caught, tried, and imprisoned by now.

Ever since she was a child, Amy had been painfully honest.

Her inability to tell a white lie had meant lots of school detentions. Kerry had often suffered through the detentions by her side, never mentioning the fact that they were only there because of Amy's honesty.

Amy liked to be an open book. She knew it made her approachable and likable, and it had served her well in her life. She recognised that she may be the only person on the run to actively tell people she was evading police capture, but it worked for her. People were helpful, they could see that she was genuine.

There had been a couple of times during the journey where she had trusted the wrong person. Now and then she'd see the tell-tale glint in someone's eye, and knew that they were eager to call the police. But she quickly evaded them, relieved that she was able to read people so well.

The train lurched forward. Amy tutted and shook her head. Beside her, Kerry slept through everything. Her coat, which she was using as a blanket, started to shift. Amy hoisted it up and covered her best friend again. The other problem with the ancient train was the lack of heating.

She had the unusual problem that, while her body was freezing cold, her head was so hot that she was sure her face must resemble a tomato. She resisted the urge to reach up and fidget with the wig. While it looked great, it was uncomfortable, and she wondered how people could stand to wear something so heavy and hot on their heads.

"Tickets please," the inspector called out.

Amy pulled out the tickets for them both and laid them on the table in front of her. Her pulse started to race. It was like this every time they encountered someone new. Despite Beryl's reassurances, she was convinced that everyone could see straight through the flimsy disguise. She felt for sure she was going to be tackled to the ground while some well-meaning traveller performed a citizen's arrest.

The ticket inspector slowly walked up the carriage, glancing at peoples' tickets and smiling and thanking them as he went. Amy held her breath as he approached her. He looked at her and gave her a warm smile.

"Edinburgh?" he questioned as he glanced at their tickets.

Amy's throat felt dry, and she didn't trust herself to speak. She slowly nodded her head.

"There's a bit of congestion on the line, so we'll be a few minutes late," he told her.

She blew out a sigh of relief. "Oh, okay, no problem."

He continued on his way. Amy took some deep and slow breaths to try to get back under control. At this rate the police wouldn't have to find her because she'd keel over from a heart attack.

∾

Amy pressed her back up against the wall and adjusted her sunglasses. She tugged her coat collar up higher, attempting to cover more of her face.

"You look crazy," Kerry called out to her.

Amy rolled her eyes. They'd arrived in Edinburgh to find that the station was swamped with CCTV cameras. Amy had wanted to leave the station as quickly as possible, but Kerry insisted that they plan what to do next rather than racing off into the city.

Amy peeked around the corner. She watched as Kerry looked up at the map, hidden behind clear Perspex.

"I'd rather look crazy than be spotted," Amy whispered.

"If they're looking for people acting suspicious, they'll be here in a flash."

"Just concentrate on finding somewhere to stay. I'll concentrate on my fashion choices," Amy joked.

Kerry ran her finger over the plastic as she read the information from the map.

"Edinburgh's full of places to stay, I can tell you exactly where they all are," Kerry said. "I just have no idea how much they'll cost. Money's starting to run out. As long as we have sleeping bags, we have to prioritise spending money on food."

"Oh, food… I'm hungry," Amy whined. "Aren't you hungry? You must be hungry. It's been hours since we ate anything."

Kerry pinched the bridge of her nose. "Amy, babe, you're a great travel companion right up until you get hungry."

"It's not that bad," Amy defended.

"It is. When you're fed and happy, then you're an angel. But the second your blood sugar dips…"

"You better feed me then."

"I'm looking for a place nearby," Kerry told her. "Keep your wig on." She laughed at her own joke.

Amy rolled her eyes and leaned back against the wall. She looked at the CCTV cameras in the ceiling. She felt so exposed, even in a station filled with people. It was as if all the cameras were pointing directly at her.

The paranoia was increasing with every hour they were on the run. Amy hated how it had changed her. Suddenly, noises were more pronounced, more likely to mean trouble. If someone looked at her for more than a couple of seconds, she was sure her cover was blown.

"Okay, I found somewhere, let's go," Kerry said. She picked up her rucksack and slung it over her shoulder.

"Great, where are we going?" Amy asked as she walked behind Kerry.

"It's a pub called The Swan," Kerry told her. "We'll sit in there and think about what we want to do next. The Swan does have rooms, so maybe you can charm the manager into giving us a room for free. We could do some chores or something?"

They exited the station, and Amy started to slow down. There was a homeless woman, around their age, sitting on the hard stone steps leading into the station. Amy stopped and looked at her. She appeared to be freezing cold.

Amy glanced down at her own coat. It was better insulated and longer than the woman's.

Amy walked over to her. "Hey, wanna switch coats?"

The girl looked up in confusion. She clearly thought it was some kind of scam.

Amy started to remove her coat. "It's freezing, you need this more than I do. We can switch... if you like?"

Amy held her coat out, hoping that the girl would be able to trust her.

The girl looked at her for a few seconds before leaping up and taking her coat off. She grabbed Amy's coat, and Amy quickly let it go. Amy smiled, wanting to reassure her.

Amy had never spent time on the streets, she'd always lived a fortunate life. Even now, on the run, she was more fortunate than the freezing girl in front of her.

"Thanks," the girl said.

"You're welcome. I'd give you money, but I don't have any I can spare," Amy apologised. She took the girl's coat and put it on. It was cold inside and out from where the air had seeped through the thin material.

Suddenly Amy remembered that she had been walking with Kerry. "I hope things work out for you," Amy said. She turned and raced down the steps to where Kerry was stood, looking around in confusion.

"Sorry," Amy said as she approached Kerry. "Sorry, I just saw this homeless woman, and she was freezing. And I thought I have this big coat and she is sleeping on the stone steps." Amy looked down at her new coat and ran her fingers over it to brush out the wrinkles. "So, I swapped coats with her. I have other layers I can put on."

Kerry smiled and pulled Amy into a hug and kissed her forehead. "You're a big softie, you are."

~

The Swan was busier than Amy would have liked. But it was also set over two floors with plenty of nooks and crannies to hide in. They had settled into a corner and thankfully removed their rucksacks and some of their layers of outerwear.

She looked at her new coat and was pleasantly surprised by the good condition it was in. Her heart sunk at the thought of the woman sleeping rough on the street. She hoped her coat would offer the woman a little more warmth.

"Breaker, breaker, do you want honey roasted peanuts or chilli-flavoured peanuts? Over."

Amy jumped at the sudden sound and put her hand to her chest. Kerry was loving the walkie-talkies that Beryl had given them. She looked over to the bar where Kerry stood watching her and laughing loudly.

Amy gave her a filthy look and picked up her own walkie-talkie.

"You don't say breaker, breaker to start a conversation, you muppet."

"Nuts, Amy. What nuts do you want?"

"Honey roasted, please."

"Honey roasted, over and out!"

Amy shook her head and put the walkie-talkie on the table. She looked around at the pub, it was buzzing with people. Which wasn't surprising, as it was a Saturday night in Edinburgh.

Being on the run was messing with her mind. When she was in the middle of a country lane in a village she'd never even heard of, she longed for the bustle of a large city. Somewhere to get lost in amongst the people. But now she was in a city, she remembered just how easy it was to be traced through CCTV. They may be in disguises, but their faces had been on the news. She didn't know if they had made the national news, if they were being sought in Scotland.

Kerry returned with two drinks. "They are sending the food over in a minute." Kerry sat down opposite her and rubbed her hands together.

"Do you want to sit nearer the fire?" Amy asked. She indicated the open log fire with a tilt of her head.

Kerry looked over her shoulder towards it. "No, I'm okay here. Just still getting over that bloody freezing train journey."

Amy took a sip of her drink, relishing the sugary rush. "It wasn't that bad." She looked over to the bar. "Did you figure out who was in charge?"

Kerry nodded. "The tall, young bloke with ginger hair."

Amy zeroed in on him and nodded her head. "Cool, I'll see if I can sweet talk him into giving us a room later. If I can't, what kind of money do we have to pay him?"

Kerry shook her head. "None. If he won't let us stay, then we need to try other places."

"We must have some money," Amy argued.

"We do," Kerry tapped her pocket. "But you have to decide if you want to eat for a week or sleep in a hotel room for a night. We can technically put our sleeping bags in a shop doorway if we have to." Kerry plucked a menu from the table and started to read through the details while she waited for the food to arrive.

Amy looked at her best friend and felt a pang of guilt. Kerry should never have been involved in any of this. It was only because she had come to the services at the wrong time that she was now on the run. Away from home, unable to speak to her family, and probably in danger of losing her job.

She had effectively ruined Kerry's life. But Amy couldn't help but be grateful that Kerry was with her. There was no way she could have gotten so far on her own.

"Kerry——" Amy started but paused when she realised two men had approached their table. Her heart started to beat in double time.

They've found us.

"Hey, ladies, we're sorry to interrupt, but we wanted to make you aware of a new gay club that's opening up. It's called Ice, and it's opening tomorrow night down on Frederick Street."

Amy let out a sigh of relief and laughed as she took the proffered flyer. "We're not a couple, but thanks, we might check it out," Amy told him.

His partner elbowed him in the side. "I told you, David, you can't just assume that two girls sat together in wigs are lesbians."

"So much for a great disguise," Kerry said. She pulled off the wig with a sigh of relief.

"Michael's a hairdresser, he can spot a wig at a hundred paces," David told her. "Sorry about the confusion. I don't mean you look like lesbians, you look very nice. Not that lesbians don't look very nice. Just that——"

Amy exchanged a look with Kerry, and they both giggled.

"I'm gay," Amy told him. "She's straight. But single and desperate, so who knows?"

"Oi." Kerry kicked her under the table.

Amy ignored her and held out her hand. "I'm Amy, and this is Kerry."

Michael stepped around his embarrassed partner and shook her hand. "Michael, and this blushing fool is my husband, David."

"Don't worry, we've been mistaken for a couple a lot," Kerry reassured him.

"So, a new gay club, eh?" Amy asked as she looked at the flyer. "Ice?"

Michael chuckled. "You have to give it a ridiculous name these days. It's got to be all cool and edgy or no one wants to be seen there. Are you visiting for long?"

"Passing through," Amy said.

"Do you know any cheap places to stay?" Kerry asked. "Like, very cheap."

"We're on the run," Amy told him.

Michael laughed. "On the run?"

David blinked and shook his head. "Like, evading the law?"

"Yup." Amy ignored the glare from Kerry. "We didn't do anything wrong, so we're kinda proving our innocence. But we have to keep moving so they don't catch us."

"Exciting stuff," Michael said. He pulled out a chair beside Kerry and sat down. "What happened?"

Amy leaned forward. "Well, we can't tell you everything, obviously. The first rule of being on the run is to trust no one. But, we've been set up by this bad guy, seriously terrible hair, you'd hate him. And now the police are looking for us. But we have a plan to get it all sorted out."

David sat down next to Amy. "How long have you been on the run?" he whispered, looking around to check that no one had overheard him.

"Two days," Amy said. "It's a lot harder than you'd think. No access to money, begging people to help you. We've been hitchhiking everywhere."

"Hitchhiking? Isn't that dangerous?" David asked.

"Yes, extremely dangerous, but someone's an idiot," Kerry said, pointing toward Amy.

Amy opened her mouth to defend herself but saw the waiter standing by the table with two plates of food. She paused and let him put the plates down and leave again.

"I'm not an idiot, I'm just doing what's necessary," Amy argued.

"You should stay with us," Michael said. He looked at David for agreement, and David quickly nodded his head.

"Absolutely! Edinburgh is massively expensive; you'll not find anywhere to stay. And it's getting late as well. We only have one sofa, though..." David drifted off.

"We have sleeping bags," Amy said. "We just need a roof. That would be so lovely of you both. Are you sure?"

"Absolutely," Michael said. "We can live vicariously through you. Harbouring fugitives sounds like fun."

Amy looked at Kerry smugly. "See? Honesty really is the best policy." She turned back to Michael and pushed her plate towards him. "Would you like a chip?"

CHAPTER EIGHTEEN
COVER UP

CLAUDIA PULLED up to the farmhouse and looked out of the windscreen at the property. To say it needed a lick of paint was an understatement. She got out of the car and walked to the door. If she was lucky, the pair were still in the building and the whole thing would be over in a few minutes.

She examined each side of the property, mapping out potential escape routes in case they ran.

God, I hope they don't run.

Once she was satisfied, she stepped forward and knocked on the door before taking a step back again. She slowed her breathing to listen for any sounds.

The door opened, and an elderly lady looked her up and down with confusion and maybe even distaste.

"Yes?"

"Beryl Taylor?"

"Who's asking?"

Claudia could tell she was in the right place. "My name is Claudia McAllister, I'm a special investigator and I'm looking for two women. I believe you may have been in contact with them."

"Nope, you have the wrong person." Beryl started to close the door.

"They are known to be working with terrorists," Claudia said quickly.

Beryl hesitated, just as Claudia had hoped she would.

"They are not at all what they seem, and it's very important for the security of this country that I find them and speak with them. I'm sure they told you that they are innocent, but I can assure you that we have hard facts to the contrary."

Claudia kept listening for any sounds inside the house. Beryl's body language and the lack of noise told her that she was too late. It was now down to finding out as much information as possible.

"They stayed here, but they're gone now. And you're wrong, they are sweet girls. Nothing to do with terrorists. I've never heard anything so ridiculous."

"I know it may seem that way, trust me, I've met a lot of people who you would never think could commit a crime. But terrorist organisations are very good at converting people. Especially if those people are sweet-natured. They play on those emotions." Claudia looked pleadingly at Beryl. The woman held answers. If only she was willing to give them.

Beryl shook her head. "No, no, I'm sorry I can't believe that. I won't believe that. Not those two."

Claudia tilted her head. "You got to know them?"

"Yes, we ate dinner together. They stayed over. They helped me with chores and things around the house." Beryl pointed to the front door. "This bugger has been jammed for over a year, I've had to use the back door. But Amy fixed it for me. Doesn't sound like a terrorist, does it?"

Claudia looked at the door. "Terrorists come in different shapes and sizes," she said.

"So, terrorists help with the washing up, do they? They teach you how to use the computer, eh?"

Claudia looked at Beryl again. "Most terrorists fight for a cause; they don't just commit random acts of violence. They believe what they are doing is right."

"Sounds like you're defending 'em." Beryl folded her arms.

"I'm not. It is a part of my job to understand who I'm looking for."

"Well, if that's your aim then I can assure you that *you* won't be finding them." Beryl started to close the door.

"What makes you say that?" Claudia asked.

Beryl stopped and looked at her through the gap in the door. "If you're looking for hardened criminals, hell-bent on hurting people and causing mayhem, then you won't find those two. They are kind and generous. They gave me money for food, which they didn't have to do. Amy saved my dog, she didn't have to do that. Kerry cleaned the kitchen so much I can see my face in the kettle—"

Claudia had heard enough. "Did they say where they were going?"

"Wales." Beryl smiled. "Or was it Plymouth?"

Claudia let out a breath. "I know you think you're doing the right thing, but people's lives are at risk."

"Yes, two young girls. They haven't done nothing wrong." Beryl slammed the door shut.

Claudia heard multiple locks and chains being fastened. She stepped forward and posted her business card through the letter box. "Just in case you change your mind."

THE PHONE ALARM BEEPED LOUDLY, indicating that it was seven in the evening. Claudia turned it off. She lay on the bed and stared up at the ceiling. Thankfully, she had managed to get three hours of sleep. A long career in chasing people down had taught her the importance of spontaneous deep sleep.

She'd spoken to the owner of the main shop in Choppington, and he'd seen the girls earlier that morning. They were heading in the direction of the nearest town with a train station, Morpeth.

Claudia had spent four hours in Morpeth, questioning everyone she came across. No one had seen or heard anything. While Mark ran projections on where they might have gone, Claudia took the opportunity to sleep in a bed in a local hotel.

As she woke up, all the case details started to filter into her consciousness. She couldn't shake the discussion she'd had with Beryl. Of course, anyone harbouring a criminal thought they were doing the right thing. The best of criminals were charming and got away with things by virtue of their personality.

It wasn't lost on Claudia that Amy was a Sociology

graduate. She could easily use that knowledge to manipulate people. Maybe she was even manipulating Kerry?

She rolled off the bed and used the bathroom to get ready. She had no idea when she would next be able to take a break, so she used the opportunity to take a shower and wash her hair. Military service had taught her to use her time wisely, and in under fifteen minutes she was ready to go again.

She picked up her overnight bag and walked out of the hotel room. The building was very old, four hundred years old, if the manager was to be believed. It was clear that it was either built by drunks or had suffered from severe subsidence since. The stairs were all different heights and often slanting in different directions. From the bed to the shower was a downhill slope. As much as she had been relieved to be in a real bed, she'd be just as relieved to be back on solid, flat ground.

She carefully walked down the rickety stairs. She wasn't surprised when the hotel manager appeared around the corner.

"Did you sleep well, Miss McAllister?"

"Yes, thank you, Mr Simpson." She handed him the key.

"Please, call me Neil."

"Neil," she offered.

"Good luck in finding your runaways," he said. "By the way, did you speak to Bert?" He walked back towards the hotel reception desk and hung up the key on the corresponding hook.

"Who's Bert?" Claudia asked, the name sounded familiar. She had spoken to so many people that afternoon.

"The train station master," Neil said.

"Oh, yes, I spoke to him first thing."

Neil handed her an invoice. "Bert Junior or Bert Senior?"

She furrowed her brow. "Excuse me?"

"Father and son, they both work as the station master. Bert

Junior works until around lunchtime and then Bert Senior takes the other shift."

"I think I spoke to Bert Senior then." She took the invoice and handed over her card. "Where would I find Bert Junior?"

Neil swiped the card and handed it back. He turned around and looked at the clock on the wall. "Oh, you'll find him in The Partridge and Pheasant around now."

She took the card. "Perfect. Thank you."

"Don't forget to rate your stay on the Internets," Neil called out after her.

Claudia didn't bother to reply, she was already on her way to the pub. The town seemed to be filled with pubs, not surprising due to the lack of anything else happening in the area. She knew there were only two ways the girls could leave the town, hitchhike or train. The buses out of town were so infrequent that there hadn't been one all day. While she knew they were partial to hitchhiking, she had a suspicion that they would have tried to get a train.

She entered the pub and approached the landlord, whom she had already spoken to once that day.

"Hello again," he greeted her warmly. "Drink?"

"No, thank you. Is there a Bert Junior here? The station master?"

The landlord nodded and gestured his head to the end of the bar where a man was nursing half a beer and reading a newspaper. She walked over to him.

"Excuse me, are you the station master?"

He closed his newspaper and looked at her appraisingly. "I am. How can I help you, young lady?"

She pulled out a poster and showed it to him. "Have you seen these two girls?"

He took the poster from her and looked. "Oh yes, I saw these two this morning. They asked how to get to Edinburgh."

Claudia felt her heart beat a little faster. "You're sure?"

"Yes, normally we run a direct service, but with the engineer works they had to go to Newcastle and catch a train from there." He looked at his watch. "If they made their connection, they would have just arrived in Edinburgh."

He handed the poster back to her.

"Thank you so much." She pulled a five pound note out of her pocket and handed to the landlord. "Buy this man a drink," she told him before turning and rushing out of the pub.

CLAUDIA YANKED the handbrake up and shut off the engine. A moment later she was exiting the car with her coat in hand.

"I'm near the station," she spoke into her earpiece.

"I'm pulling the CCTV footage now, but there's a lot to go through and the connection is lagging," Mark replied.

She shrugged on her coat and descended the stairs two at a time to enter Edinburgh Waverley Station through the side entrance. The journey from Morpeth to Edinburgh had felt much longer than it was. In the back of her mind, Claudia knew that every minute was a minute her subjects could spend evading her. Ten minutes was a reasonably small amount of time unless it was in the hands of a desperate person fleeing.

"I'm searching the station now, call me as soon as you get anything concrete."

She paused as she entered the station. Hurrying was sometimes the biggest mistake a hunter could commit. A second or two surveying the landscape could be the potential difference between a successful capture and a loss.

The train station was undeniably beautiful in its

architecture and retained a lot of original features. It was also extremely busy. Claudia knew that Waverley was the second biggest train station in the UK, and right now it felt it.

A glance at the departures board demonstrated what a busy station it was, even later in the evening. Claudia wondered if this was the girls' destination or if they were simply using it to get elsewhere. The station was a major junction. It would be very easy for someone to head in any direction in a matter of minutes.

She shook her head and walked down a flight of stairs towards the main concourse. She couldn't worry about that now. Her best course of action was to assume they had remained in Edinburgh and to search the surrounding area, until she knew otherwise.

The concourse was quiet due to the late hour. Claudia walked purposefully, looking into each shop and coffeehouse as she went. She stood under a large clock and turned around, taking in every corner of the large station. Each person was quickly analysed and categorised. A couple of times she paused and brought up the pictures of the girls in her mind before moving on.

The station was clear. She pulled her gloves out of her pocket and put them on. She headed towards the exit and into Edinburgh itself. Outside the station, the dim street lighting made it harder to scan the crowds. Claudia stood by a pillar and carefully looked around. There was a chance that they were waiting for a train, or planning to hitchhike. The last thing she wanted to do was spook them and send them running off.

Someone caught her eye. Her heart beat a little faster, and her muscles began to twitch. She pulled out her phone and accessed the last few CCTV stills that Mark had sent her and then looked up again. Amy Hewitt was just across the street.

She pocketed the phone and stepped out into the road.

Weaving around cars, she zeroed in on her target. The girl seemed none the wiser as she slowly walked along the pavement.

Claudia was right behind her, easily within grabbing distance if the girl decided to run.

"Amy Hewitt," she said loudly.

The girl kept walking.

"Amy Hewitt, you're under arrest."

The girl turned around and looked confused. "Are you talking to me?"

Claudia paused. She felt her adrenaline drop. This was not Amy Hewitt. The woman in front of her was around the same age but unkempt and presumably living rough. From behind she was the spitting image of Amy. Her mind raced. It was the hair and the coat. A very distinctive coat.

"Where did you get that coat?"

"Who's asking?"

Claudia handed over a ten pound note. "I am."

The girl eagerly took the money. "Some posh girl. Came out of the train station and switched coats with me."

"So, she has your coat?"

The girl shrugged. "Suppose so."

"Can you describe your coat?" Claudia asked.

The girl stuck out her bottom lip and looked up at the sky. "I'm not sure I remember it."

Claudia rolled her eyes. She took a twenty pound note out of her pocket. "I will give you this if, and only if, you give me a full description of your coat, a full description of the girl who took it, tell me exactly what she said to you, and where she went."

Claudia knew it was cruel. The girl clearly needed the money. But she was on a mission, lives were at stake if she didn't find Amy and bring her in soon.

"It's a black pea coat, I bought it in ASDA about three

years ago. It's got hardly no padding and there's a rip on the left sleeve. The posh girl was about my height, she had an auburn bob, short like. But it totally looked like a wig to me. She was walking past when I was sat outside the station. Then she stopped and asked if I wanted to swap coats. She said hers was warmer." The girl shimmied a little inside the thick coat. "And it is. I asked if she was kidding. She said no, by then she was already taking her coat off. I didn't want to say no because my coat was bloody freezing. We swapped and that was it."

"Where did she go?"

"She didn't say. She walked up towards the Royal Mile. She was with another girl, but she'd walked off ahead. I really didn't get a look at her at all."

Claudia looked at the girl for a moment. She was satisfied that she was telling the truth. She reached into her pocket and pulled out another twenty pound note.

Handing the girl both the notes, she said, "Okay, look after yourself."

The girl took the money. She turned and hurried away, clearly keen to put some distance between them. Just before she crossed the road she turned back and muttered a thank-you before vanishing.

Claudia tapped her earpiece and waited to be connected.

"Bad news, they're disguising their appearance," she said.

Mark let out a breath, and she heard a mug angrily hitting the desk through the line. "Well, that explains why I'm having so much trouble finding them."

"Amy is using a wig, auburn and styled into a short bob. I don't know about Kerry. Also, after they left the station, Amy exchanged her coat with a homeless girl. She's no longer wearing that coat; she now has a black pea coat with a rip on the left sleeve."

"Okay, I'm going to go back through the CCTV with this new information."

"Good man. I'm going to ask around and see if anyone else has seen them. If we can't track them on CCTV, then we'll need to get new posters done with an identikit picture."

She hung up the call and started heading towards the Royal Mile. She knew Edinburgh well, the hilly capital having been a place she'd holidayed in the past. Edinburgh was split into two parts. One part was the elegant Georgian New Town, the other the medieval Old Town. Unluckily for her, Amy and Kerry were in the Old Town, complete with its narrow streets and alleyways, arcades, and many, many pubs.

The only way to do this was methodically. She approached the first pub she saw and stepped around the group of men standing just outside its door. Inside she pulled off her gloves, using the delay to have a good look around the large building as she blocked the main exit. The pub was moderately busy but not rowdy, and she set about walking around the area. Once she had completed a full circle, and she was reasonably satisfied that the girls were not there, she headed towards the bar.

She leaned on the bar and continued to look around.

"Hi, what can I get you?"

Claudia turned to the young bartender. She unfolded the poster and handed it to him.

"Have you seen these two girls?"

"Yep." He smiled and handed the paper back to her.

She blinked. "You have?" She couldn't believe her luck.

"Yeah, they were talking to David and Michael a while ago. They had some food, and then they all left," he told her.

This might be easier than I thought. "Who are David and Michael?"

"David and Michael Chapman. They are regulars, great guys. They live down in Niddrie."

"How long ago did they leave?" Claudia was already walking away.

"About two hours ago, I think."

Claudia didn't wait to hear anymore. She headed out of the pub and jogged back towards where she had parked her car. She tapped her earpiece.

"Hey," Mark answered.

"David and Michael Chapman, living in Niddrie, I need an address now," Claudia said.

"On it."

She heard Mark typing in the details. Her heart was racing. She was right behind them, and they had no idea she was coming for them.

"Got it, number seventeen Mountcastle Drive. Sending it to your phone now."

"How far is it from my current location?"

"About a fifteen-minute drive."

"Perfect. I have a solid lead; I'll call you back when I know more."

CHAPTER TWENTY-ONE
SUSPICION

AMY GRIPPED the blanket in her fingers. She slowed her breathing and listened. The house was quiet apart from the usual house noises. In the garden, she could hear the leaves on the trees rustle. Upstairs she could hear the whir of the heating pump.

But there was something else bothering her. Something she just couldn't put her finger on. It wasn't a new sensation, but it had been building all day. Uncertainty ate away at her.

She pushed the blanket away.

"Kez, we have to go." She sat up from her makeshift bed on the floor and started to roll up the sleeping bags.

"I'm comfortable and warm. Why on earth do we have to leave?" Kerry asked her from her cocoon on the sofa.

"We have to go," Amy repeated. She shed her pyjamas and started to get dressed. She knew she would feel better once she was dressed. At the moment, she felt vulnerable, wearing her duck print pyjamas with damp hair from the shower.

Kerry sat up. "Why? What's going on?"

"I don't know," Amy said honestly.

"Okay, calm down and tell me what you're thinking." Kerry stood up and gently took her shoulders.

Amy took a deep breath. She knew she could always rely on Kerry to listen to her. Even when she was having a freak-out for no reason.

"I just feel... wrong. Something is wrong. We have to get out of here. I can't explain it."

"Are you sure you're not just wigging out for no reason? I know you've been on edge for a while now."

"I know, I know I have. But this is different. I feel like I'm having a panic attack or something. I just need to get out of here."

Kerry stared into her eyes for a couple of seconds. She nodded. "Okay, let's go then."

Amy sighed in relief. She threw on her thick sweater. Her breathing was still coming in short pants, but at least they were going to be on the move soon.

Kerry started to get changed.

"I'm sorry," Amy said.

"Don't be sorry," Kerry reassured her. "We're best mates, this is what best mates do. If you're having a freak-out, then we're going to deal with it. Don't forget to grab the rest of that bottle of water."

Amy was reaching for the bottle when a bright light illuminated the living room. Kerry froze what she was doing as both girls looked towards the curtained window in terror.

"That's someone parking on the driveway," Kerry whispered.

"It's midnight," Amy whispered back. She hopped on the spot as she pulled her boot on.

Kerry crossed the room and stood with her back to the wall. Without moving the curtain, she looked through a tiny gap out of the window. "Black car, posh looking. We should run. Now."

CHAPTER TWENTY-TWO
FIRST CONTACT

CLAUDIA LOOKED at the large cottage as she pulled onto the Chapman's driveway. To each side of the house was a large brick wall and wrought iron gates. Getting around the property to the back would be impossible without the help of the owners.

Stealth wouldn't work here. She needed speed. She exited the car and walked towards the front door. She rang the doorbell and then knocked loudly a second later for good measure. The lights in the hallway turned on, and she heard someone rushing down the stairs.

She unfolded the poster and held it up ready. The door opened, and a man in a dressing gown looked at her in confusion.

"I believe these two girls are in your property," she said quickly. She knew she had to use the element of surprise. "They are known terrorists, and they are linked to a substantial terror plot. It's essential that they are arrested as soon as possible."

"Michael, who is it?" A voice called from upstairs.

Michael looked speechlessly from her to the stairs and then back again.

"Mr Chapman, I know they seem innocent, but the truth is these girls are dangerous. If you know anything about their location—"

Michael opened the door fully and silently pointed towards a closed door. Claudia stepped into the house and opened the door. She rushed into the living; it looked like whoever was here had just left. The back door into the garden was open, and the curtains blew in the wind.

"They must have just left," Michael said.

"Michael, what's going on? Is she the police?" David had come downstairs. His disappointed tone was clear.

"Amy and Kerry are terrorists, David," Michael explained to his husband. "All the bull about being innocent, they are bloody terrorists. Involved in some plot."

She heard David gasp at the information. She'd question the couple later; with any luck she was moments behind the girls. As she walked towards the door, something caught her eye. She looked under the coffee table, which had been moved to one side to make room for a bed. She saw something black and reached for it. She turned the walkie-talkie over in her hand.

"Is this theirs?"

"Yes," Michael said.

Claudia pulled a small torch out from her jacket pocket and headed through the back door into the garden. She shone the light and started to run. A large perimeter wall surrounded the garden. Towards the back were some high trees which could be used to climb. She ran towards them and could see a fresh muddy footprint on one of the branches.

She clipped the walkie-talkie to her belt and reached up to haul herself onto a secure-looking branch. She climbed high enough to safely get to the wall and stepped onto it. The garden backed onto a large area of parkland. Everything was pitch black. She surveyed as much of the area as she could while she was at this vantage point.

With care, she lowered herself to the ground. She unclipped the walkie-talkie. "Amy Hewitt, my name is Claudia McAllister. I need you to give yourself up and let me take you in."

She took a few steps away from the wall into the darkened area. She looked at the walkie-talkie, barely illuminated by the full moon. *I wonder if it even works? Would they bother to carry it around if it didn't? Maybe that's why they left it?*

"We're innocent," a voice came through the speaker.

"Amy?" Claudia asked.

"Yeah. And we haven't done anything wrong."

"No? Then come and talk to me about it, and we'll get it all sorted out."

There was a pause until, "Do you think I was born yesterday?"

Claudia smirked. "No, but you can't run forever. If you come and talk to me, this will all be over."

"I'm not coming back. You'll arrest us." This time Amy sounded breathy, and Claudia concluded that she was running.

"Then let's talk," Claudia suggested. She looked out into the darkness and waited for a reply. She knew the girls were out there, running away, but she had no idea of the direction.

"No way," Amy replied. "You probably have dogs coming after us. And drones."

Well, the paranoia has certainly kicked in.

"It's just me here, Amy. I promise you that. No dogs, no drones."

The silence stretched on. "But that won't last forever," Claudia spoke again. "You can't keep running. You're being monitored, we know your tactics, we're in communication with your network. I've found you once, and I'll find you again. Or maybe someone else will find you, someone less forgiving than me."

"I don't have a network," Amy replied bitterly. "See? You think we're guilty, don't you? You have no intention of helping us. What did you say your name was?"

"Claudia McAllister."

"Well, I have one thing left to say to you, Claudia," Amy said.

Claudia waited, but nothing came.

"What do you want to say, Amy?" Claudia finally asked.

She cocked her head closer to the device. Suddenly a loud raspberry sound crackled through the speaker. Claudia blanched backwards.

"Really," she mumbled to herself. She held down the button. "Received, loud and clear. But I'll keep this walkie-talkie on me. When we're close enough, we can speak. So, if you change your mind the next time I come for you, just let me know."

"Yeah, wha—" Static filled the speaker.

They were out of range.

"AMY, WAIT!" Kerry shouted.

Amy didn't wait. Her heart felt like it was beating out of her chest and all she could hear was the rushing of blood. Even though she felt like she might pass out, she kept running.

It had been a close call. Too close. She'd never climbed a tree in her life, she was sure that Kerry hadn't either. But through sheer adrenaline, both launched themselves into the tree and were over the wall, crashing down into the mud below. They had both picked themselves up and kept running.

Amy didn't dare turn around. In her mind, they were right behind her. If she turned around then she'd see them, panic, and it would be game over.

"Amy!" Kerry tried again.

Amy slowed down and turned around. No one was behind her but Kerry. But she didn't want to give them the chance to catch up. "Come on!"

"I can't," Kerry admitted. She slowed to a jog.

Amy looked at the road behind them. It was lit with street lamps for as far as she could see. They were alone. She let out a long sigh and leaned forward to put her hands on her knees as she gasped for breath.

"We can't hang around here," Amy said. She stood up again. "She's coming."

"She who?" Kerry said between panted breaths.

"Claudia. Come on," Amy urged.

"Who's Claudia?"

"The woman who's chasing us, come on." Amy turned around and started to walk quickly. It was real now. They were being chased by a person who had a name.

"How do you know her name is Claudia?"

Amy thrust her walkie-talkie into the air. "She spoke to me."

"Shit, she has my walkie-talkie," Kerry said. "Can she track us by that?"

"I don't think so."

"But you spoke to her?"

"Yeah."

Amy heard Kerry take a deep breath and jog a little to catch up to her. "And? What did she say?"

"Give yourselves up, you're terrorists, I'll find you, blah blah."

"Shit."

"Yeah." Amy pointed towards the end of the road. "There's the main road, we need to get out of here."

"What if she's there?" Kerry asked.

Amy stopped and spun around to glare at Kerry. "What if she's following us? We don't know. We don't know anything. She's a professional man-hunter, she's probably got all kind of tricks and... and robot things that are looking for us. She could be anywhere. But I think we need to get in the first car that we see and get the hell out of here."

Kerry looked at her nervously. It was the first time that Amy had really panicked since they had been on the run. She's been paranoid, over-cautious, but this was pure panic. Amy could tell from the look on Kerry's face that she was just as scared.

Kerry was always the practical one, the one with the plan. Amy was the happy-go-lucky one, the one that always said everything was okay. Except for now. Amy really knew that everything wasn't okay now.

"We need to get out of here, right now," Amy demanded.

"Okay, you're right," Kerry said. "We'll get out of here. We'll go down to that road, and we'll get in the first car we can. But I need you to take a few breaths and chill. No one is going to give us a lift if you look as panicked as you do now, okay?"

Amy couldn't calm down. All she could hear was Claudia's voice. The calm, sensible tones of a woman who had been sent to find them. And had somehow managed to do it. Amy's mind swam with theories on how Claudia had found them. She wondered if it was technology, if they had been found by camera. Or if someone had given them up.

"Amy," Kerry said harshly. "Focus. Take some deep breaths. Give yourself thirty seconds now so you can get us out of here."

Amy slowly nodded her head and focused on taking a few breaths. She looked over her shoulder and peered into the darkness. She didn't think she could see anyone, but she couldn't really be sure. Her senses were playing tricks on her. Everything sounded louder, noises she usually ignored were suddenly like a brass band in her ears.

"I'm okay," Amy whispered.

"Sure, babe?"

"Yeah, let's go."

The two of them jogged towards the main road. As soon as they got to the road, Amy started to wave her hands about to flag down cars. One car went by, followed by another. But a third stopped, and a middle-aged woman opened the window.

"Are you okay?"

Amy rushed over, Kerry closely behind her.

"Hi," Amy said, a friendly smile on her face. "I'm so sorry about this, but is there any chance you could give us a lift?"

The woman looked unsure.

Amy continued quickly. "Anywhere is fine, I just have this nasty boyfriend—well, ex-boyfriend—and we want to just get away. We won't be any bother. I know it's late and we probably look a bit of a state, but we're good people, honestly—"

The woman held up her hand to stop Amy's speech. She nodded. "Okay, get in the back. I'm only going to Musselburgh."

"Musselburgh is fine," Kerry said as she opened the back door.

"I love Musselburgh, always wanted to visit," Amy said as she got in the car.

CHAPTER TWENTY-FOUR
UPPING THE PRESSURE

CLAUDIA QUICKLY REALISED that she needed to get back to the car and continue the search from there. She ran towards the wall and launched herself upwards, grasping the top and easily pulling herself over. She dropped to the ground and raced back towards the house.

The Chapmans were still standing around in the living room, looking dumbstruck and useless.

"I'm going to go and look for them," she announced. She handed her business card to Michael as she walked towards the front door. "If they come back, call me immediately. I'll be back shortly to question you."

She opened the front door and ran to her car, throwing it into reverse and speeding off the driveway and into the street. The satnav system pinged to life, and she looked for the quickest route around the parkland, hoping to head them off.

Once she was in the right area, she drove up and down every street. She meticulously checked the residential streets for any sign of the girls. After fifteen long minutes, she realised they had either found a hiding place or they had managed to get away.

"Call Mark," she instructed tersely.

"Hey," Mark greeted.

"They were there, I was right behind them, but they got away. There's a park behind the Chapmans' house and I lost them in the dark."

"I'll map potential escape routes, but they are close to the city which means it will be a wide area."

"I know. I spoke to Amy; it seems they were communicating with each other via walkie-talkie. But one got left behind in their hurry to leave."

"What did she say?"

"She said she was innocent, she thought we were coming after her with dogs and drones. Really paranoid."

"Did she say anything else?"

"That she didn't have a network backing her up. And she blew a raspberry down the line."

"Seriously?"

"Yes." Claudia frowned. This just wasn't adding up.

"Sounds weird," Mark commented.

"Yes. Something's not right. Can you use this walkie-talkie to track them?" Claudia asked, she knew she was grasping at straws.

"Probably not. Send me a picture of it, and I'll see what brand it is. But it's probably not going to be possible."

"Fine, I assumed as much." She pulled the car over and took a deep breath. "Listen, we need to stop making this so damn easy for them. Call Andrew, tell him that I nearly had eyes on them but they have escaped. Last seen in the Edinburgh area."

"You want to give him that information?" Mark sounded surprised.

"Yes, if these girls are as dangerous as we've been led to believe, then it's high time we started working together and getting serious. Tell him that we need to leaflet the local area, preferably the whole county. We need posters of them, stills of them in their disguises and without. The local communities are hiding them, and they seem to have the gift of the gab so people are trusting whatever they say. We need to get their pictures out there; flyer drops and even local news. The sooner we cut off their support network, the sooner we can flush them out."

"It will take them a day or two to get that kind of campaign together," Mark said.

"I know. But we need to start now. They are always one step ahead, and that needs to stop. Now."

～

"So, you saw them in the pub?" Claudia asked. As interviews for this case went, this was by far the nicest. When she had returned to the Chapmans' house, she had been greeted and offered a hot drink. Now she sat on a sinfully comfortable sofa and held a cup of coffee in her hands. She looked at the two nervous-looking men sat on the sofa opposite her.

"Yes, we were drumming up some interest in a new gay bar in town," the short one, David, said. "I spotted them and thought they were a couple."

Michael rolled his eyes. "He sees two women together, and they're a couple. Every time."

"Oh, now, come on, you agreed!" David turned to Michael.

Michael ignored him and continued to address Claudia. "They had these fake wigs on. Clearly had never worn wigs before in their lives. They stood out like a sore thumb."

Claudia cursed her timing. She had been hunting for the girls for ages, and these two just stumbled across them in the local pub.

"Anyway, we got talking," David continued the story. "They asked if we knew any cheap places to stay."

"They told us they were on the run," Michael said. "Just like that, blurted it out."

David hooked a thumb towards Michael. "So, this one offers them to stay here."

"They had just said they'd been hitchhiking," Michael explained. "Which I thought was dangerous. I couldn't live with myself if something happened to them just after we left."

"Anyway, they agreed to come back here, and we had coffee. The girls wanted to use the shower and then they set up in here to go to bed," David said.

"What else did they talk about?" Claudia asked. She sipped at her coffee, relishing its bitter aftertaste.

Michael leaned back on the sofa and scrunched up his face. "It's hard to remember. I think we talked about television mainly. Amy spoke a bit about coffee, she works in a coffee shop. And some of the stories she told me means I'm never setting foot in another one ever again."

"Which will save us about a thousand pounds a year," David added.

Michael gently elbowed him.

"They were just nice, ordinary people," David said seriously. "They said they were on the run, but they didn't go into any details. I suppose we thought it was a bit of a joke. They were down-to-earth and funny, and we didn't think anything of it."

"You said they are terrorists?" Michael asked.

Claudia inclined her head. "I'm not permitted to give you specific details, but they have been linked to terrorist activity, yes."

"Are we in trouble? Do I need to contact my solicitor?" Michael asked.

"Not unless you are withholding information which could

assist in their timely arrest." Claudia swallowed down the rest of her coffee. It was clear that the men weren't in possession of any useful information. Not that they were aware of now anyway.

She placed the coffee mug on the table in front of her.

"It's late and you're both tired and have had a shock. If anything comes to mind later, then please call me, no matter what the time. Any further information you have, whether or not you think it might be relevant, could help bring these girls in."

"Of course, absolutely," Michael agreed. He stood up and walked with her towards the front door. "We're just sorry we weren't more use. I can't believe we got caught up in all this."

"You're not the only ones who have been taken in by them," Claudia reassured him.

"They seemed so nice, so genuine."

"Yes, I'm hearing a lot of that." Claudia shook Michael's hand. "Thank you for your help, and the coffee. As I say, if you think of anything at all, don't hesitate to call me."

CHAPTER TWENTY-FIVE
KNOW YOUR ENEMY

THE SOUND of the industrial sit-on cleaner pulled Amy from her sleep. She opened her eyes and watched as the service station employee drove the cleaner across the concourse, performing a fast and tight turn before the entrance. He performed another tight turn and then another straight after, clearly enjoying riding the large, noisy machine.

Well, he's having the time of his life, Amy mused.

She looked up at the large clock on the wall. It was approaching nine o'clock in the morning. They'd been there for eight hours. Two people had kindly given them rides, each in opposite directions. Amy was happy that if Claudia tracked one then she certainly wouldn't expect the second to take them back past the scene of the crime. She'd heard that criminals never returned to the scene of the crime. Or they always returned to the scene of the crime. Either way, she remained certain that Claudia wouldn't expect it.

The second person had left them at the deserted service station just outside of Coatbridge near Glasgow.

Once they had cleared Edinburgh, the adrenaline had quickly given way to exhaustion. So, the quiet services were a blessing as it forced them to rest. Sitting on the hard benches, Amy was convinced that she wouldn't be able to sleep. But eight hours had passed, so clearly she had.

She turned to see Kerry hugging her rucksack, asleep with her face planted in the top of the bag. Deciding to let Kerry sleep a while longer, she shucked off her coat and stood up. She rolled her head and lifted her arms to stretch her body out, then pushed her things close to Kerry before taking a stroll around the services.

The car park was starting to fill up. She looked at the people coming into the services to determine whom she might approach. Hitchhiking was their only way away from the services. It was in the middle of nowhere with no public transport. It was essential that Amy found someone to charm. That person also had to be travelling in the right direction, and not a murderer.

Amy might not let on to Kerry, but she knew how dangerous hitchhiking was. She'd taken a "needs must" approach so far, but she'd be happy when they arrived at Aberdeen and could finally get the data off of the USB stick.

She put her hand into her pocket and nervously rolled the stick over in her hand. Hoping that Kerry's friend would be able to help them was a leap of faith. But with the wrath of the intelligence services coming down on them, they had no choice. Amy knew she needed a plan B. She had been wracking her brains for one, and nothing had presented itself to her yet. The stress of being chased was doing strange things to her mind. Her thought process was all over the place. She took a deep breath and continued walking, hoping to clear her head.

A bank of computers with free Internet was in the corner of the services, and before she knew it her feet were walking her towards them. Before she pulled the chair out, she peered over to check that Kerry was still asleep. She knew what she was about to do was, potentially, very stupid. She didn't know how the powers of the state worked. So far she just assumed that they could see and hear everything. She assumed that every single camera had facial recognition and would instantaneously ping up at headquarters. But logically she knew that was unlikely. Otherwise there would be no criminals on the run. Crime would be a thing of the past. Surely, they couldn't be as advanced as they looked on television?

She sat down and looked at the computer screen. After a moment's indecision, she pulled the keyboard towards her. She wiped it down with the sleeve of her jumper in one long stroke. She glanced back up at the screen and watched the flashing cursor. After another look over her shoulder to check Kerry was asleep, she typed in a search.

Claudia McAllister

A second later, thousands of search results were compiled. She scanned the list until she saw a business profile. Amy clicked the link. Her eyes were immediately drawn to the photograph. A strict and unsmiling work picture gazed at her. Long, dark hair was swept back into a practical ponytail. Hazel eyes bored into her. Amy quickly scrolled down, feeling the intensity of the stare looking into her soul. Claudia, if this was the same Claudia, was beautiful in an ethereal way that Amy had never experienced. Just a couple of seconds of looking at the image, and Amy felt a strange connection.

She shook her head to refocus her thoughts and started to read the business biography on the screen. It was short and to the point; Amy wondered if it was Claudia's own words.

"Used to work with MI5 counter-terrorism. Now runs her own agency," Amy mumbled to herself. She sat back. "She's not with them, she works alone."

"Who works alone?"

Amy jumped out of the chair, crashing her thighs into the desktop.

Kerry ignored her drama and leaned forward to look at the screen.

"Jesus, Kerry, don't sneak up on me like that." Amy rubbed her thighs.

"You left me on my own over there," Kerry said without looking at her. "Then I find you, and you're chatting away to yourself like a lunatic. This is the woman who found us?" Kerry reached for the mouse and started to scroll up and down the webpage.

"Yeah," Amy muttered, unsure if Kerry was about to berate her for doing the online search.

"She's independent, so she was telling the truth when she said she was on her own," Kerry said.

"I think so. Now I'm wondering why she's found us and they haven't. Are they even looking for us? Maybe they aren't even looking. Maybe they... don't care? Or gave up? Or they just farm out the silly cases to people like her. Surely they don't think we're important if they gave the case to her?" Amy knew she was clutching at straws.

Kerry pulled a chair over and sat down. She focused on the screen, returning to the search results and looking at other pages.

"Maybe. Perhaps we're full of ourselves and they aren't coming at all?" Kerry suggested.

"Either that or she is, like, elite, and she's found us and they haven't," Amy guessed.

Kerry let out a sigh. "Which would mean we have two groups of people looking for us." She leaned back and pinched the bridge of her nose.

"Three, if you count Spiky." Amy reached for the mouse and navigated back to the original webpage. She hesitated a moment as Claudia's photograph appeared again and then scrolled down. "What's she got that they haven't? How is she tracking us, almost finding us, and they don't seem to be?" Amy asked.

"I don't know, babe. But I don't think you're going to find the answers on there."

Amy scrunched up her face and sat back in her chair. "It was weird. Speaking to her, I mean. Like it already felt real, but then it felt one hundred percent more real."

Kerry just nodded and looked at her sympathetically. "What do you want to do?"

Amy knew that Kerry was asking a wider question. Kerry wasn't just asking what she wanted to do next, but what she wanted to do overall.

Amy looked at the floor, ignoring the hustle of the services that was gradually becoming busier. She wanted to be proved innocent. She wanted to go back to her life, where everything was simple and easy. She wanted her bed, her home, her mum.

"Nothing's changed," Amy said. "They still think we're... the t-word... so we have to prove that we're not. We have to get this USB stick to an expert."

"I agree," Kerry said.

"I think we need to focus on the goal. So far, we've been running. We've vaguely tried to get to Aberdeen, but we've been all over the place. If we'd stuck to our plan, we might already have got there by now."

"You're right, we've been focusing on running. What do you suggest?"

Amy looked out into the car park. "Someone here must be going Aberdeen. I think we wait to find someone who is travelling there. It might take a while to find that person, never mind a person who is willing to let us travel with them. But it's better than potentially travelling backwards."

"Yeah, speed is of the essence now. We don't know how this woman found us, so we need to crack on."

"Exactly, she may know that we're hitchhiking, but how's she going to find us? There's a lot of space between here and Aberdeen. It will take her a while to find us. Surely?"

Kerry nodded. "Yes, we'll spend more time here finding the right person, going to the right place. In the long run, it will save us time."

Amy reached for the mouse and closed the search window.

"Amy, it's more important now that we remember what we agreed."

Amy sucked in a breath. "If we get split up?"

"Yeah. We've split the money, but we can't split the USB. You're carrying that, and I'm fine with it, but I have to know that you'll carry on. If I get caught, I have to know that you're going to keep going. I need to know that you'll finish what we started. If this woman..."

"Claudia."

"Claudia, if she finds me, I need to know that you're already running. I'll be able to deal with it all better if I know that you're okay."

"But, what if I'm not okay without you?" Amy asked softly.

"You've always been okay without me." Kerry swept her into a one-armed hug. "It's me who needs you. You're..."

Amy waited to hear what she was. She felt Kerry stiffen. "Don't keep me in suspense, Kez. I'm what?"

"Holy shit."

Kerry loosened her grip and Amy turned around. She followed Kerry's gaze to one of the big screen TVs mounted on the services' wall. A cold tingle of air swept up her spine. They were on the news. The TV was muted, and the subtitles were slowly catching up with what the newsreader was saying. But the image on the screen was of them, the screenshots from the CCTV the day it all started.

"We need to get our wigs," Kerry mumbled. She looked around to see if the few people in the services were paying attention to the screens. Luckily, everyone seemed to be too busy going about their business to notice.

"Agreed." Amy casually walked over to the seats where she'd left Kerry sleeping and hauled her rucksack onto her back. Kerry joined her and grabbed the handle of her own bag.

"Let's head for the bathroom," Kerry suggested. "Nice and slow."

"I'm freaking out," Amy whispered.

"I know. Just... look normal. We're just travelling. Like everyone else. Everything will be fine."

Kerry sounded calm, but Amy could detect the underlying panic in her tone. She tried to swallow down her fear. It wasn't the first time they had been featured on the news. But this was different, now they were the subject of a nationwide manhunt. Finding people they could trust had just become a hundred times harder.

AMY FELT her hand rise subconsciously and quickly lowered it again. The wig was great at disguising her appearance, she could hardly recognise herself in the mirror, but it was uncomfortable. It made her head hot, and it was starting to give her a headache where it fit tightly over her unruly hair.

To add to her discomfort, there was the added problem that she was convinced that everyone was looking at her. The news article featuring them was running every thirty minutes inside the service station. When the article was running, they headed outside and stayed away from people. Once it was finished, they stayed in the car park, only speaking to people who had just arrived. Now and then, they would head back into the services, but only with their hoods shielding their faces.

Amy could feel the sweat trickling down her back. The pressure was on, and she mentally cursed Claudia for it. She couldn't know for certain that the mysterious huntress was the one who had set the media on her. It felt like it must have been her.

Them had now turned into *her*. Claudia McAllister, elite hunter who had been so successful she had set up her own business. She'd already found them once, and Amy felt as if she lurked behind every corner, waiting for them. The cat and mouse game now felt more claustrophobic with the stark knowledge of just how sharp the cat's claws were.

A motorhome pulled into one of the large spaces at the end of the car park. Amy walked over to the vehicle and waved towards the male driver who sported a hipster look. He was in his mid-thirties. He smiled and waved back to her as he manually wound down the window on the old motorhome.

"Hey," she greeted him. "I'm Amy."

"Stuart, and this is Alice." He gestured behind him with his thumb.

Amy looked into the back of the motorhome and saw a little girl, no older than eight.

"Hey Alice, I like your braids," Amy said warmly.

Alice smiled. She blushed and looked down at her feet, clearly embarrassed by the attention.

"Me and my friend Kerry are kinda stranded and looking for a lift to Aberdeen," Amy said. She pulled her shoulders as high up as she could and shivered a little as the wind blew. She wasn't cold, her heart was beating too fast to be cold. But she knew the pathetic look may tug at a heartstring or two.

Stuart looked her up and down, weary to say the least. Amy remained silent; she knew that silence was the most powerful weapon when it came to bartering.

"Well..." Stuart trailed off, uncertainty warring on his features.

"We are so quiet, you won't even know we're here. Unless you want us to sing, we're great at singing. And we bring our own sweets, because every road trip needs sweets." Amy winked towards Alice who was looking at her curiously.

"I've never picked up hitchhikers before," Stuart admitted.

Amy had picked up on the unsaid signal that he was going

to Aberdeen. This was her chance to get out of the services and on the road to their final destination.

"We're not hitchhikers, we're Amy and Kerry. And we're dead nice. You'll even miss us when we're gone, when you're driving alone you'll think, 'Gosh, I wish Amy and Kerry were still here'. I promise, we're no trouble."

Stuart laughed and then nodded. "Okay, okay, I'll give you a lift. I warn you, it might take a while, the van is a bit clapped out. We can only do fifty on the motorway, so it will be about a four hours' drive."

"Better than a three-day walk," Amy replied. She turned around and waved her arms to get Kerry to come over.

~

Stuart wasn't exaggerating when he said that the motorhome was clapped out. The engine was making a noise that echoed throughout the vehicle. Kerry and Alice sat in the back, Kerry keeping the girl entertained with the travel games set that Amy had brought along. Alice had seemed sombre when they first started the journey, but it only took Kerry a few minutes to win her over.

Stuart smiled as he chanced the occasional look in the rearview mirror. Amy watched him with interest. He seemed relieved; he had been concerned about Alice for some reason.

"She's a great kid," Amy fished. The music was playing loudly enough to cover their conversation.

"She is. She... um, well, we lost her mother, four months back."

"I'm sorry to hear that, was it sudden?" Amy chanced a look back to check that they were speaking privately.

After another glance in the rearview mirror, Stuart nodded. "Yeah, cancer. She was gone in five weeks. It really hit Alice hard."

Amy took in his taut body language and looked towards her window to give him some privacy. "I'll bet, it must have hit you hard, too. You're lucky you have each other."

She caught Stuart's reflection in the glass. He wiped at his eye quickly. "Yes, she's my life. She's all I have left of Sam. When Sam got sick, everything fell apart. She was the breadwinner, so we lost that income straight away, we lost the house, and we've been living in this motorhome ever since. But it's not sustainable. I'm going to Aberdeen so I can drop Alice off with my mum while I look for work and try to get back on my feet."

Amy continued to look out of the window, not wishing to crowd Stuart while he confided in her. "That sounds like a good idea. It will give her stability."

"Yeah, it's best for her."

Amy detected the tone and understood immediately. Stuart felt guilty. "It's best for you, too," she said. "You need time to grieve."

He was silent for a few moments, and Amy knew he was struggling with the ocean between managing personal grief and the responsibilities of being a single parent.

"You need to be the best parent you can be for Alice, you've clearly done that in the immediate aftermath," Amy continued. "She's loved, safe, and as happy as she can be. She needs time and stability to process what has happened, but you need that, too. Dropping her off with your mum, so you have some time to grieve, is best for both of you."

"I hope so," Stuart replied softly. "I feel like..."

"Like you're abandoning her?" Amy guessed.

"Yeah..."

Amy turned to face him. "You're not. You're clearly a devoted dad, but even the best parent needs some time to breathe and think about what has happened. What you're doing is giving Alice a loving family environment while you get some time to get yourself back together. Losing a partner is huge."

"So is losing a mother," Stuart pointed out.

"Alice is young. Kids are resilient and she will bounce back in no time. Losing a mother is hard, but with a great dad and a loving grandmother, she'll be okay. But you need to look after you, to make sure you can look after her."

Stuart glanced at her and offered a tight smile. "Thanks, I needed to hear that." He looked back at the road. "It's been hard, just the two of us."

"I can't imagine what you've been through," Amy confessed, "but I do know that you can't saddle yourself with guilt. You need your own time to grieve so you can get back to Alice as the best person you can be."

Stuart chuckled. "You know, when we get to Aberdeen, I have a feeling I'm going to be saying, 'Gosh, I wish Amy and Kerry were still here'."

Amy laughed. "I warned you about that."

CHAPTER TWENTY-SEVEN
WAITING

CLAUDIA RUBBED HER EYES. She rolled her shoulders to try to release some of the tension in them. She'd headed towards a lay-by and was waiting for further information. Waiting was the worst part of the job; so much time was spent in the car—waiting. At least eighty percent of her time was spent anticipating information, the remaining twenty consisted of racing after her prey. The feeling of a large hourglass over her head never went away. At a moment's notice, she could be tasked with tearing off in any direction, but for the moment, and for the last few hours, she had sat in the car waiting for a scrap of information.

People always assumed the life of a professional hunter was glamorous; little did they know that huge amounts of time were spent in solitude, often in a car. Claudia knew every single centimetre of the inside of her car. Within a day of owning it, she knew what every lever, knob, and button did. Before working in intelligence, she wouldn't have known how to turn her rear fog lights on. The stitching on the steering wheel was slightly frayed at the bottom where she had pulled on a minuscule thread a day after receiving the vehicle. She looked at the thread, dying to pull on it some more. With a sigh, she turned her head towards the window and looked out at the traffic that passed by. It wasn't a particularly busy road, but it was slightly more interesting than the inside of the car.

She hated relying on other people. Back when she worked for MI5, it was waiting for a team of analysts to find something, check it, report it to a higher level, double-check it, verify it, have it sent to the commanding officer, and then, finally, receive it herself. By the time she got information it was usually out of date. Nowadays she had to wait for Mark, which was far quicker and much more efficient, but still mind-numbingly tedious.

Amy and Kerry had managed to evade her at every opportunity. The analysts and profilers were stumped. Every time they had a lead on a direction, they ended up being wrong. The girls didn't fit with any profiling. Nothing about them seemed to make sense. It seemed as if they were always ten steps ahead, and no one knew where they were going or what their end goal was.

It physically hurt to have been so close to catching them. She knew that for the sake of five minutes, she could have arrested them. She should have been happy; it was the closest she had been to them and it was enough to spook them. The more spooked they were, the more pressure they felt. And with pressure came mistakes. No matter how well trained.

The car dashboard lit up with an incoming call from Mark. She sat up a little straighter and mashed the answer button on the steering wheel.

"Mark?"

"Get to the M80, northbound," he instructed.

Within seconds, she was speeding out of the lay-by and up the road. "What have you got?"

"I've been through reams and reams of footage. Knowing they like hitchhiking and service stations, I had a look at the local service stations where they were last seen. It took me a while, but I found them. I have a visual of them getting into a Mercedes Compass Motorhome number plate P726 JIQ. I plugged that into the ANPR, and they are currently on the M80 heading north. You're about an hour and a half behind them, if you hurry."

CHAPTER TWENTY-EIGHT
GOTCHA

"ARE you sure you don't mind?" Stuart asked as he fussed with the petrol pump. He looked clueless at why the screen was blank and the card slot was blocked.

"Not at all, we're disastrously low on road trip sweets," Kerry said. She leaned forward and pressed the button to start the pump. The machine whirred into action.

Stuart looked slightly embarrassed and shoved his bank card into the machine. He put his hand in his pocket and handed Kerry a ten pound note. "Can you get her a drink, nothing too sugary, and then some sweets. Maybe some real food, too, like a sandwich?"

Kerry took the money. "No problem, so you want me to get her a couple of bottles of wine and about twenty bags of crisps?"

Alice giggled. Kerry held out her hand, and Alice grabbed hold of it.

Stuart smiled. "Yeah, but no beer," he joked.

"Of course not, we're more refined," Kerry said.

"I'm going to use the bathroom," Amy called out from the front of the motorhome.

"Okay, Alice and I are getting some snacks," Kerry shouted back.

"Ooh, get me a Twix."

Kerry rolled her eyes. "She'd eat nothing but Twix if she was allowed," she told Alice. They started to walk towards the services. "And then she'd basically be a Twix. Two giant chocolate legs, wrapped in gold foil."

Alice laughed. "And with biscuit instead of bones!"

"And caramel instead of blood!"

Alice made a face, and Kerry chuckled. Alice was a darling girl, clearly devastated by the loss of her mother and her home life. But she was bright and kind, and Kerry was enjoying talking to her.

Some of the stress was beginning to lift after watching YouTube videos of Alice's favourite bands and talking about the latest talent contests on television. It had only been an hour, maybe two, and Kerry felt better.

Kerry held Alice's hand tightly as they crossed the car park. Being responsible for the young girl was the first time in a long time that she had to look after someone other than herself. He problems seemed less important now she was effectively the guardian of Alice.

They entered a shop, and Kerry looked at the sandwiches.

"I thought we were getting sweets?" Alice asked.

"Oh, we are, but we need to get some real food. Because then the sweets are so much tastier, like a dessert," Kerry told her. "Besides, if you just eat sweets you'll feel sick, and your dad won't be very happy either."

"Okay," Alice agreed.

They picked out a sandwich for her, a drink, and two bags of sweets. Kerry offered Alice the money to pay the checkout staff, but Alice squirmed behind her, unwilling to let go of her hand. Kerry smiled and told her it was fine, then turned towards the checkout and paid for the items. The assistant placed them in a plastic carrier bag and handed it to Alice before giving Kerry her change.

"Kerry Wyatt."

Kerry felt cold fear shoot down her back. The woman's voice was calm and professional, and right behind her. Kerry gripped Alice's hand a little tighter, hoping that she wouldn't be the reason for any further stress or horror in the girl's young life.

She slowly turned around. A woman in a suit, with long, dark hair swept into a ponytail, stood with her hands clasped in front of her. She was looking kindly at Alice with a small smile on her face. Kerry felt relief. She'd always imagined that the moment she was caught would include screaming and shouting, weapons being waved about, and it ending with her being pushed face first into the floor. This was almost serene.

"My name is Claudia McAllister. I need to speak with you." Her hazel eyes bore into Kerry; the message was clear that they were going to do this with as minimal fuss as possible. "Where is Amy?"

"Probably back at the motorhome," Kerry answered honestly. Fear was giving way to relief. Relief that it was over, and it wasn't nearly as awful as she'd thought it would be. "We're travelling with Alice and her dad. He is filling up with petrol."

"We should probably head there," Claudia said. She smiled down at Alice. "Do you have some sweets for the road trip?"

"Yes." Alice thrust her hand into the carrier bag and produced the two bags. "One for dessert, and one for later, in case we hit traffic."

"Always good to plan ahead," Claudia said. She stood to one side and gestured for them to exit the shop. Kerry walked Alice towards the motorhome.

Claudia walked beside them. Her hands were in the pockets of her long, black trench coat, and she looked around as they walked. "They are lovely shoes," Claudia indicated Alice's pink Barbie trainers.

"My daddy got them for me." Alice smiled widely, very happy with the compliment and not at all fazed by Claudia's sudden appearance.

Kerry had to admit that the woman obviously knew how to handle the situation. While her heart was beating like a drum in her chest, she could also feel the weight lifting off of her shoulders. Claudia felt safe, put-together, and competent. And there was only one of her. No black SUVs with men and semi-automatic machine guns. Just one woman, who seemed keen to put a young girl's mind at rest.

"Who are you?" Alice asked.

"I'm a friend of Amy's," Claudia replied. She was all smiles and disarming pleasantries.

They got to the motorhome, and Stuart was sitting in the driver's seat reading a magazine as he waited for everyone to return.

"Where's Amy?" Kerry asked.

He lowered his magazine and looked from Kerry to Claudia with a frown. "Dunno, she's still not come back."

"Where did she go?" Claudia asked.

"Who are you?" Stuart put his magazine down and stepped out of the motorhome. He held out his hand towards Alice, sensing that something was wrong.

"She went to the bathroom," Kerry answered.

Claudia blew out a breath and looked around the car park. "Get your things," she told Kerry. She turned towards Stuart. "I'm a private investigator working with the government. Miss Wyatt and Miss Hewitt are helping me with an investigation. I need your name and contact details."

Kerry leaned into the back of the camper van and pulled out her rucksack while Stuart relayed his information to

Claudia. He was obviously confused, but Claudia's manner gave him no room to query what was happening.

"Thank you." Claudia handed her business card to him. "I'll be giving Kerry a lift from here. If you hear from Amy, please call me immediately."

Claudia took hold of Kerry's elbow. "Let's go."

Kerry pulled back slightly and gestured her head towards Alice. Claudia looked at her curiously for a moment before realisation set in. She nodded and let go of Kerry's elbow.

"Hey, it's been real fun, but I have to go and help Claudia with some things. Sorry I can't come with you the rest of the way."

Alice looked sad but slowly nodded. "It's okay. Maybe I'll see you around?"

"I hope so, I'd really like that." Kerry gave Alice a quick one-armed hug and then turned towards Claudia. Claudia gestured towards the services with her arm, indicating that they both start moving. Once they were out of earshot, Claudia spoke, "Can you communicate with Amy? Can you tell her to give herself up?"

"No, we don't have a way to talk to each other. We had walkie-talkies, but I left one—"

"I'm aware." Claudia unclipped the missing walkie-talkie from her belt and held it out to Kerry. "Tell her it's over, and she needs to give herself up."

Kerry took the device. "I'll try, but Amy doesn't really listen to me."

"We'll walk while you convince her, she might still be around here." Claudia walked into the services, her eyes scanning every part of the room.

"We're innocent, you know, we haven't done anything wrong."

"I've heard that a few times before."

"I mean it, we were set up," Kerry implored.

Claudia stopped dead. She took Kerry's arm and thrust the walkie-talkie closer towards her mouth. "I need you to get your friend to give herself up, now."

Kerry let out a breath and pressed the button down. "Amy? You there?"

Claudia got her mobile phone out of her pocket and dialled a number. She held the phone to her ear while she continued to look around the bustling service station.

"Amy, come on, please talk to me." In her heart, Kerry didn't want Amy to answer. While Claudia seemed to be a better option than the black ops guys they had seen before, she was still the enemy, and Kerry had no idea where her loyalties lay. Part of her wanted Amy to stick to the plan, to get away and decode the USB data.

"This is Claudia McAllister, I need a local pick-up for Kerry Wyatt," Claudia spoke into her phone.

"Amy?" Kerry tried again even though her heart wasn't in it. All she wanted now was for Claudia to give up, give Amy a chance to get away before more agents descended, and all hell broke loose. She feared that Amy had no idea what was happening. She worried that she was actually buying a Twix somewhere and would any moment now plod around the corner with her mouth full of chocolate.

"I'm still looking for Amy, she can't have gone far. I suspect she's aware that her friend has been apprehended and is making her own getaway, but there's not much I can do about it until I can hand off this asset."

Asset. That's all she was now. An asset. A way to get information, information that would probably fall into the wrong hands.

"I need them here sooner than that, I'm losing valuable time." Claudia looked at Kerry and raised her eyebrow, gesturing towards the walkie-talkie.

"Amy?" Kerry tried again. "She might not even have it on," she told Claudia.

"Tell them to call me the second they arrive." Claudia hung up the call and started to make another. "Where would she go? Do you have a plan? A pick-up? Who are you working with?"

Kerry chuckled. "Working with? No one."

Claudia pressed the phone to her ear. "Is it Green Falcon? ISIS? Al-Qaeda?" She turned her attention back to her phone call. "Mark, I need CCTV of Bonnybridge Services now. I have Kerry Wyatt in custody, but Amy has slipped away."

"Al-Qaeda? Are you out of your mind? I'm an accounts clerk from Wakeham, not Jihadi Jane."

Claudia turned the mouthpiece of the phone away from her mouth. "We have intelligence that says otherwise."

"Then it's wrong," Kerry argued. "I don't know where you guys get your intel from, but come on. You must have looked into us both, do we seem like terrorists to you? Really?"

Claudia looked at her silently for a moment. She turned the phone back towards her mouth. "Call me the second you have anything." She hung up the call.

"Terrorists know how to appear ordinary. That's how they are so difficult to uncover," Claudia pointed out.

Kerry stared at her. She was serious. This woman seriously thought she was a terrorist. "How can you possibly think that Amy and I are terrorists? We have bumbled our way up and down the country. We've gotten lost, we've been at the mercy of anyone who would help us, we're hungry, scared, cold, and alone."

"You conned your way into people's homes in order to seek refuge, you exchanged clothes with homeless people in order to disguise your appearance—"

"Whoa, whoa, wait a minute." Kerry held her hand up. "We didn't con our way into anyone's homes. We have been invited in. We have left money in the places we've stayed. We've helped people. Amy gave her coat to a stranger because it was a cold night, not to change her appearance."

"Where is the USB stick?" Claudia asked.

"Amy has it."

"You will be searched when you get to the local station," Claudia explained.

"And they won't find the USB, because I don't have it." Kerry folded her arms.

Claudia shook her head. She looked around, probably scanning the services again for any sign of Amy. Kerry wanted to keep her talking to distract her, but she somehow felt that Claudia wasn't the sort of person who got distracted.

"You will be questioned," Claudia told her. "Your helpfulness during your questioning will directly relate to the sentence you will end up serving."

"Sentence?" Kerry gasped.

"The more help you are now, the less time you will serve." Claudia twisted her phone in her hand, the only indication of her stress. Her voice was slow, clear, and methodical. "We will find Amy, with or without your help. But your actions from hereon will dictate your future. I suggest you think long and hard about what you say."

"I am not a terrorist. I don't know any terrorists. I don't support them. I know nothing. I am just an accounts assistant, I watch *X Factor* and go to the pub occasionally with my mates from work, I read cheesy romance novels, I once forgot to tax my car for a couple of days, and I put fifty quid into a charity box as some kind of retribution for my crime. I am not a criminal."

Claudia regarded her silently.

Kerry swallowed. The last time she felt this nervous was when she had been falsely accused of stealing money from her mum's purse when she was eight. She'd been completely innocent, but still the fear of being found guilty ate at her and caused tremors to start throughout her body. This was bigger than the wrath of her mum. This was bigger than anything. Claudia had a poker face, and Kerry had no idea if she was getting through to her or not.

"Amy is innocent," she repeated. "If she's running, it's because she's scared. She found the USB stick under a table at work. A guy came in looking for it, she didn't trust him, and then he produced a knife and threatened to kill her if she didn't give it to him. As a good citizen and a decent human being, she wasn't about to give it up to him in case it had something important on it. He threatened us, he told us that he would set us up and convince your lot that we were terrorists. We ran because we didn't know if he was telling the truth or not, seems he was!"

"Where would she go?" Claudia asked.

Kerry sighed and shrugged. "I don't know. Amy's... kinda unpredictable. Normally, I'd say she'd charm her way into a lift with someone. But we were in the car park so she wouldn't take that risk." Kerry held out the walkie-talkie. "You ask her, she's not talking to me."

Claudia took the device. She looked around the concourse again. "Where were you heading?"

Kerry bit her lip. She wanted to be honest, wanted to show that she could be trusted. But the truth was, she didn't know if Claudia could be trusted. She couldn't put Amy in harm's way. "Just... away. We were looking for someone to help with the USB stick, but we didn't know where to go. We were just so scared about being caught."

Claudia didn't look like she bought it. She opened her mouth to speak but quickly closed it again as she looked behind Kerry.

Kerry peered over her shoulder. A local police officer was rushing towards them.

"Take her to the station. I'll be back in touch later," Claudia instructed him.

Kerry felt cold metal touch her wrist and looked down in surprise at the handcuff being clicked into place. She glanced up again, but Claudia was already rushing further into the services, searching for her prey.

CLAUDIA EXITED the women's toilet area and marched towards the first shop in the services centre. She'd already mentally calculated a plan to search the building in the most efficient order. The key was to be swift but thorough, sweep every part of the building in as little time as possible. Amy could well be unaware of what had happened and simply be going about her business.

Claudia knew she needed to capitalise on that if it were the case. However, she knew it probably wasn't. Too much time had elapsed, and the local police arriving would surely have tipped her off. It was most likely that there were only two options left. She was either hiding out in the services, or she had left and was making a getaway on foot.

She tapped at her earpiece to contact Mark. Every second not moving in the right direction was now a second wasted, and she needed immediate support to make the right decisions.

"I'm still searching for that CCTV. It's an old system, so it may not be accessible online," Mark replied.

"Fine," Claudia growled. "Then I need a map of the

surrounding area. I'm assuming she is on foot and hasn't braved the car park and isn't trying to hitchhike."

"I'm on it now," Mark replied. "Also, MI5 are on their way."

Claudia knew that investigators would dispatch the ground teams as soon as they heard of Kerry's capture. She also knew that the flat-footed oafs would just make a huge mess of the whole thing. MI5's way was loud, brash, and heavy-handed. They'd no doubt swarm the surrounding areas with armed personnel. In Claudia's experience, that was no way to capture anyone. Methodical, thoughtful, and considerate was the best way to seek and capture. Especially if you were seeking terrorists who were known to quickly go to ground at the first sign of trouble.

She couldn't shake off Kerry's words. Of course, it wasn't the first time that someone had desperately tried to convince her of their innocence. No one ever held their hands up and told her they'd done it all. Everyone had reasons. Excuses. But the passion of Kerry's denial, accompanied with her own doubts, flew in the face of the intelligence that MI5 had provided her. It wouldn't be the first time that MI5 had been wrong, but it would be a substantial blow to their reputation to be wrong by this magnitude.

"There's one hotel on-site," Mark said. "The petrol station is a little way from the main services building; it contains a small shop which has bathrooms. To the south is the motorway, to the east are fields, to the north and west is a canal. There are moorings for narrowboats just beside the back of the services."

Claudia moved on to the last shop inside the main building, already calculating the most efficient route to check the outer buildings before making her way to the canal.

"Thank you, Mark. I need to know if Kerry Wyatt says anything. Something is off about this case."

"Like what?"

"I'm not sure, I'm not one to usually take notice of a plea of innocence, but there was something about Kerry..." Claudia shook her head, not wanting to bring any further doubt into her mind. She needed cold, hard facts. "Just see what you can find out."

"I'm on it." He disconnected the call.

Claudia exited the main building and took a slow and careful look around the car park. There were a number of people who believed in hiding in plain sight. She had to admit, it was a brilliant tactic. Trying to blend into a crowd or just standing still and not bringing attention to yourself was a fantastic way of remaining undetected. Though she suspected that Amy was a little too manic for such tactics.

"H-hello?"

She looked down at the walkie-talkie that had crackled into life. She unhooked the device from her belt and held it to her mouth. "Amy?"

"Kerry is innocent," Amy said, through the static.

Claudia started to walk around the car park, trying to ascertain a direction where the connection would be stronger. It seemed that the device was nearing the edge of its range. Finding a stronger signal would help her pinpoint a direction of travel.

"Amy, you need give yourself up."

"No, I just need you to know that Kerry hasn't done anything wrong." The voice crackled weakly.

"Amy, it's over." Claudia headed in the opposite direction, not caring how ridiculous she must have looked to passers-by. "Tell me where you are and I'll come to you. I promise you that everything's going to be okay."

There was a pause. Claudia bit her lip and waited. She needed Amy to speak again, to get a direction.

"I-I can't trust you. Or anyone."

Claudia cupped her elbow in her hand and rested the

device on her forehead as she thought about her next words. "Why can't you trust anyone?"

"I've been framed."

"I can help you," Claudia said. The voice was starting to clear. She continued walking around the services and came to the hotel building. Amy was either inside the hotel, or she had taken the side path through to the canal.

"Just make sure that Kerry is okay."

Claudia thought for a moment. "I will. But you're the one who says you can't trust me." She hoped the slightly confrontational comment would encourage more conversation. Partly to find a direction on Amy's location and partly because she was curious. She'd never had such a conversation with a suspect before.

"Promise me that Kerry will be okay. I'll believe you then."

Claudia chuckled. The naivety was almost cute. "I promise," she said. "She is in custody with the local police. The task force will be too busy looking for you to take her out of the local station."

"They won't find me, I'm getting quite good at this."

Claudia laughed outright. "Yes, yes, you are," she admitted. "But that won't last forever. Come on, Amy. You must be tired? Cold? Hungry?"

"I'll figure it out." Amy sounded determined but uncertain. "Are Michael and David in trouble?"

Claudia frowned. "Who?"

"The gay guys back in Edinburgh. Are they in trouble for harbouring fugitives?"

"No, they weren't aware of your status."

"We told them we were on the run," Amy explained. "But we told them we'd been set up. Because we have."

Claudia shook her head in disbelief. Amy really didn't know when to stop talking for her own good. "Well, still, they didn't know your actual status."

"Which is?" Amy questioned.

"Wanted on terrorist charges."

"I'm not a terrorist," Amy denied quickly. "I don't know what it is about me that makes you think I am. Is it the hair? I do try to control it, but seriously, in this country, with this wind? No chance."

Claudia couldn't help but smile. She could see how Amy had managed to charm her way up and down the country. "Yes, it's the hair," she played along. "Maybe some hairspray?"

"Nah, I don't control my hair. It kind of has a timeshare agreement with my head. It just lives there."

"Amy... you can trust me. Please, tell me where you are?"

Claudia waited. And waited. She bit her lip and leaned in close to the walkie-talkie.

"Bye, Claudia," Amy whispered.

AMY TURNED the walkie-talkie off and clipped it onto her belt. She turned around to check if she was being followed, relieved to see that the canal path behind her was empty. She turned back and wiped at the tears which lay on her cheeks before shoving her hands back into her coat pockets.

She'd let Kerry down. When she'd walked around the corner and seen Claudia standing behind Kerry, she'd frozen. There was nothing she could have done, but still she felt guilt streaming through her. Kerry had been arrested. She was probably on her way to a cold prison cell somewhere, and it was simply because she knew Amy. Because Amy had made a stupid decision to run rather than to stop and seek help.

Although Amy was pretty certain that her decision was still the right one, if only because she had no idea who to trust. Clearly they had been set up. By whom and to what extent, she didn't know. And without that information she'd decided to Mulder it and trust no one.

She'd watched from behind a pillar as Claudia spoke with Kerry. She could see the terror in Kerry's eyes but was relieved to see Claudia was being calm and collected. She'd even taken the time to talk to Alice. Amy didn't want anyone to get caught, but if they had to be, then she had to admit that she was thankful that it was Claudia doing the catching.

But now she was alone, and her bravery had suddenly left her. Kerry was her best friend, and Amy always felt like she could do anything if Kerry was with her. Alone, she felt useless and silly. She had no idea how she was going to get to Aberdeen. A difficult journey had grown utterly impossible.

"Is everything okay, dear?"

She looked up to see a woman in her seventies. She was standing on the canal path with a small watering can, having been watering the plants that hung on the side of a narrowboat. The woman looked at her in concern. "Has something happened?"

Amy let out a bitter laugh. "Yeah, kinda."

"Well, you tell me all about it. I'll see what I can do to help."

Amy took a deep breath. She wasn't in the mood to come up with a reasonable lie. Everything felt like it was crashing down around her ears.

"I'm on the run from the police. I was with my friend, but my friend was just caught and now I'm on my own and I don't know what to do."

The woman walked towards her and looked sympathetic. "Well, why don't you come on board and have a cup of tea? I'm sure we can figure it out together."

Amy looked at the friendly face and slowly nodded. This had been her experience the whole time; everyone was so kind and helpful. She was pretty sure she could say she murdered someone, and people would offer her a digestive and a shoulder to cry on.

"You might get in trouble for harbouring a fugitive, though." She felt it best to warn her.

The woman laughed. "Well, let's see them try. I'm Lesley, by the way."

"Amy."

"Come on board, Amy, you should meet my husband."

Amy wiped at the tears on her face before nodding again. Lesley climbed on board the prow of the narrowboat and walked down a few steps into the galley. "Fred? I have a visitor. Put the kettle on."

Amy followed her down more steps and into the living quarters of the boat. She'd never been in a narrowboat before and was surprised to see it resembled her nan's bungalow. At the bottom of the steps was a proper sitting room, with two small sofas and an armchair, all in a floral pattern. Separating the sitting room from the dining area was a display cabinet filled with glassware and ornaments. Beyond the dining area she could see a tiny kitchen and a corridor off that that must have led to a bedroom. She looked around with a smile. It was a little house on the water. Everything was miniature, but there was everything you could ever need.

"This is so cute," she said. "And beautiful," she added, not wanting to offend her hosts.

"Thank you," Lesley said. "It's small, but it suits us, doesn't it, Fred?"

Fred walked into the living room, drying his hands on a tea towel. "It certainly does." He smiled at her and held out his hand. "Fred, lovely to meet you."

Fred looked to be a similar age to Lesley. He had glasses and thin, greying hair. He looked like a typical grandfather, and she instantly felt comforted. She shook his hand. "Amy."

"Would you like some tea, Amy?" he offered.

"Yes, she's lost her friend, and she's running away from the police," Lesley told him.

Amy held her breath and watched Fred's wrinkled face. She

waited for an argument to begin about harbouring fugitives. She was surprised when he laughed. "I'll get the biscuits as well, then."

Amy held the mug in a two-handed grip, appreciating the warmth of her second cup of tea. Lesley and Fred were telling her about their children and grandchildren. Their daughter lived at one end of the country, and their son at the other. Not wanting to play favourites, they bought the narrowboat upon retirement. They'd spend a few weeks moored near one child, before heading off to see the other. They repeated the procedure several times a year, using the travel time between the two as some much-needed respite.

She'd told them about her run-in with the police, about the USB stick, about Cara, and about Claudia. Fred had immediately agreed that she had been set up. He said he'd seen a television program about MI5 and had decided the whole lot of them were useless. He said that it was a miracle that the country hadn't been bombed to oblivion by the "bad guys", as he called them. Amy didn't have the heart to tell him that he'd been watching a drama and not a documentary.

Lesley was about ready to phone the Prime Minster and tell them, in no uncertain terms, that Amy was innocent and that the whole saga was ridiculous. It was only Fred reminding her that Amy was being set up that had stopped her from pacing.

An hour had passed since she had been invited on board, and she was starting to calm down and formulate a plan. She wondered if it was essential to her British DNA to have a cup of tea to instil a sense of calm within her. Or maybe it was the biscuits. She'd eaten a hell of a lot of biscuits.

It was obvious to Amy that she needed to get to Aberdeen,

to speak to Jason, and to prove both her and Kerry's innocence. Kerry wouldn't tell anyone her plan, so she felt fairly confident that no one would know where she was headed. She just needed to think about the best way to get out of the area and on her way to Aberdeen. Lesley was already looking at a map of canal paths and seeing how long it would take them to get there.

Amy was usually more cautious about telling people her destination, but losing Kerry had changed that. She wasn't even sure where she was, so finding Aberdeen was going to be impossible without help.

The problem was that narrowboats travelled at a similar pace to the average person walking. And canals didn't go in straight lines. It would take many days to get anywhere near to Aberdeen via the canals. Not to mention that canals didn't criss-cross the country like motorways and railway lines. Sometimes they stopped, and you had to travel via another mode of transportation to get to the next canal.

A knock on the door sounded.

This is it, Amy thought. Her heart started to race. She lowered herself down onto the sofa as Fred got up and open the door.

Amy held her breath. She wondered if it would all end on a floral sofa, on a narrowboat, feeling sick because she'd eaten too many ginger nut biscuits.

"Hello, Fred," a friendly female voice said. "I just wanted to let you know that some woman is asking all of the boat owners if we've seen that young girl that you took in a while ago. Of course, I didn't say anything to her. Not my place. But she's on George's boat at the moment, and then she'll be coming here. Just thought you should know."

"Right, thank you, Margaret. We better get moving."

Lesley stood up. "I'll untie us, you start the engine."

"Will do," Fred quickly headed towards the back of the boat. Amy watched him in confusion. She sat up and looked at Lesley. "What are you doing?"

"Performing the slowest high-speed getaway on record," Lesley explained. "We're not beaten yet."

CLAUDIA KNOCKED on the window of the narrowboat. Why anyone would choose to live on a narrowboat was beyond her. No one had a front door or a doorbell or a letterbox. She wondered how people had post delivered.

"Yes?" A man in his eighties walked through the hatch at the front of the boat. Claudia walked along the canal path to meet him.

"I'm looking for someone, Amy Hewitt." Claudia held up a poster with a selection of photos of Amy on it. "Have you seen her?"

As she approached him, he snatched the piece of paper out of her hand and raised his glasses to look at the image. "Hmm," he sighed.

Claudia noticed the woman she had previously spoken to, Margaret Chapel, was now walking along the canal path. Claudia looked at her curiously. Margaret smiled, and Claudia smiled in return. Something was up.

"Why are you looking for her? She in trouble?"

Claudia returned her attention to him. "Yes, she is, Mr?"

"Perry. George Perry."

"Mr Perry. My name is Claudia McAllister, and I am working with MI5 to track down that woman. Have you seen her?"

George returned his attention to the paper. Scrunching up his face as he peered at the picture. Claudia rolled her eyes and returned her attention to Margaret Chapel who was boarding the narrowboat in front of them.

When she was questioning Margaret, a loud yapping sound had come from within her narrowboat home. Margaret had invited Claudia aboard to continue their conversation, while she attended to her dog, Mrs Boo. Mrs Boo was an awful, yapping terrier who was clearly doted upon. The loud barking was deafening, but it gave Claudia the chance to scope out the narrowboat and ascertain that Amy was not hiding on board. She'd already been allowed to board and search two other narrowboats, which were occupied by holidaymakers. She knew she was close.

Having searched the hotel, the petrol station, and a couple of caravans, Claudia's last chance was the canal. As she had rounded the corner from the services she had sighed. A row of narrowboats all along the canal path were moored up, at least eight of them. Knowing Amy's talent for making friends, she surmised that the girl could be in any one of them.

"No, not seen her. What's she done?"

Claudia watched as Margaret hurried from the narrowboat in front of them and rushed past, not wishing to make eye contact. Suddenly, the boat was being untied from its mooring ring by a woman who then pushed the boat out into the canal, leaping on board as it moved. The engine sprung to life.

"Mr Perry, we need to follow that boat," Claudia told him firmly.

"Fred's boat?" He looked at the boat with a confused look.

"Yes, that boat," Claudia told him. "Now."

"It will cost you."

Claudia glared at him. "Fine, fine, just do whatever you have to do to make this thing move and follow them." She looked from George to the departing boat.

"A hundred pounds."

Claudia looked at him and raised her eyebrow. "Mr Perry, if you don't move this boat immediately, I'll have you arrested," Claudia threatened.

He mumbled something as he stepped from the boat and untied the rope mooring it to the bank. He looked at her. "You might want to get on board then."

~

"Is this as fast as we can go?" Claudia asked in frustration.

Initially, she had stood at the front of the boat, expecting that any moment they would speed up, and she would be able to jump to the other craft. It quickly became clear that they were travelling at exactly the same speed and wouldn't be closing the gap any time soon. When a woman walking her dog on the canal path overtook them, she made her way to the back of the boat to speak to George.

"The speed limit on canals is four miles an hour," George said.

Claudia stared at him, open-mouthed. "Four?"

"Yup."

"This thing can only do four miles an hour?"

"This thing? Thing? I'll have you know that *Ermintrude* has a GreenLine 43 HP diesel engine." George stood up from his stool on the tiny back deck. He pointed at the narrowboat in front of them. "They only have a Barrus 38." He let out a derisive snort.

"*Ermintrude?*"

"The name of this boat, didn't you see it when you got on board?" George sounded offended by Claudia's disinterest.

"Clearly not." Claudia sighed. "If we have this super engine, why are they so far in front of us?"

"Speed limits are speed limits." George shrugged.

Claudia let out a deep sigh and rested her head in her hand for a second. She looked up. "I get that we're not going to do a James Bond and fly through the air in a stream of machine gun fire, but is there a possibility that we could go a tiny bit faster? So that I could maybe see the boat in front of us? Maybe push it to, say, four and a half miles an hour? Five would be nice."

George let out a sigh and shook his head. "Fine. But if we get fined, then you're taking the blame."

"Trust me, I will take any and all blame. Just get us nearer to... whatever that boat is called."

She walked through the boat, back towards the bow. She looked at her phone and cursed the lack of signal. This was probably the one and only time she would consider ringing for backup, and she was on a narrowboat in the middle of the countryside with no signal.

～

It was another fifteen minutes before they were any closer. Claudia stood at the bow, watching the waves between the two boats. She'd attempted to call out to the man on the back of the other boat, but he had ignored her as he held the tiller and softly steered his vessel. She looked at her phone for the twentieth time in the last couple of minutes. There was still no signal, no way for her to tell the ground team that they were now far away from the services and on their way to god knows where.

She looked up from her phone and blinked in surprise. Amy stood on the small back deck. She had a cup of tea in her hands and looked directly at Claudia.

"Hi," Amy shouted.

"This is ridiculous," Claudia shouted back.

Amy shrugged. "You're just saying that because you're losing. And your boat is named after the cow from a children's TV show."

Claudia couldn't help but smile. She turned back to look at George who, at the back of the boat, was too far away to hear. She turned back to Amy. "What's yours called?"

"*The Kingfisher*. Cool, huh?"

"Very."

Amy spoke with the man steering the ship and then looked up at Claudia. "Fred says you're speeding."

"I'm chasing a fugitive."

"Fred says you're not supposed to make waves." Amy pointed at the waves coming from the boat.

"You can tell Fred that I wouldn't be making any waves if he stopped and let me arrest you."

Amy sipped her tea.

"This has to end eventually," Claudia called out.

"Is Kerry okay?"

Claudia shrugged. "I don't know," she said honestly. She held up her phone. "No signal."

Amy's brow knit in frustration. "I don't suppose it will help to say it again, but, you know, I'm innocent."

"So everyone tells me. It's not up to me to make a judgement on you, Amy. My job is to bring you in so you can be questioned."

"How did you get into this job?"

The narrowboat surged a little, and Claudia put her hands onto the rail to keep herself from falling. She glared at George who shouted an apology. She looked back at Amy. "I don't think that's really appropriate."

"Sure it is, you're chasing me. We're going to be here a while, unless you want to try swimming. You might as well tell me what made you start chasing people. Not judging or anything, but it's a bit of a weird job. It's like competitive speed-stalking."

"I signed up after the London bombings on Seven Seven." Claudia could tell by Amy's expression that she'd given away more than she had been willing to. Somehow, Amy had seen right through her.

"I'm sorry."

"For what?" Claudia tried to brush it off.

"For whatever loss you suffered. You did, didn't you?"

"Not exactly," Claudia confessed.

"But you saw something."

Claudia opened her mouth. How did she explain? Did she even want to? The boat surged a little again, and she was reminded where she was. On a narrowboat, about to shout out her sob story to a woman she was hunting. She closed her mouth and swallowed hard.

Amy offered a kind, understanding smile.

Claudia took a couple of steps back and leant on the roof of the boat behind her. She needed to remind herself, this was just a waiting game. It wasn't like Amy could go anywhere.

CHAPTER THIRTY-TWO
HOW DOES SHE DO IT?

IT HAD ONLY BEEN AN HOUR, but Claudia was starting to think of herself as something of an expert on narrowboats. It seemed that it was normal practice to keep to the middle of the canal. Until another boat approached from the opposite direction, then Fred and George would steer to the right and allow the other boat to pass on the left side.

Fred was obviously speeding, more so than George. But George was keeping up as best he could. The many turns in the canal were causing problems as both men had to slow down; the waves from the narrowboat in front were pushing *Ermintrude* back slightly. Claudia knew that they needed a long stretch of quiet canal so that George could really put his foot down, or whatever you did in a boat. Otherwise, a lock or a bridge would soon bring them both to a standstill anyway. It was just a matter of time.

They were approaching a large, sweeping corner. Another narrowboat was approaching from the other direction as Fred steered into the bend. It wasn't unusual, they'd performed this manoeuvre several times before. But something felt wrong. Fred looked shifty.

The Kingfisher was in the middle of passing the other narrowboat when suddenly Fred performed a hard turn, straight into the other boat. The front of *the Kingfisher* crashed into the back of the other boat. Fred shouted out an apology and held up his hands as if he didn't know what to do. Claudia could tell it was all an act.

The other boat was effectively pushed in between *Ermintrude* and *the Kingfisher*, wedged sideways between the two. Claudia spun around.

"They are going to shore, get to the bank," she shouted to George. George was way ahead of her, steering *Ermintrude* as best he could against the choppy waters and the narrowboat that was now drifting towards them.

Claudia climbed onto the roof of the narrowboat to get a better view. She saw Amy make a leap for the canal path. A moment later, Fred threw her rucksack to her. She waved goodbye to them and ran into the woods that lay just beyond the canal path.

"How does she do it?" Claudia murmured to herself.

~

Claudia stood in the middle of a clearing in the forest and looked around. She held her breath and listened intently for any sounds other than the birdsong that surrounded her. Amy only had a five-minute head start at best. But it seemed like it was enough.

As soon as she was free from the narrowboat, she ran into the forest, following the footprints Amy had left in the muddy floor for as long as she could. Soon it had become a game of guesswork, and now she was calmly trying to get a bearing on where Amy could have gone. She'd tracked suspects in wooded areas before, the smallest thing could send her in the correct direction. A smell, a sound, even a feeling.

Her phone rang. She hadn't even thought to check it once she'd entered the forest.

She tapped her earpiece. "McAllister."

"I have the CCTV footage from the service station," Mark told her. "You know, from when they first went on the run. It's... surprising."

"Surprising?"

"I've sent it to you, you should have it now."

"I'm kind of in the middle of something," Claudia told him. She crouched down to examine a cluster of leaves.

"You're going to want to see this right now," Mark told her.

Mark was rarely wrong about these things. If he was encouraging her to drop what she was doing and view the footage, there was a reason for it. Not that it didn't annoy her to be wasting the time she should be spending hunting for Amy. She got her phone out of her pocket and unlocked it. She quickly accessed the file and hit the correct button.

"It's downloading," Claudia told him.

"These girls are not professionals," Mark explained.

Claudia furrowed her brow. "Are you sure?"

"When you see the footage you will see what I mean. If these girls are part of a terrorist cell, I'll give up eating takeaway for a month, a year, even."

Claudia watched the loading circle with interest, willing it to speed up. "You sound pretty confident." She started to walk in a direction out of the clearing. The kicked-up leaves looked as good an indication of Amy's direction as any.

"Claudia, these girls have been set up. I don't know where MI5 have their information from, but it's wrong. Anyone looking at this footage, without bias, will easily see that these two are just average civilians."

She looked at the screen to see that the footage was about halfway downloaded. "I'm in the middle of the woods, my connection is terrible," she explained.

"The woods?"

"Long story. If you can get my location, I need you to ping it to MI5."

"You sure?"

"Yes, I've nearly lost Amy a couple of times now. If she goes to ground, we'll have no hints to work on. I need back up."

"I'm on it."

A piece of paper speared through a small branch caught her attention. She approached and cocked her head as she read the scribbled writing on it.

Rabbit traps, be careful. A x

She looked around the ground and saw a painful-looking metal trap which she hadn't noticed before in her hurry. She looked back at the note and shook her head. Amy had stopped in her getaway to leave a note. A note warning Claudia of danger. This girl was unbelievable.

Her phone beeped, indicating that the footage had downloaded. She held the screen up. "I'm playing it now," Claudia said.

The video started to play, and she watched with interest. Amy and Kerry were talking to someone off camera. They looked terrified, their line of vision moving quickly from one direction to another as they calculated their next move. Amy spoke again, and Claudia wished she knew what was being said. Suddenly the girls ran. The camera tracked them for a while before showing them vanishing into the ladies' toilet.

"Safe to assume it was a man they were talking to," Claudia commented.

"Yes, I'm looking for other angles to see if we can figure out who they were speaking with, but I'm coming up blank."

"What am I seeing now?" Claudia asked, the view having changed to an empty road.

Mark laughed. "Just wait for it."

Claudia let out a sigh. She didn't like waiting, and so far this entire case had been about waiting and near misses. And waiting at this particular moment was bordering on painful, knowing that she was so close to catching Amy and closing the case. She watched the empty road, her finger itching to slide along the trackpad and hurry time along a little. Just as she was about to do so, a car came into view. The shaky picture on an old CCTV camera made the scene all the more unbelievable. The car bounced heavily over speed bumps, the boot door open to the elements with two legs sticking out and flailing helplessly.

"What the..."

Mark laughed again. "Great, isn't it?"

Claudia scrolled the footage back so she could see it again. "Is that... Amy?"

"Sticking out of the back of the car and being driven over speed bumps? Yep, that's Amy. Why she's laying in the back of the car like that, I have no idea. But it's them. I have something else, too."

It sounded serious. "What have you found?" she asked.

"I've found footage of Tom's Café, going back months. The woman you asked me to look into, Cara, well, she comes in every morning without fail. She makes a drop, places something under one of the tables. Every evening a man comes in and picks it up."

Claudia raised her hand to her head, massaging at the stress that was forming. "Some kind of data drop," she mused.

"Exactly. Cara must obtain the information; she puts it on the USB and hides it in the services. In the evening, it's picked up. Same thing, every weekday."

"What about Amy?" Claudia asked.

"Oblivious," Mark said. "She chats to Cara, but she is unaware of the data drop happening under her nose. Until Thursday. She vanishes for a while, and when she returns she checks the tables and finds the USB stick. A while later she presumably accesses it, and then all hell breaks loose."

"She was investigating Cara's disappearance; she must have seen what you saw."

"It proves that these two aren't evading us because they are master criminals. They are just stumbling along. Somehow keeping ahead of us by luck, and probably bad judgement."

"We've been profiling them all wrong," Claudia whispered. She watched the footage again. Her mind swam at how someone could possibly get themselves into that predicament. "We're calculating what their next step might be based upon information that they are part of an elite terrorist cell, but... they're idiots."

"Exactly," Mark concurred. "Everything that seemed random was probably just random."

"Which means someone has set them up," Claudia said. "The information came from MI5; we have to assume that someone in-house is creating the lie. External information would have been counter-checked and discarded by now."

"Which means that someone inside MI5 planted false information about them," Mark said.

"And now, presumably, someone in-house is using MI5 analysts and software to find them so they can get there first. Probably to get the USB data they have, and kill them."

"That's my guess, too," Mark said.

"Cancel what I said before, don't tell MI5 where I am. Not until we know who we can trust." Claudia leaned against a tree. A potential spy within the agency was serious business. As incompetent as she knew MI5 could be, this was unheard of. She needed to think quickly, work out what information she could trust. Who she could trust. And, most importantly, who was in danger.

"I need you to come up here and get Kerry Wyatt," Claudia said.

"Me?"

"Yes, you."

"How do I do that?"

"I'm sure you'll figure out a way to fool the local police. You did used to work for MI5 after all. You know the drill," Claudia said. "I don't know who else to trust. We can't let MI5 take her in."

Mark was silent for a moment. "Okay, okay, I can do that. I can forge something. We just need to get the real MI5 away from her."

"Tell MI5 we're following a lead, send them somewhere away from here. We need to throw them off the scent so I can find Amy. I don't know what these girls are mixed up in, but I'm not about to let them get killed simply because they were in the wrong place at the wrong time."

"Right, okay, lie to MI5... got it." Mark sounded hesitant.

"I believe we just call it an 'alternative fact' these days, don't worry."

"Okay, I'll get on it."

"Call me with an update," she instructed and tapped her earpiece to disconnect the call.

She snatched the note from the branch. Amy was as innocent as she seemed. All this time she had been telling the truth, she was innocent. Someone had set them up. It was a one in a million chance. Now she had to find Amy before anyone else did.

She guessed Amy's most likely direction of travel and took off into the clearing.

"Amy!" she shouted.

She paused as the paths split into two directions and looked at the ground for any clues.

"Hands up."

Claudia froze at the sound of the male voice behind her. She slowly raised her hands, the note still gripped in her right.

"Now, slowly turn around."

She took a breath and slowly turned around. A man in his late twenties with short, black, and spiky hair pointed a gun at her face.

"You're Claudia McAllister?"

Claudia nodded. He was professionally trained; his stance and his handle on the weapon were military. But he was nervous. Something that Claudia knew she could use to her advantage. She took in a deep breath, judged the distance between them and then made her move. Snapping her head up she looked beyond his left shoulder. She watched as he quickly turned around to see what had caught her attention.

She launched herself at him, sending him flying face down into the ground. The gun clattered away. Before she had a chance to get a hit in, he was on his feet and elbowed her in the ribs, winding her. As he turned, she kneed him in the stomach and he fell to his knees.

She tried to make a move for the gun. He grabbed her foot, roughly twisting her ankle and causing her to cry out in pain as she felt the muscles twist in directions they ought not.

She crashed to the ground, her face heavily impacting the hard forest floor. Things moved slowly. Her vision blurred. She tried to push herself up, but her body refused to respond. She felt blood streaming down her nose, blocking her airway. Turning onto her back to get some breath, she opened her eyes to see him standing over her. He'd managed to retrieve the gun and was again pointing it at her face. He wore a furious expression.

Claudia knew that she was no use to him. There was no

need to keep her alive. She was a loose thread, nothing more. She resigned herself to a quick and painless death. Her eyes fluttered closed. She waited for the sound that she knew would be coming.

A sound did come. But it wasn't the sound she had expected. There was a scream, a woman's scream, but it wasn't her own. Then the sound of something solid hitting flesh. She opened her eyes to see Amy stood over her, a large, bloodied branch in her hand. The man was unconscious on the forest floor.

"I hit him really hard," Amy explained, staring down at his body. "I didn't know how hard to hit him. Like, what if I didn't hit him hard enough? And I just pissed him off and he shot me? But now I'm wondering if he's dead. Because I thought go big or go home." She looked at Claudia. "Is he dead?"

Claudia struggled to sit up and look at the man. She blinked a little to clear her vision. "No, he's not dead," she said upon seeing the leaves under his nose twitching. "Get his gun."

Amy stepped over him and picked up the gun between her thumb and forefinger. "What do I do with it?"

Claudia held up her hand expectantly, and Amy handed her the weapon. She quickly disarmed it. Putting her empty hand on the ground, she attempted to stand up. She winced at the shooting pain in her ankle.

Amy noticed and rushed to her. She pulled Claudia's arm over her shoulders and gently helped her to her feet.

"He might not be alone," Amy pointed out. "We should get out of here."

Claudia was struggling to focus her thoughts. She distantly recognised the disorientation of a head injury but pushed it to one side. The situation was too dangerous to fall apart now. They had to get to safety.

"Why were you here?" Claudia asked.

"I got turned around, I saw you and ended up following

you. I figured you'd never be able to follow me if I was already following you. Then I realised he was following you as well. You're pretty easy to follow. Like, you were following me, but two of us were already following you. It's funny when you think about it."

Claudia rolled her eyes. The girl really was an idiot. "I'm sure I'll laugh about it at some point."

"Come on, we have to get going," Amy told her.

"We?" Claudia asked. "You're... helping me?"

"Yeah, you're hurt. And he had a gun. And despite that hair, he might have friends."

"Have you forgotten that I'm supposed to be arresting you?" Claudia asked. Of course, she had no intention of doing such a thing now she knew the truth of the situation. But Amy wasn't to know that.

"I thought you might overlook it, seeing as I saved your life. But if it makes you feel better, you can arrest me later," Amy joked. "Can you walk?"

Claudia tested her weight on her ankle. "Kind of."

"Kind of will have to do," Amy told her. "Put your weight on me."

Claudia wasn't used to relying on anyone else. She attempted to let some of her weight rest on Amy.

"More than that, I'm a big girl." Amy shifted her into position. "Come on, let's get clear of the woods."

CHAPTER THIRTY-THREE
OUT OF THE WOODS

CLAUDIA WASN'T FAT. Not at all. In fact, Amy thought she was probably the perfect body shape and size. She was tall, but not too tall. And she was well built but not stupidly muscular or too big. Amy shook her head to rid herself of thoughts of the perfectness of the body that she was helping to support. Claudia wasn't fat, but she was getting heavier the further they travelled.

"Are you sure you're okay?" Amy asked, for the eighth time in the last twenty minutes.

"Yes, fine," Claudia replied through gritted teeth.

Amy knew that she wasn't okay. The way Claudia limped indicated the ankle was far more painful than she was letting on. Amy was also a little worried about a possible concussion. She'd seen Claudia hit the ground hard, and her replies claiming good health were becoming more and more slurred.

Luckily, Amy had a St John's Ambulance badge. It was fifteen years old, but she'd earned it fair and square on the away day with school. Although, the more she thought about it, the more she realised that everyone had gotten one that day. Maybe they were a whole class of soon-to-be doctors.

"I hear traffic," Amy said. "We'll head for the road and then hitchhike."

"Dangerous," Claudia mumbled.

"Yeah, but is it really more dangerous than being in the woods with a guy I clobbered with a branch?" When no answer came, Amy paused and looked at Claudia. "Should we rest a bit?"

Claudia took a couple of deep breaths. When Amy had first supported her, Claudia had been careful to not lean her weight fully on her. Now, Amy felt that Claudia would crumple to the ground if she wasn't holding her tight.

"No, we should get out of the woods," Claudia admitted.

"But a minute or—"

"We should go now," Claudia cut her off.

Amy understood. Claudia was worried about how much longer she'd be able to keep up the pace. She was pushing herself to get them both to safety, and when she was there, she'd rest. If she stopped now, she was worried she might not be able to start again.

"Okay, but before we do…" Amy reached into her coat pocket and rummaged for what she was looking for. She pulled out a bag of M&Ms. "Eat these."

Claudia stared at her.

"Seriously, a little sugar hit." Amy held out the M&Ms with no intention of taking them back.

Claudia sighed. She held her open palm out, and Amy shook a few of the sweets into her hand.

They started to walk again. Claudia put a couple of M&Ms into her mouth.

"I'm not bad for a terrorist, am I?" Amy grinned.

"You're not a terrorist," Claudia said around a mouthful of chocolate.

"Oh, you admit that now?" Amy couldn't hide her surprise.

"I saw the CCTV footage of your getaway at the services in Wakeham."

"And that made you believe that we're not terrorists?" Amy frowned.

"No terrorist would get them self into the predicament you got yourself into." Claudia chuckled. "How long were you dangling out the back of the boot?"

"Hey, I was doing my best." Amy smiled.

"How long?"

"The longest thirty seconds of my life," Amy admitted. "I did tell her to go, go go."

"Oh, well, then you got what you deserved because she certainly did that." Claudia looked up. "I can hear traffic."

Amy wondered if Claudia remembered that Amy had already pointed that out just a few moments ago. "Do you have any money with you?"

Claudia shook her head. "No, I have my bank card, but I'm loathe to use it. They'll track it immediately. Same with my phone... but I have to call Mark."

"Who's Mark?"

"I usually keep some cash on me, but I've spent it," Claudia continued.

Amy scrunched up her face. It shouldn't be relevant, but she needed to know. "Who's Mark?" she repeated.

"My colleague. He's an analyst, but he is on his way up here. To keep Kerry safe."

They were nearing the edge of the woods. Amy smiled. "You kept your promise."

"I kept my promise," Claudia acknowledged. "But I need to tell him what's happened and arrange a coded message so he can pick us up. Preferably just before we get a ride out of here. We have to assume they're tracking my phone."

"Won't they know what you say to him? They'll target Kerry..." Amy started to worry.

"They can't listen to the details of the call, just triangulate where the call was made from geographically."

"Oh." Amy suddenly realised how little she knew about the spying powers the government had. As far as she'd been concerned, everywhere had facial recognition and everything was powered by androids. She wondered just how little she knew.

Just a single line of trees stood between them and the main road. She'd been watching the traffic flow, seeing how many cars went by a minute. Judging how quickly she could get them out of there.

"Make the call," Amy said. She gently extracted herself from Claudia and helped her to lean against a sturdy tree.

Claudia frowned. "Once I make the call, it will only be minutes for them to get a location on us..."

"Are you doubting my ability to convince someone to give us a ride? Have you learnt nothing these past few days?" Amy chuckled and lowered her rucksack to the ground. "Make the call, I'll get us a lift."

Amy turned and climbed up the small bank towards the road. She stood on the edge of the road and waited for a car.

As she waited, she replayed in her mind the memory of Spiky standing over Claudia, pointing a gun at her face. Amy had been in no doubt that he was about to kill her right there. She'd rushed in without thinking about herself or her own safety. Spiky had terrible hair, but he was definitely some kind of elite-trained secret agent. Amy knew she was lucky that she had managed to knock him out. She still felt sick to her stomach when she recalled the sound of the thud that had rung out when branch and head collided.

Amy shivered at what would have happened if she hadn't got turned around. If she hadn't found herself suddenly behind Claudia and following her, allowing her to see Spiky and his attack. Claudia would surely be dead. And Amy would be skipping through the woods being pleased as punch at her evasion skills, not knowing that a cold-blooded killer was getting closer with each passing minute.

A car appeared over the hill in the distance, and she took a step forward so she was more visible. She waved her arms in the air and looked pleadingly at the driver. As often was the case, the car started to slow down and stopped beside her. The male driver was in his forties and wore a business suit. He opened the passenger window and leaned over.

"Hey, everything okay?"

Amy plastered her biggest relieved smile onto her face. "Hi, thank you so much for stopping," she gushed. "My friend and I were walking in the woods, and she's hurt her ankle. Could you give us a lift to civilisation?"

The man looked her up and down, and Amy did her best to look safe and a little pathetic. It always helped to look like a kicked puppy.

"Just the two of you?" he checked.

"Yup, and my rucksack which is as big as a ten-year-old child, but I swear, it's just a rucksack."

He laughed. "Sure, I'm heading to Airth. Is that okay?"

"Perfect," Amy said. She had no idea where she was and no clue where Airth was, but it wasn't here so that was fine. She jutted her thumb towards the tree. "I'll get my friend; I'll be one minute."

~

Claudia was quiet in the car. Amy kept talking to their driver, Darren, and occasionally looked over at Claudia to check that she was doing okay. Of course, Claudia maintained that she was fine, offering a tight smile at any enquiry as to how she was doing.

Darren was thankfully happy to talk about his work. He

sold something, Amy hadn't been listening. Of course, Darren thought she was intrigued by the way she leaned forward and made all the right noises. But she couldn't really bring herself to listen, she was far too busy watching Claudia from the corner of her eye. Not that Claudia didn't know exactly what she was doing. She suspected that nothing passed Claudia by.

"So, I can drop you off on the high street?" Darren's voice caught her attention.

"Oh, no, could you drop us on the edge of town? I have a friend who lives near there, and we can get her to pick us up," Amy lied smoothly. She didn't want to be dropped off in the middle of a CCTV-filled high street.

"Sure, you mean by the hotel by the roundabout?"

"Yes, that's perfect," Amy said. She hoped it was the right answer. Judging from Darren's silent nod, it was.

She chanced another look at Claudia.

"Stop fretting," Claudia mumbled to her.

"You definitely have a concussion," Amy murmured in return.

Claudia looked away, gazing out of the window. Amy surmised that being perceived as weak wasn't one of Claudia's strong points. If Claudia wasn't about to admit that she was ill and needed to rest, then Amy was going to have to take charge.

"You know what? Here is perfect," Amy told Darren.

"Here?"

"Yup, here's great. I recognise it now. Right here is great." It was a deserted country lane, but there were empty fields on either side of the road and Amy had a plan.

Darren looked confused but pulled the car up regardless. Amy opened the door and got out. She dragged her rucksack out, and, waiting for Claudia, she leaned in through the open passenger window. "Thanks for the lift."

Darren looked around the quiet country lane. "Are you

sure you want to be dropped here? It's a fifteen-minute walk into town."

Amy indicated the old post office building on the other side of the road. "My friend works there."

"You sure?" Darren asked as he looked at the building.

Amy looked at it again and realised it was completely derelict. It had probably been closed for fifty years.

"She's, um, a decorator. Doing it up." Amy added.

Claudia snorted a small laugh.

"Okay, get home safe," Darren said. He drove off, and Amy waved until he was out of sight. She turned to Claudia and let out a breath. "Okay, how far do you think you can walk?"

"As far as we need to, what's your plan?" Claudia replied, leaning on a stone wall for support.

Amy knew that Claudia wouldn't be able to get far, which was why she had asked Darren to stop the car where they were. The road was lower than the open fields on either side. A short hike to the top of one of the hills, and they could easily set up Amy's tent away from sight of the road. It wasn't ideal, but she didn't want to take Claudia into town in her current condition. She was doubtful how much further Claudia would make it; the woman clearly needed a rest, whether she was up for admitting to that or not.

"We're setting up my tent, over that ridge," Amy explained.

Claudia's head snapped up to look at the field. She looked back at Amy, as if half-expecting her to be joking. "What?"

"We're setting up my tent, over that ridge," Amy said slowly.

"I've twisted my ankle, not had a lobotomy, you don't need to speak like that."

Amy rolled her eyes and heaved up her rucksack onto her back. "You may not want to admit it, but you're in a lot of pain and you need to rest. Your Mark person won't be able to get up here for hours. We have very little money. There's at least one man after us, probably more. If we go to town, then they will probably find us, or we'll be trying to avoid CCTV and whatever for hours. This way, we get off the beaten track, off the radar, and we can sit and wait it out in a safe location, where no one will find us."

"You... want us to camp?"

"Yes, we need to set up now. It's going to get dark soon."

Claudia looked at the sky as if only just realising it was coming up towards the end of the day.

"I'm just trying to be sensible and get us—well, you—somewhere safe. So, we can wait it out. Because I kinda need you and you kinda need me. We're in this together now." Amy finished tightening the rucksack straps around her waist. "We need to set up for the night. You said Mark won't be here for another nine hours. Well, I hate to break it to you, but that is tomorrow morning."

Claudia continued to look around the country lane, seemingly still surprised by the turn of events. Her reaction made Amy worry more.

"And I'm exhausted. If I don't rest soon, I'm going to pass out," Amy added. If Claudia wasn't going to rest for her own sake, she could rest for Amy's instead.

CHAPTER THIRTY-FOUR
CAMPING WITH DUMMIES

CLAUDIA LEANED against the large tree and watched Amy prepare the tent. She would never admit it, but she was glad they were stopping. It was extremely painful to put pressure on her ankle, and her head was throbbing. Having a break would have been the very last thing she suggested, but going along with Amy's suggestion was easy considering the pain she was in.

It was obvious that Amy was hardly an expert when it came to camping. Claudia smothered a smile when Amy started referring to a large, yellow dummies guide for information on putting up the tent. It might have been the headache and the hazy vision, but she was seeing Amy in a very different light. If she were honest with herself, she had always had doubts about Amy being involved in terrorism. At the back of her mind, something gnawed away that it hadn't seemed that likely. But she had a job to do, and that always came first.

Trying to analyse what was real and what was fake, who to trust and who not, wasn't helping her headache. The facts of the matter were clear; Amy and Kerry had been set up.

Someone was willing to kill her, and presumably them, to get the USB stick.

"Do you know what's on the USB stick?" Claudia asked.

Amy lifted her head up. "No, I didn't get much time to look at it before Spiky came in and threatened to make me a human knife rack."

"Spiky?"

Amy gestured to her head. "You know, bad hair job, had a gun."

"Ah." Claudia understood now. "So, it was Spiky at the services?"

"You saw that, too?" Amy asked.

"No, Mark did, he told me what was happening. Well, as much as he could tell from the CCTV footage anyway. Tell me in your own words?"

Amy sucked in her cheek. She stood up and brushed the dirt off her hands. "So, I work... worked... in a coffee shop in the services. Just temporary, you know?" She looked at Claudia expectantly.

Claudia nodded even though she knew there was nothing temporary about the job. Amy was settling for something comfortable rather than casting herself into the real world.

"Cara came in every weekday morning. We'd chat a bit..." Amy turned around and started fussing with the tent. "We got on, or I thought we did anyway."

"You liked her?" Claudia asked.

Amy looked at her. "Does my file say I'm gay or did you guess? Do I look gay?"

"Your mum told me," Claudia admitted.

Amy rolled her eyes like only a daughter frustrated with her mother could. "She outs me every chance she gets, I swear."

"Mine, too." Claudia pretended to let it slip, but in honesty, it was a calculated move. She wanted Amy to be able to confide in her, and, for a reason she couldn't quite place, she needed Amy to know.

Amy's eyes bugged, and Claudia tried to keep her smile in check.

"Oh... well, yeah, I guess I like her. She'd never like me, I know that, but it's nice to pretend."

Realisation hit Claudia like a brick. *She doesn't know.*

"Anyway, she was just distracting me to place a USB stick under her table. I checked out the CCTV and saw that a guy came in every night to pick it up, Spiky."

"You checked the CCTV yourself? Were you allowed to access that?"

"Well, not exactly," Amy admitted. "But Cara had gone missing and I wanted to see if I could track her down myself. The police were useless." She put her hands on her hips. "One even said he didn't like my coffee. Can you believe that?"

Claudia fought back a smile, but before she had a chance to answer, Amy had turned around and was unrolling a sleeping bag inside the tent. "Anyway, I saw what she was doing. Realised that she obviously isn't interested in me, she was just using me, distracting me. Which makes sense because she is way, way out of my league."

"Maybe she was doing both?" Claudia murmured.

Amy popped back out of the tent. "Hmm?"

"Maybe she did like you. There would be other ways to distract you if that's all she wanted to do."

Amy seemed to mull that over. The way she scrunched up her face and considered the matter was bordering on cute. Claudia knew that she must have a concussion.

"Maybe. Doesn't matter now, anyway. You need to rest," Amy told her. She pointed into the tent.

Claudia decided to not argue with her. She pushed away from the tree and started to limp towards the tent. Amy met her and helped her along. After some manoeuvring, she got into the tent and slid along until she was laying on the sleeping bag. It was surprisingly comfortable. Either that or her standards had considerably lowered following the last couple of hours.

Amy threw her coat down on the polythene tent groundsheet and undid her boots. As she fiddled with the laces she started to laugh.

"What?" Claudia asked.

"I'm just remembering the narrowboats."

Claudia smirked. "That was ridiculous."

"We were going, like, six miles an hour," Amy said.

"Four, there's a speed limit on the canals. George told me."

Amy turned around, a full smile on her face. "George? Mine was Fred."

"Oh, I would have much preferred a Fred. George was miserable. And I had to pay him."

"No way, really?"

"Yes, he was a wily old sod," Claudia said.

"Huh." Amy turned her attention back to her boots. "Lesley and Fred were really nice."

"You seem to stumble across really nice people," Claudia commented.

"I think most people are nice."

Claudia shrugged out of her coat and balled it up to act as a pillow. "I can't believe you managed to evade us by just bumbling around."

Amy pushed off her boots and edged into the tent. "Hey, we didn't bumble around." She turned an electric light on and closed up the tent flap, zipping it securely.

"You did."

"Just because it was so easy to evade you and all your drones and spy shit doesn't mean we were bumbling around," Amy said. She smiled as she sat cross-legged and looked at Claudia.

"Drones and spy shit?"

Amy wafted her hand around. "Yeah, I know your tactics."

"Clearly." Claudia chuckled. She took a deep breath. She had to tell her. "Amy?"

Amy looked at her. "Hmm?"

"Amy, I'm sorry to be the one to tell you this, but... Cara's dead."

The colour drained from Amy's face, and Claudia wished she was better at these kinds of things. She'd been through sensitivity training like everyone in her job had. But telling people repeatedly that friends and colleagues were dead made it commonplace.

"We don't know the extent of her involvement in the plot, but she was murdered."

"I knew it," Amy whispered. A tear fell down her cheek. "I said she might be dead, to the police."

"There was nothing you could have done."

Amy reached into her pocket. "Did she die for this?" She held the USB stick.

"Possibly," Claudia allowed.

"Spiky said that there was a tracker on this, that when I plugged it into my laptop, it signalled to you lot that I had it. That's why they came for me. Is that right?"

Claudia licked her lips. Giving out information pertinent to national security wasn't something she'd normally ever do. But Amy deserved to know some of the truth.

"Yes. It was known that information was being taken. A piece of code with a tracker was added so the next time it was accessed, the location would be broadcast. Sadly, it was you who accessed it."

"Why did they bring you in? You're freelance, right?"

Claudia let out a sigh and laid down, snuggling her throbbing head into her makeshift pillow.

"I am self-employed. They contacted me because of my reputation; the stakes were very high and they needed results."

"Why are the stakes so high?"

"I can't tell you that." Claudia was only going to go so far on the information train. There was a slim chance that this was an elaborate double bluff. The very thought hurt her head more.

"But you used to work for them?" Amy persisted.

"I was an MI5 agent, yes."

"Cool."

"Not really."

"Why did you leave?"

"Why does anyone leave a job they loved? Because of management." Claudia closed her eyes and massaged the bridge of her nose with her thumb and forefinger in an attempt to relieve the pressure.

"Ew. Did he try it on?"

Claudia barked out a laugh. "No, no. My immediate boss was my girlfriend's father, he's a nice man. Too nice for the service. He's a fall man, and he doesn't even know it."

"What do you mean?"

Claudia opened her eyes and turned her head slightly to look at Amy. "The intelligence services are about seeking out information and deciding what to do with it. It's not like a factory where they produce, say, cars. It's intangible. Decisions have to be made, often based upon hunches. Mistakes are made all the time. Sometimes those mistakes are catastrophic, and, in those cases, government require an answer as to what went wrong. And the service needs someone who is in a position of power but not too important, so they can throw them under the bus."

Amy scrunched up her nose. "That sounds awful."

"It is. So, I left."

"You said *was*, what happened?"

Claudia furrowed her brow.

"You said he was your girlfriend's father, what happened?" Amy repeated the question.

Claudia attempted a shrug. "We split up."

Amy regarded her suspiciously. "Something happened. You said he was your girlfriend's father. Not he is your ex-girlfriend's father."

"Semantics."

"No, it isn't," Amy assured her. "She hurt you, you're distancing yourself from her. You don't have to talk about it, it's okay."

Claudia chuckled bitterly. "How very kind of you." She lowered herself back down and settled her hands over her stomach, concentrating on slowing her breathing. It was a relief to be off her ankle, but her mind was racing with information and the chance of sleep seemed slim.

"Affair?" Amy guessed.

Claudia rolled her eyes.

"Yep, affair," Amy confirmed to herself. "That sucks, sorry."

"I didn't say that she had an affair," Claudia argued, sitting up and leaning on her elbow.

Amy looked at her for a few moments. "You should rest."

Claudia opened her mouth to argue but didn't have the energy. She flopped back down onto the ground, wincing at the jolt.

"If it helps, she was an idiot," Amy mumbled.

Claudia smiled. "Thank you," she whispered.

"What happened on 7/7?" Amy asked.

Claudia sighed. "You don't let up do you?"

"People say I talk a lot," Amy confessed.

"People are right."

It was silent for only thirty seconds before Amy spoke again.

"So?"

Claudia sat up again. "Are you seriously going to badger me about this? A concussed woman?"

"You've been telling me you were fine for the last hour," Amy replied with a smirk. She reached into her bag. "Besides, you shouldn't sleep yet. You need to eat and drink. Luckily for you, I have a lot of supplies."

AMY WATCHED the steady rise and fall of Claudia's chest. Promising herself that she was just checking her breathing, nothing more. The woman had quickly fallen into a deep sleep, and Amy itched to check her mobile phone for medical advice. She was sure that someone with a suspected concussion was supposed to rest. But the self-doubt within her wondered if that was completely wrong, and the advice was to absolutely not rest under any circumstances. It seemed unlikely.

She felt blessed to be in Claudia's presence while the woman soundly slept. Claudia didn't seem like the kind of person who would ever let her guard down. Amy had to remind herself that the only reason Claudia was doing this was because she was in pain.

Over the past hour, Amy had sat like a guard dog. She'd listened for any sounds outside. Sat stock-still so as not to disturb Claudia and watched her, occasionally wondering about the woman's life.

She was an ex-spy. She was a lesbian, or bisexual, but she was definitely into women. She had an ex-girlfriend who had been foolish enough to cheat on her. Amy knew that she would never cheat on someone as strong, confident, and beautiful as Claudia. She shook the thought out of her head. Now was not the time to develop a silly crush on the woman. Amy could feel the heat rising in her cheeks as she admitted to herself that her thoughts about the unconscious hunter hadn't been entirely pure.

She bit her lip as she fiddled with the loose thread on her thick socks. In her mind she replayed the events of her rescue, that's what she called it; a rescue. She had rescued Claudia from Spiky, his gun, and his crimes against hair gel. A smile crept across her face, and she felt herself beaming with pride. Claudia may think of her as a bumbling idiot, with flyaway hair and no prospects, but at least Amy would be able to say that she rescued her. She saved the life of a spy. Ex-spy. Whatever, she'd done it.

"You look smug."

She turned around to see Claudia sleepily looking at her.

"Good morning to you, too," Amy said softly, not wanting to break the spell just yet.

"How long was I asleep?"

Amy looked at her watch. "Nearly three hours."

"Have you slept?" Claudia enquired, seemingly already knowing the answer.

Amy shook her head. "I was guarding you... us, the tent. You know, the lookout."

"What happened to being exhausted and possibly passing out if you didn't rest soon?"

Amy felt heat on her cheeks. "Might have lied."

Claudia chuckled. "Might have, huh?"

Amy continued to play with the loose thread on her sock. Anything to distract from Claudia's sleep-mussed appearance and throaty laugh. She wanted to scream into the thick padding of her gloves. What was it about her and successful women who were completely out of her league? Was she so starved for attention that she was doomed to crush on whomever fate put in front of her?

"You should probably sleep." Claudia looked at her watch. "It's just turned midnight, and I'm not due to contact Mark until ten. That should be enough time for him to get up here, establish a safe location, and secure Kerry." Claudia sat up and rubbed at her eyes. She brushed her fingers through her hair.

Amy licked her dry lips and looked away. It seemed somehow private to watch Claudia waking up. Intimate.

"I don't think I could sleep," Amy said.

"I understand."

I don't think you do, Amy thought. She needed to change the subject. Claudia was an ex-spy and was going to easily figure out Amy's not-so-subtle crush.

"How are you going to contact Mark?" Amy asked. She fussed with her bag, pretending to be looking for something within its depths.

"We have a one-hit way to communicate," Claudia explained. "My phone is being tracked, but I have software to mask the signal briefly. I can make one call before they reverse triangulate it and figure out the new signal."

Amy blinked and looked up at her. "In English?"

"My phone, all phones, have a unique identifier. That identifier is being traced. I'm going to change that identifier and make a call to Mark, which means they won't be able to tell my phone has been used. However, they will be tracking Mark's phone as well. So, they will see a new call come in from a new identifier and figure out it's me. They will triangulate the location of the new identifier and find us, but it will take time. Hopefully enough for Mark to get here."

"Why will they be tracking Mark's phone?"

"The second they started to investigate me they would have pulled my phone records, they would see that Mark and I communicate frequently, and they will have put a trace on him, too."

Amy shivered at the thought of it. "Scary stuff."

"It is when you are on this side of things. But when you have a terrorist cell planning to kill as many people as possible, preventing them from communicating, or knowing you can find them if they do, is essential. Yes, I know all the arguments for civil liberties. But, personally, I would rather this than have innocent people being murdered because we had the technology but couldn't use it."

Amy nodded slowly. Claudia clearly had strong feelings on the subject. Amy couldn't blame her; she couldn't imagine the things she had seen in her line of work.

"I'm sorry, that was a little harsh," Claudia admitted.

"It's okay. I get it." Amy's eyes met Claudia's. She swallowed and quickly returned to digging in her bag. She wasn't looking for anything, just trying to defuse the situation. She'd decided that Claudia's eyes were hypnotic, and she'd spill all her secrets if she stared into them for too long.

"Amy?"

Amy felt her heart beating out of her chest. "Yes?" She risked a sideways glance at Claudia.

"I need to make a splint, or some kind of a brace for my ankle, something to support it. Do you have anything I could use? You seem to have packed everything." She gestured towards Amy's rucksack.

Amy looked at the rucksack and then at Claudia. "Sure, what do you need?"

"I don't suppose you have—"

Amy was already unloading her bag. "I have a couple of small towels, I have a first aid kit, travel Scrabble, which is stupid and won't help you with a sprained ankle so ignore I said that... God, I'm stupid." She sighed and carried on unpacking. "Clothes, clothes, you're welcome to use whatever you need. Bottle of water, food, um..." Amy felt the blush in her cheeks burning. She was at the awful stage in her crush where she constantly said the wrong thing and embarrassed herself. She continued unpacking. "A small toolkit, wash bag, um... tape... extra socks—"

"Can I have a towel, the water, the tape, and the Pocket Scrabble?"

Amy looked up at her. She nervously licked her lips. She didn't want to be mocked, but she had a feeling it might be coming.

"Sure..." She handed the items over, one at a time. "What are you going to do?"

"I'm going to use the towel and the water to cool the ankle and reduce the swelling. Then I'm going to tape it up, using the tape as sort of outer ligaments to keep things where they should be. Then, I thought we'd play a game of Scrabble to kill some time until you felt ready to sleep? But we don't have access to a dictionary, so I'm relying on you to let me cheat when I make up words."

Amy bit her lip and nodded. "That sounds fun."

∾

Amy jumped. She sat up and looked around, trying to figure out where she was and what was happening. A hundred thoughts raced through her mind in a split second.

"It's okay," a familiar voice whispered.

She looked down to her side to see Claudia laying in the sleeping bag and looking up at her with concern.

"Sorry," Amy said. "Didn't mean to wake you."

"I was awake. Nightmares?"

Amy couldn't remember. She couldn't even remember falling asleep. The last thing she could remember was scowling at her Scrabble vowels. She'd wanted to show off a little.

Display her intelligence to Claudia. But she'd been tired and dealt the worst letters. The only move available to her was to add two O's to the P in 'occupied' that Claudia had put down.

She looked down and realised that Claudia's long trench coat had been placed over her like a blanket. No matter how she scanned her brain, she couldn't remember the events leading up to her falling asleep. Nor the reason for her waking up.

Her shoulders felt tense with stress. Her whole back ached from tensing her muscles throughout the last few days. With a sigh, she laid back down. The chill from the cold night permeated the tent. She pulled the coat back over herself.

"Thanks for the loan."

Claudia chuckled. "You loaned me your sleeping bag, it was the least I could do."

They lay side by side. Amy's mind was spinning so fast with questions that she was starting to feel dizzy. She needed to talk. Release the tension in her mind, as well as in the tent.

"What do you think is on the USB?" Amy whispered.

"I don't know. Sensitive government information," Claudia suggested.

"Do you think Cara stole it?"

"I think that's very likely."

Amy sighed. She was usually an excellent judge of character, but apparently not when it came to Cara. She'd been blinded by a good-looking woman wearing a fancy suit and speaking in an exotic accent. In her mind was a fantasy world where Cara could do no wrong. She'd even imagined Cara doing charitable events at the weekend. How wrong she was.

"And she was passing it on to... who?" Amy asked. She turned her head to look at Claudia.

Claudia was lying on her back, staring up at the ceiling. It was only then that Amy realised the torch they had been using to play had been dimmed. It was just light enough to make out Claudia's facial features, but dark enough to sleep.

"A terrorist group?" Amy asked at Claudia's prolonged silence.

"Maybe."

Amy licked her lips. Part of her didn't want to know, but the bigger part of her simply had to. "Do you think she was a terrorist?"

Claudia turned her head and looked at her. She smiled softly. "I don't know, there's a chance. Or she might have just been caught up in something that got out of control. They might have been blackmailing her."

"I hope so," Amy whispered. "I don't think I could stand finding out that she was a terrorist all along. I trusted her." She swallowed. "I liked her."

"If she was a terrorist, then she may well have been recruited for her personable nature. Being trustworthy is a key skill."

"I feel like an idiot."

"Don't," Claudia instructed. "You're not."

"I am. I trusted her. I would have done anything she asked me. That's probably why she chose me. To her, I was just a pathetic minion in a coffee shop. Maybe she was grooming me? Maybe I would have been a terrorist in the end. Following her blindly, like some lovesick puppy."

Claudia reached out her hand, taking Amy's and gripping it firmly. "Don't underestimate yourself, Amy."

Amy felt a blush rising on her cheeks. She hadn't meant to blab about her feelings for Cara. It all just burst out. "I just serve coffee... I don't know anything about the real world."

"Do you really feel that way?" Claudia asked.

Amy slowly nodded.

"Then maybe it is time to get back into the real world? If that's truly how you feel? There's nothing wrong with serving coffee, but if you feel that you aren't valued because of it, then that's a problem."

Amy opened her mouth to reply. She furrowed her brow and closed her mouth again. She turned her head and stared at the ceiling of the tent. In that moment, she had felt all her usual excuses building in her brain. Ready to explain that she loved the services, it may not be conventional, but it was the life for her. But she knew in her heart that it was all lies. Claudia had called her out, concisely and with kindness.

She'd watched her university friends go on to bigger and better things. But she had just stopped. The fear of failing had stopped her from even trying. Tom's Café was safe. Boring, predictable, and safe. She even convinced herself that she enjoyed the quirky nature of the job.

Claudia squeezed her hand once more and then removed it. Amy keenly felt the loss.

"Having chased you across the country for the last four days, I honestly believe that you can achieve anything you put your mind to," Claudia said. "Now, get some sleep. We only have a few more hours until we meet Mark."

THE CAR PASSENGER door was flung open, and Kerry raced towards Amy with a huge smile on her face. Amy dropped her bag and embraced Kerry in a hug.

"Oh my God, you're okay? You're okay? Right?" Amy asked in panic.

"Me? What about you? You've been missing for hours!" Kerry replied. "I'm just the idiot that got caught."

Amy relished the warm hug of her best friend. "I missed you so much."

"Missed you too, babe," Kerry replied. She leaned in close. "Have you seen the totty in the car?" she asked in an excited whisper.

Amy took a step back and glanced at Mark who was speaking with Claudia. He was tall and blonde, just the kind of thing Kerry drooled over.

"Ooh la la," Amy said and nudged Kerry in the ribs. "You like?"

"I like," Kerry sighed. "What do you know about him?"

Amy shrugged her shoulders. "His name is Mark, and he works with Claudia."

Kerry looked at her and sighed. "Seriously? *I* know that. What else?"

"I don't know, we didn't really talk about him," Amy admitted.

"Ladies, we have to go," Claudia called out to them. "They'll have tracked the call by now."

"Ladies." Kerry snorted a small laugh. "Who's she kidding?"

Amy shrugged. "She's just being professional, she's nice..." Amy picked up her rucksack and started to drag it towards the car. She stopped when she realised that Kerry wasn't following her. She stopped and turned around to see Kerry smiling at her.

"What?" Amy asked.

"I've seen that look before," Kerry said as she walked up next to her and took her arm.

"There's no look," Amy argued. Sometimes she hated how perceptive Kerry was.

"There's a look."

"Kerry, there's no look," Amy denied. She wondered how obvious her look was. Why did she even have a look? How did she get rid of the look?

"Girls," Mark called out to them.

"Girls." Amy chuckled. "We've been demoted."

"Hey, we were ladies a minute ago," Kerry shouted back towards Mark.

Mark looked at her and then turned to Claudia who just shrugged and got into the car.

"You think they're really going to help us?" Kerry asked.

"Yeah, I do. They believe us now, which means they've finally worked out that someone on the inside is setting us up."

"How do we know it's not them?"

Amy shook her head. "Don't start. I'm fragile enough as it

is. I trust them, if they end up being murdering terrorists then... tough."

~

"If this doesn't look weird, I don't know what does," Amy complained as she released her rucksack and sighed in satisfaction as it dropped to the floor. "Four people checking into one hotel room."

"We look like swingers," Kerry pointed out.

"I don't have any car keys," Amy complained.

Claudia put a hand on Amy's back and gently pushed her away from the door.

"Mark booked the room for himself. I'm sure no one looked, or cared, who checked in," Claudia assured them.

"If anyone did see, they'd think that Mark looks like a very lucky boy," Kerry added.

Mark blushed as he edged around the three women with several messenger bags slung over his shoulder. He walked over to the desk and started to unload laptops and cables.

Amy stood behind him to see what he was doing. "Why four laptops?"

"Oh, um, to clean the signal through them and transfer data from a non-networked machine onto a patched—"

Amy held up her hand. "Yeah, got it. Techie stuff, I shouldn't have asked. Is this going to help us access the USB without half the government knocking on the door?"

"Yes," Mark disappeared under the desk with the end of a cable. "When you accessed the USB, the signal was picked up on the Wi-Fi network and broadcast out. Two of these machines are not on any network and have no broadcast ability whatsoever. We'll be able to access the data without any chance of it being picked up."

A cable poked up from under the desk and Amy grabbed

hold of it. "Are you sure? Because last time wasn't really a blast for me."

"I'm sure, don't worry, I know what I'm doing." Mark stood up and took the cable from her. "Thank you." He plugged it into the back of his machine.

Amy turned around to say something to Claudia but stopped dead when she saw Claudia getting changed. Her suit jacket and blouse were discarded on the back of a chair and she stood in a white tank top as she searched for the opening of the long-sleeved, roll neck top she was about to put on. Amy felt her mouth open and close before tearing her eyes away from the woman. As she snapped her head away, she made eye contact with Kerry who was smirking smugly at her, trying not to laugh.

"Do you have the USB?" Mark asked.

Amy reached into her pocket and briefly held the small rectangle. She'd gone to hell and back to keep it out of the wrong hands. She still wasn't one hundred percent sure whose hands were the right ones. She glanced up at Claudia, now thankfully dressed. Claudia offered a comforting nod. She placed the USB into Mark's waiting grasp.

"If we all die, I'll be really pissed off," she joked lightly.

"Me too, I'm halfway through a brilliant book," Mark replied. He took the USB and sat at the desk. After a deep breath, he removed the cap and put it into the laptop. Kerry sat on the edge of the bed and watched. Amy stood behind him with her arms folded and waiting. Claudia stood beside him and looked at the screen.

"It's a standard widespread data grab," Mark explained. "Some is encrypted. This may take a while."

"What's a widespread whodymaflip?" Kerry asked.

"Hackers who steal data rarely take just the data they need," Claudia explained without looking away from the screen. "They take large chunks, either because they don't know what it is they're looking for, because they don't have time to pick out the exact thing, or, often, because they are trying to throw people off the scent of what they are doing."

Mark turned to face a different laptop and started to type strings of commands that Amy couldn't identify.

"So, they steal a lot of stuff, and you have to figure out what it was they actually wanted?" Amy asked.

"Exactly." Claudia smiled at her.

Amy smiled and felt like she had been praised by her favourite teacher.

"So, what now?" Kerry asked.

Claudia looked at her. "We crack the encrypted data. Have a look at what they took and see if we can figure out what their plans are. I would have to assume that there is a large-scale attack planned. A lot of time, effort, and money will have gone into whatever it is they are planning. They won't want to throw it away, or make big logistical changes."

"Easier to kill the people who have the information." Kerry looked at Amy. Amy nodded slowly in agreement.

"Exactly. You both were very lucky," Claudia said. "I'm in awe that you managed to keep ahead of them for so long."

"You said we bumbled around," Amy argued, another grin forming on her lips.

"You did, darling." Claudia winked at her before turning her attention back to the laptop.

Amy looked at Kerry, and Kerry smirked at her. Was Claudia flirting? Did she call everyone darling? Whatever was happening, Amy needed to get out of the confined space.

"Does anyone want to use the bathroom? I'm in desperate need of a shower."

All three shook their head. Amy quickly grabbed her rucksack and disappeared into the hotel bathroom. She locked the door behind her and let out a big sigh.

MARK HAD QUICKLY REMOVED the encryption. Now, Claudia mindlessly doodled a picture of a flower on the hotel room notepad as she stared at the freshly revealed data on her screen. There was no discernible pattern, and most of the data on the USB stick seemed to be pointless garbage that she couldn't imagine a possible use for. She accessed a different folder and started to stare at a different batch of seemingly pointless data sets.

She chanced a look over at Mark's corner of the room. Claudia had grown tired of the casual glances that Kerry and Mark offered each other. Normally, the blossoming attraction would have made her agitated, but knowing that the object of her own affections was nearby caused her to indulge in a little matchmaking of her own.

She had given the pair an important task and set them up in the corner of the room. It was a two-fold attack. Firstly, they would be able to get to know each other while working on something. But secondly, she would be alone to concentrate on the data sets and see if a meaning could rise from them.

Sadly, her pattern-seeing ability was currently at sea as her mind kept flipping to thoughts of Amy. The girl had been showering for over an hour, and Claudia thought for sure that the water would have run cold by now. No matter how she tried to pull her thoughts away from Amy, she found her mind drifting back to her.

She could no longer blame her concussion; the headache and subsequent fog had cleared. There was no use in denying it, she was smitten with Amy. To deny it would just clog up her brain. Acceptance allowed her to move on to more important things. Besides, Amy wasn't interested in her. She was too old, too cold, too... *her*. Amy was young, vivacious, funny, and flighty. Claudia was none of those things.

Knowing that nothing would happen between them made everything easier. Claudia was free to accept her own attraction and get on with her work. She stared at the data set in front of her again and shook her head. Nothing about this made any sense.

"Figured it out yet?"

Claudia jumped in her seat. Amy stood behind her, wrapped in a towel with damp hair clinging to her bare shoulders.

"Um, no... no, it's..." Claudia swallowed. She turned back to the laptop. "There are various sets of governmental information, but nothing that seems useful."

"Maybe another set of eyes will help?" Amy asked. Claudia looked at her in the reflection of the laptop, watching as her eyes drifted over to Mark and Kerry in the corner of the room. "Aw, that's cute."

"I couldn't stand it anymore. I set them a task and forced them together," Claudia explained.

"Good." Amy pulled out the chair beside Claudia and sat down. Claudia couldn't help but look at the bare thigh on show while Amy continued to look at Mark and Kerry.

Claudia managed to tear her eyes away and refocused her

attention on the laptop screen. She clicked the data set closed and looked at the root directory of folders.

"What is all this then?" Amy asked.

"A lot of it is old emails from various people, various departments with nothing in common. This is a common hacker plot. Take large amounts of data that mean nothing, throw us off the trail. Have us spend ages looking at every single file to see if there is anything of use in there."

"A million red herrings," Amy mused.

"Exactly." Claudia clicked a button and previewed some files to explain her point. "These are old emails, these are flight times, these are in Russian, but it's just recipes and weather reports."

"You speak Russian?"

"*Da.*"

"Cute." Amy bumped her shoulder with her own naked one.

Claudia hoped the blush that she felt on her cheeks wasn't visible. She clicked to preview some more files. "These are old news stories with no connection, and then this is gibberish train information."

"Wait." Amy put her hand over Claudia's on the mouse to prevent her from moving on. She leaned forward and stared at the screen.

"It's just misleading data. It talks about stations that no longer exists and trains that don't even run," Claudia assured her. She looked at Amy's hand on hers, wondering if she should shake her off. "See, this one, Croxley Green? According to my records, that was permanently closed in 2003. So, this is either old data or gibberish."

"These are the ghost lines." Amy removed her hand and pointed to a line of data. Claudia felt cold at the loss of contact. "I've heard about this; John comes into the services sometimes and he told me about them."

"Ghost lines?"

"Yeah, basically train companies run certain trains just to keep the lines open. So many train lines were closed in the sixties and seventies that train companies and enthusiasts wanted to fight back. To confuse government, they ran trains on those lines, to pretend they were in use. But the trains would never be used. They'd go to the most ridiculous places at the worst times, they'd go only once a day, and they'd have no return journey. Anything to discourage people from actually using them. They still run today but mainly to move stock around. They pass through miles of track that's not known about, go through stations that have been abandoned for decades. I recognise these station names. Wedgwood, Brigg, Peartree. You don't forget names like that."

"So, these train times might be real," Claudia mused as she looked at the data again. "I'd discarded it as rubbish data because of the strange times and locations that don't seem to exist. But if these trains do run then it would be a fantastic way to move people or items around the country."

"Oh my god." Amy slammed her hand over her mouth. She stared into nothing as a memory seemed to hit her.

"What is it?"

"Cara warned me. One day, she told me that she'd read a report about really poor maintenance on trains. She asked me if I ever took trains, and I said sometimes. She told me to avoid trains at all costs, that they were all death traps. Disasters waiting to happen." Amy blew out a breath. "She was warning me."

Claudia's pulse started to race. "Did she say anything else?"

Amy shook her head. "Nothing specific. Just that."

"I think this is it," Claudia said.

"But, wait, if these are just train times of ghost lines... then no one would be on them," Amy said. "That's the whole point in them, they never get used."

Claudia brought up a map. "The trains may not get used, but they go into mainline stations. They pass through major cities. Just think of the damage that can be caused by filling a train with explosives."

Amy paled. "That's... horrible. Why would someone do that?"

"Someone with a point to prove, someone who wants to be heard." Claudia leaned back in her chair. It felt right. Out of all the data on the USB, the ghost lines seemed the most likely target. But she still had the question of which train, at which time.

"Why would MI5 help with something like that?" Amy asked. "Like, isn't it their job to keep people safe? Not help to blow them up? And how does a mole get into MI5 anyway? Isn't there a test or something? I went to America years ago, and I had to tick a box to say that I'm not a communist. Don't you have to fill in a form to say you're not a terrorist? Not that anyone would be stupid enough to say they are a terrorist. But, surely there are some safeguards?"

Amy's waffling had focused Claudia's mind on the right question. And the answer was becoming blatantly clear. She couldn't believe she hadn't seen it before.

"I know who it is," she whispered. She stared blankly at the screen, everything coming together in her mind and rendering her still.

"Then we need to call it in, tell... whoever it is you tell."

Claudia shook her head. She looked at Amy. "This person, they are high up. They control a lot of the data. If they think we are on to them, they'll wipe everything. They must have put some kind of failsafe in place to protect them. We have to catch them in the act."

"How do we do that?"

"I have no idea; I need to think." Claudia jumped to her feet. She started to pace in front of the window. It was

Miranda, had to be. Miranda had spent every day of her working life, for the last ten years, explaining how flawed the MI5 systems were. An attack would shake the service to its core. Procedures would have to be overhauled.

She'd seen enough people decline into extreme beliefs to know that it could happen to anyone who was passionate about something. Miranda was passionate about MI5 having more power. Not only was Miranda the most likely candidate, she was also in the position to provide a fake dossier. Her department oversaw profiling and information retrieval. If she said someone was part of a terrorist organisation, then no one questioned it.

"Do you trust your old boss?" Amy asked.

Claudia stopped pacing and looked at her. "Yes, I trust him. Why?"

"Arrest me. Arrest us." Amy waved between herself and Kerry. "I mean, let me get dressed first. But then arrest us. Set them up."

"No, Amy, I can't put you in that kind of danger. Who knows what her plan is? I can't—"

"You can," Amy insisted. "We haven't been missing for that long. You rock up at spy school HQ with both of us. Everyone is like, whoa, she caught them, awesome. Then the mole is bound to make some kind of a move, but you and your boss will be watching their every move."

"What about Spiky?" Claudia asked.

Amy scrunched up her face as she thought. "He didn't see me clobber him."

"True." Claudia smiled at the memory. "He presumably doesn't know we're onto them, and he doesn't know that you immobilised him. Which means I can report that one of the terrorists, who you were working with, threatened me with a gun and a kindly passer-by assisted me."

"Dog walker." Amy nodded her head. "It's always a dog

walker. Dead body found? Dog walker found it. Someone being attacked? Dog walker saw it. Missing person? Dog walker was the last person to see them."

"Okay, a kindly dog walker," Claudia agreed. "But I'm still not happy with the idea of putting you in harm's way."

"I trust you," Amy told her. "Besides, I went on this whole journey to prevent a terrorist attack from happening. I've not done that yet, but I can if we do this."

Claudia took a step forward and knelt in front of Amy. She put her hand on her knee and looked into her eyes. "Are you absolutely sure about this? I don't have jurisdiction at MI5. I can't guarantee your safety."

"I trust you," Amy repeated.

Claudia looked at her for a moment. She nodded and stood up. "We better talk to Kerry about this. Considering you just offered to have her arrested without her knowledge."

Amy shrugged and looked over her shoulder to Kerry and Mark. "What are best friends for?"

~

Claudia paced the hotel room's small bathroom. She held the burner phone Mark had brought with him to her lips as she considered the plan from all angles. She wasn't happy about it, but it was the best way to catch Miranda in the act. Maybe the only way.

She dialled the number she knew from memory, held the phone to her ear, and waited.

"Andrew Barr?"

"It's me," she said softly.

"Claudia? What the hell? You disappear off the face of the earth, your associate poses as one of my officers and kidnaps a suspect? My team are dispatched to Edinburgh on your information. What is going on?" Andrew was livid. She could picture him now, pacing his tiny office and gesturing wildly.

"Amy Hewitt and Kerry Wyatt are both with me. I have the data, and I know what the plan is. But there is a mole in your office." There was no point in sugar-coating it.

"A-a mole?" Andrew hesitated. The anger seemed to start to wane. "But... that's impossible. You know how closely everyone is vetted here."

"I do. I also know that those who design the systems, or frequently complain about them, are the ones most likely to be able to break them."

Andrew was silent for a few moments. Claudia gave him time. Allowed the enormity of the situation to sink in. He needed to be calm and collected. No one could suspect that he had any doubts.

"Andrew," she continued, "we need to act now, and we need to not give any indication that we know about the mole. We can't give them the opportunity to cover their tracks. There's a window of opportunity here, and we need to grab it."

"You have a plan, by the sounds of it?"

"I do. It's... unconventional."

"Sounds just like you." Andrew chuckled.

"I'll need your help."

"You have it. Always."

CLAUDIA WATCHED as Amy and Kerry were handcuffed and led into the cells. She swallowed at the sight and hoped she was doing the right thing. Trusting the famously incompetent security service wasn't something that came naturally to her.

"Well done, McAllister."

She turned to see Miranda Haynes. "Thank you. It was a little harder than I'd anticipated, but I got them in the end."

"I'm still awaiting the final briefing report," Miranda mentioned. "I heard you were attacked? In the woods?"

That information had been included in the brief round-up of information given to the team. Though it was suspicious that it would be the first thing Miranda would bring up.

"Yes, a man, I didn't get a good look at him," Claudia lied. "It all happened quite fast, and I was shocked when a passer-by hit him over the head."

"Dog walker?" Miranda guessed. "They are always in the wrong place at the wrong time."

"Exactly."

"You were missing for a while?" Miranda fished.

"Have you tried getting a signal in the middle of Scotland?" Claudia joked.

"Did you speak with them much? Get any intel on their organisation?"

Claudia shook her head. "No, it was quickly apparent that they had a story and they were sticking to it. I thought I'd leave the interrogation to you lot."

Claudia wondered how Miranda had managed to remain under the radar all this time. Her barrage of questioning was eliminating any doubts Claudia might have had.

"You have the USB stick?" Miranda asked.

"It was destroyed."

"Destroyed?"

"Yes, destroyed. Nothing left of it. As I began to close in on them, they took the decision to destroy it. Presumably to cover their tracks so they can maintain this ridiculous story of their innocence." Claudia turned to walk away. "I suppose that was something they were briefed on. As I say, they adamantly stuck to their story."

"They are professionals, highly trained," Miranda reminded her. It was all Claudia could do not to chuckle. Seeing Amy refer to a dummies guide in order to put a tent up and only managing to put down 'poo' on a Scrabble board didn't exactly scream terrorist genius.

"So, when you say destroyed?" Miranda quizzed.

"Completely destroyed, nothing but cinders left."

"I see." Miranda pressed the button for the lift, and they both waited.

"Will you be questioning them?" Claudia asked, hoping she sounded casual.

"Yes, I'll leave it for tomorrow. Separate them and give them time to stew, see if that makes them a little more open to questioning."

More like give you more time to forge whatever documents you need,
Claudia thought.

"Good idea." The lift doors opened, and they stepped in.
Claudia pressed the button for the top floor. Miranda looked at
her curiously. "Need to speak to Andrew," Claudia explained.
She rolled her eyes. "I just want to get paid and get out of here."

"Not been encouraged to come back?" Miranda asked.

Claudia laughed. "No, definitely not. After the last few
days, I'll be glad to get back to my own office."

~

Claudia paced Andrew's office. The trap was set and now they
were just watching and waiting for someone to fall into it. It
was the early hours of Monday morning, but the office was as
busy as always. The MI5 offices were in the centre of the
building. With no access to natural light and officers working
shifts, it was always a hive of activity.

But this time the office was buzzing with tension. Or
maybe Claudia just felt that way because she was stressed and
sleep-deprived. She itched to go down to the cells and check on
Amy and Kerry, but Andrew had only allowed her to remain in
the building under the proviso that she keep a low profile.

"This had better work," Claudia said, not for the first time.

"It will. If you're right and she is the mole, then everything
is set up nicely. We just need to wait." Andrew sat at his desk
with his fingers steepled as he waited for news.

"And you're sure of the officers you have working on this?"
Claudia pressed.

"Absolutely. None of them have ever had contact with her.
They have all performed undercover counterterrorism work
before, two of them from within the service. When she makes
her move, we'll know."

Claudia sat on the sofa and put her head in her hands. She hated the idea of Amy and Kerry in the cells, separated from one another.

"Which one is it?" Andrew asked.

Claudia looked up at him. "I'm sorry?"

Andrew drew a finger in the air in her direction. "You don't get like this. You like one of them. Is it Amy?"

Claudia blinked. "What... I don't know what you mean. Don't be ridiculous, I'm just—"

"If you were worried about the mole, then you would be angry. You're not, you're nervous. That indicates to me that you are concerned about something going wrong. And I'm willing to bet it's related to our two new additions to the cells. You only spent around fifteen minutes with Kerry, but Amy... well, I'm still waiting for the full story there."

"You'll be waiting a long time." Claudia chuckled. She didn't work for Andrew; she didn't have to provide him with a blow-by-blow report of what happened.

"I see." Andrew grinned knowingly.

Claudia smiled in return. "You spend too much time around the profilers."

"And you just basically told me that I'm right." Andrew looked smug. He leaned back in his chair. "Amy, then?"

"It's nothing," Claudia assured him. "She's very sweet and innocent, and I feel guilty for putting her in this situation."

"What happened after you arrested Kerry? I didn't quite get the whole story between the services and your attacker in the woods."

Claudia raised an eyebrow.

Andrew put his hands up. "Off the record, just two friends talking."

She flopped back on the sofa and looked at the ceiling. She'd have to tell someone, keeping it bottled up was driving her insane.

"She boarded a narrowboat, which pulled away and started to sail along the canal. So, I boarded a narrowboat as well. We were travelling at something ridiculous like four and a half miles an hour, it would have been quicker to walk. Hell, it was quicker to walk. We were overtaken by dog walkers!" She laughed at the memory.

"I have a wonderful mental image of this," Andrew admitted.

"I'm able to see the humour with hindsight. I was infuriated at the time. And then Amy came out onto the rear of the boat with a cup of tea in her hands and started chatting to me. Unbelievable."

Andrew laughed. "This gets better and better."

"They waited for another boat to get in the way, and then Amy ran into some woods. It took forever to get our boat to the path so I could follow her. Gave her an enormous head start. But somehow she got turned around in the woods and ended up behind me."

Andrew sat forward with interest. "Wait, she was running away from you but ended up behind you?"

Claudia looked up at Andrew's smiling face. "Yes, I wasn't kidding when I told you she bumbled her way around the country. But thank God she was behind me."

The smile vanished from Andrew's face. "Yes. She was very brave."

"Very stupid more like it," Claudia added. "Attacking an armed man. She could have been killed."

"Sounds like she didn't care much at the time."

"No, she is quite foolhardy: act first and think later." Claudia smiled.

"Quite the opposite to you," Andrew pointed out. "Maybe that's what you need in life?"

Claudia shook her head. "She's a child, Andrew."

Andrew opened his desk drawer and pulled out a folder. He

put his glasses on and opened the folder. He ran his finger along the first piece of paper. "No," he said, "no, not a child, she's twenty-five."

Claudia rolled her eyes. "Practically a child."

"You're not exactly ancient," Andrew argued. "You speak to me when you get to this ripe old age."

"There's just over ten years between us," Claudia pointed out. "That's a lifetime." She shook her head; the conversation had diverted somewhere she wasn't comfortable. "Besides, I like her. Respect her. I can worry about her without it being anything else."

Andrew held up his hands. "Okay, if you say so." He looked at her with a smirk.

"Don't give me that look," she warned him.

"It's my face." He shrugged.

Before she had time to reply, his phone rang. Claudia got to her feet, unable to sit when it looked like things might be happening.

Andrew answered the call and listened to the other person in silence for a few moments. Claudia started to pace, unable to hear the other end of the conversation and getting little from Andrew's poker face.

"I see," he eventually said.

Claudia let out a frustrated sigh.

"I see. Thank you for letting me know."

"Know what?" Claudia whispered, unable to stay quiet much longer.

Andrew put the phone down. "It worked. The telecoms team managed to successfully listen to Miranda's calls. She just contacted an external source. She told him that the necessary data was missing and a new asset needed to be deployed. She also said that she would arrange for the two decoys to be removed."

"Removed?" Claudia placed her palms on Andrew's desk

and stared at him. Any joy at Miranda implicating herself in the plot was eradicated by the thought of Amy and Kerry being hurt.

"I have authority to go and make the arrest." Andrew stood up and gestured towards the door. "Shall we?"

Claudia spun around and stalked towards the door. She opened it and quickly walked across the open plan office. Miranda just stood there, chatting with one of the secretaries. Claudia had to admit that she had courage. Standing in the middle of the secret service, discussing BBC dramas, all the while planning a terrorist attack. If it weren't so horrendous, Claudia would have been impressed.

"Miranda Haynes, you are under arrest," Andrew said as he approached her, flanked by three internal security officers.

Miranda looked at him in surprise. She looked around the room, which was starting to fill with officers—some ready to make the arrest, some ready to search through her office and personal effects for any information.

"Is this some kind of a joke?" Miranda laughed. "My birthday isn't for three months."

"Unfortunately, this is no joke." Andrew gestured for the officers to restrain her. "We have evidence of your collusion with terrorist organisations with the goal of planning a mainland attack with loss of civilian life."

Two officers stepped behind her and took her arms firmly. Miranda glared from Andrew to Claudia. Handcuffs clicked in place. Claudia could hear the rest of the office whispering about what they were witnessing.

"Ah, I see," Miranda nodded. "You've become aware of the training exercise. I'm sure once you investigate it, all will become clear, and we'll laugh about this."

Claudia wouldn't put it past Miranda to have concocted a paper trail proving her innocence. Her computer skills were legendary, and if she had assembled a like-minded team, who knew what they could have put in place.

Miranda didn't seem worried. Claudia was hit by a strange sinking feeling. Of course Miranda would have an exit strategy.

"The exercise is simply to demonstrate how weak our security is. How our processes are too slow, and our methods don't work. It's highly classified, but I have proof."

Claudia scoffed a laugh. "Of course you do."

"Claudia," Andrew warned.

"We found the explosives," Claudia blurted out.

It was a gamble; they hadn't quite deciphered all the aspects of the plan. Claudia had her assumptions and was keen to fast-track the interrogation process. Miranda was a master strategist; she wouldn't break easily under the intense lights of the interrogation room.

The look of terror in Miranda's eyes told her that she was on the right track.

"And we've already linked you to the supply of explosives. Your man, in the woods, he's working with us."

"Claudia," Andrew said again.

Miranda's face was practically turning purple as she struggled to breathe. "The plan wasn't mine."

"Oh, well, that's all right then." Claudia laughed. "Phew. For a minute, I thought you were the mastermind. But you were just a sheep."

"Nothing would have happened," Miranda said. "You've got it all wrong."

"Are you seriously telling us that you wouldn't have let an actual attack happen? Or that you'd be able to stop one? You would have been in your element if an attack had taken place. You would have been able to throw Andrew under the bus, and you would have taken control of this division. Shaped it into what you have always wanted. A spy state where everyone is guilty until proven innocent, where you weren't accountable to anyone. A large-scale attack on UK soil is exactly what you want to happen."

"I have to read you your rights," Andrew began. Claudia knew the tone. He was on board. He wanted her to push to see what they could get out of her in the heat of the moment.

"You're up to your neck in it, Miranda," Claudia continued. "If you want to help us with some of the finer details, maybe you'll get a cell with a window. Although I doubt it. In the Miranda Haynes world of justice, you'd vanish from sight, wouldn't you?" She turned to face Andrew. "What do you say, boss?"

Andrew drew himself up tall and turned to look at Miranda with disgust. "I don't think we need anything from her. We've already picked apart the relevant details," he lied smoothly.

"I can help you," Miranda assured him. "For immunity".

"What makes you think we need your help?" Andrew asked. "Your network has turned on you. We have everything we need."

"I can give you names. All of them. I know things, things that you need to know. Just give me a chance," Miranda pleaded.

Andrew sighed and rubbed his forehead. "Fine." He turned around. "Get an interrogation room set up."

Claudia imperceptibly nodded at Andrew and turned on her heel. She trusted his skills to get the details from Miranda, and either way they had suspended all trains operating on the so-called ghost lines pending a search of all vehicles.

Her suspicions of Miranda's involvement had been spot on. She'd never liked Miranda. As much as she hated the red tape within the service, she had always felt that Miranda toed too harsh a line. Miranda had always claimed that an apocalypse was just around the corner, and every conversation quickly descended into a discussion about the softness of the agency.

Claudia just wished that she had considered the idea of doubting the intelligence handed to her by Miranda's team long before she set off searching for Amy and Kerry.

~

Claudia pushed on the heavy metal door and winced at the loud screeching as it opened. She looked apologetically at Amy who was lying down on the cell bed.

"We pay millions of pounds in taxes, but it's impossible for someone to oil that door?" Amy asked. "Then again, I should be happy it's you and not the mole. Whoever that is. Did you catch them? Can you even tell me? I mean, you should, considering I agreed to this plan."

Claudia smiled. "Do you ever stop talking?"

Amy pushed herself into a sitting position and smiled sweetly at Claudia. "Yeah, but only for tops thirty seconds."

Claudia stepped into the cell and closed the door behind her. "We did catch the mole. They will be questioned and their network taken down. So, on behalf of Her Majesty's government, thank you."

"Does Her Majesty's government pay compensation?" Amy asked, with a wide grin. "Because I'm suffering serious emotional distress."

Claudia chuckled. "You will be compensated for the inconvenience."

"Sweet. It's pretty inconvenient being called a terrorist and having a shit picture of you plastered all over the news. And I gave my favourite coat away. And I think I lost a Q from my travel Scrabble, and that's the best letter."

"A retraction has been issued. We contacted your work and gave them the basics of what happened, so your job is still yours if you want it. Of course, you'll have to sign a non-disclosure agreement. You can't speak about what happened here."

Amy rolled her eyes. "Fine, fine. I was going to write a book about my daring escape, overcoming insurmountable obstacles in order to evade the stunning huntress."

"Stunning huntress?" Claudia raised an eyebrow.

"Yeah." Amy blushed fiercely.

Claudia blanked for a moment. Was Amy flirting with her?

"So, I get a retraction, but my Q remains lost?" Amy shook her head. "The stuff I do for Queen and country."

"Can't you draw a line on an O?" Claudia suggested with a smirk.

A knock on the door sounded, and it noisily squeaked open. Andrew stepped into the cell. "Miss Hewitt, I wanted to introduce myself and apologise for the events of the last few days. And to go over a few pieces of paperwork, if I may?"

Suddenly, the cell seemed so much smaller. Andrew's awkward appearance had interrupted something, but Claudia wasn't sure what it was. Had Amy being flirting with her or just letting her mouth run unchecked as she so often seemed to do?

Whatever it was, Claudia felt the need to get out of there quickly.

"I have to go, I have some things to finish up," Claudia said. "All the best, Amy."

She turned and left before anything else could be said.

AMY HUMMED a tune to herself as she wiped down the work surface. She'd been back at work for two weeks, and it was like nothing had changed. Which was a positive and a negative thing. On the bright side, she could dive back into her daily routine. On the down side, she'd slid back in with astonishing ease. Thoughts of changing her life and doing something different had vanished.

Arriving home had been a strange feeling. Her mum had hugged her long and hard and berated Andrew, who had brought her home. Within an hour, everything had been said, at least everything Amy was willing to say. A couple of hours after that, they watched a movie with tea and biscuits, and it was like nothing had changed.

The following day, she had gone back to work. Tom had turned up to welcome her back, and to tell her that she had a choice of not being paid or having her holiday allowance docked for time away. She chose to have her allowance docked. It wasn't like she'd be going on holiday anyway.

Days quickly took on their normal pattern. She woke up horribly early to go to work. She came home exhausted and went to bed in the early evening. It amazed her how fast she had fallen back into her old lifestyle.

"Could I have a latte, please?"

Amy turned around and smiled at the woman. "Sure, in here or to go?"

"To go." The woman fished around for coins in her purse, not bothering to make eye contact with her.

Amy quickly made the drink and took the payment. She even thanked the woman when she left a measly five pence tip in the cup and saucer by the till.

She turned around and carried on cleaning the work surfaces. The place had gone to hell while she'd been gone.

"Is the coffee here any good?"

She knew that voice.

She dropped the cloth and spun around.

Her heart started to beat faster as she stared into the familiar eyes of Claudia McAllister.

"Y-yeah," she stammered. "It's the best you'll ever taste."

Claudia raised an eyebrow. "A bold claim. I'll have a black coffee, then."

"Here or to go?" Amy asked. She couldn't move. Her feet were rooted to the floor.

"Here." Claudia sat on a stool and placed her briefcase on the counter next to her.

"You just vanished," Amy said. "I know we didn't agree to meet up or anything, but I didn't even get a chance to say goodbye."

"I was called away onto the clean-up operation, the mole left a lot of mess behind," Claudia said. "And... and then I didn't know if you'd want to see me. So, I decided to stay away."

Amy frowned and gestured to where Claudia sat on the stool. "But you're here?"

"I couldn't stay away."

Amy couldn't help but grin at the admission.

"So, you came for the coffee?"

"Of course, I hear it's the best coffee around."

"How have you been?" Amy asked. It wasn't lost on her that Claudia had become her new Cara. Her older, exciting crush. But this time she wasn't going to stammer while she wiped sweaty palms on the back of her trousers. This time she was going to be brave.

"I've been good. Bored, but good. You know, one of the people I caught, they didn't even know what a narrowboat was. Didn't have a painting by number kit either."

Amy shook her head. "Those terrorist bastards. Travel Scrabble?" She asked seriously.

"No. And no M&Ms."

"Amateurs," Amy muttered. "What would they do if they had a blood sugar drop?"

"That was probably why I managed to catch them so soon." Claudia chuckled.

Amy let out a contented sigh. She just stared at Claudia. She was back, she was actually back. And for no other reason than to see her.

"Amy?" Claudia questioned after a few moments of silence.

Amy shook her head. "Sorry, it… this just reminds me of Cara, you know?"

Claudia looked around the café in understanding. "Ah, I imagine it would. Don't worry, I'm not here to make a drop."

"Something's been bothering me," Amy confessed. "Why did Cara place that USB under a different table that last time? If she didn't want them to have it, then why come here at all?"

Claudia put her chin in her cupped hand as she thought. "It's hard to say. Maybe she had a last-minute change of heart. Or maybe she had been followed here, her tail remaining just out of sight, allowing her to choose a different table? Maybe false information had been given to her?" Claudia looked Amy in the eye. "Or, maybe it was you."

"Me?" Amy blinked.

"Maybe she knew you'd find it and know what to do with it."

"But, I… no, it couldn't have been that."

Claudia sat up straight and looked at her. "And why not?"

"I'm just… me. If Cara needed help, she would have asked someone else."

Claudia shrugged. "If you say so. Personally, I think it's reasonable that she would come to you. Someone she knows, someone she trusts. She'd seen you every day for ten months. If she were being blackmailed to take part in a plan she didn't want to be involved with, it would be a way of preventing the plan from succeeding. Speaking of which." She opened her briefcase and held out a piece of paper.

"What's that?" Amy asked.

"It's an application form."

Amy stepped forward and took the form. "To join the intelligence agency as an officer?" She looked up at Claudia.

"The agency needs good people. It needs intelligent, caring women who really understand how people work. I think you would be perfect for this role. I also think you want to be more than you are now, but you're scared. So, I'm going to sit here and drink the best black coffee I'll supposedly ever taste, and I'm going to either watch you fill this form in or I'll fill it in for you and drag you to the interview myself."

Amy chuckled. "I… don't know what to say."

Claudia reached into her briefcase, pulled out a pen, and handed it to Amy. Amy looked at the form and the pen and then back up to Claudia. "Why are you doing this?"

"Because you won't," Claudia said. "And you saved my life so now I'm saving yours."

"Pfft, I'm fine, I don't need—"

"Maybe you don't. But other people do. Amy, you enriched people's lives when you went on the run. You were a criminal, on the run, being chased by the police, and you actually told people that and they still let you in, fed you, and protected you. Lied for you. You are an amazing person. Keeping that amazing person locked up here serving some of the slowest coffee I have ever known..."

Amy laughed. She lowered the form and the pen to the counter and quickly served up a black coffee from the jug on the hot plate. "There, stop whining," she joked.

"At last, I was dying of thirst," Claudia replied with a smirk.

Amy pulled the cap off the pen and looked at the form. She was buzzing with excitement to see Claudia again. Her palms were indeed sweaty, and her heart was beating fast and hard in her chest. She couldn't believe that Claudia had taken the time to come and see her, to bring her a job application form. She believed in her, really believed in her. To the point where she was willing to blackmail her in order to realise her true potential.

She lowered the pen and looked up at Claudia. The woman was looking at her phone, her brow knitted in an adorable manner as she read from the screen.

When Cara had vanished, all Amy could think about were the opportunities wasted. The times she could have said something, could have told Cara how she felt. If anything had come from the events of the past month, it was a sincere promise to herself to not let opportunities go to waste.

Claudia looked up from her phone, obviously sensing Amy's eyes on her. "Yes?" She asked with a crooked smile.

Amy reached forward. She grabbed the front of Claudia's shirt and drew her closer, placing a firm kiss on her lips. She briefly cast a thought to the fact that Claudia could possibly be armed, and may end her there and then for kissing her. So, she put all of her feeling, all of her passion, into the kiss. If she was only going to get one chance at it, it would be a good one.

She ended the kiss and pulled her head back slightly. She stared with wide eyes at Claudia, letting her go and gently straightening out her shirt front for her.

"So..." Claudia whispered. "I... I didn't imagine it. There was something between us?"

Amy smiled in relief. "Yes, yes, there was. Is. If you want there to be? I mean, I know we're very different and I'm not sure you wanted that kiss, but I just kinda gave it to you anyway. It was really presumptuous and probably rude. And I have totally ruined your lipstick. Which means I probably look a complete mess. And—"

"Amy?"

"Yes?"

"Shut up and kiss me again."

REVIEWS

I sincerely hope you enjoyed reading this book as much as I enjoyed writing it. If you did, I would greatly appreciate a short review on Amazon or your favourite book website. Reviews are crucial for any author, and even just a line or two can make a huge difference.

ABOUT THE AUTHOR

A.E. Radley is an entrepreneur and best-selling author living and working in England.

She describes herself as a Wife. Traveller. Tea Drinker. Biscuit Eater. Animal Lover. Master Pragmatist. Annoying Procrastinator. Theme Park Fan. Movie Buff.

When not writing or working, Radley indulges in her third passion of buying unnecessary cat accessories on a popular online store for her two ungrateful strays whom she has threatened to return for the last seven years.

Connect with A.E. Radley

www.writingradleys.com

FLIGHT SQA016 - BOOK ONE IN THE FLIGHT SERIES

Spurred on by overwhelming and ever-increasing debts, Emily White takes a job working in the first-class cabin on the prestigious commuter route from her home of New York to London with Crown Airlines.

On board she meets Olivia Lewis, who is a literal high-flying business executive with a weekly commute, a meticulous schedule, and terrible social skills.

When a personal emergency brings them together, will Emily be able to swallow her pride and accept help from Olivia? And will Olivia be able to prevent herself from saying the wrong thing?

GROUNDED - BOOK TWO IN THE FLIGHT SERIES

City professional Olivia Lewis is coming to terms with her latest romantic failure by attempting to throw herself into her work. But with clients suddenly leaving Applewood Financial in their droves it becomes clear that old enemies have decided to strike and Olivia realises that she is losing everything.

Meanwhile the world of flight attendant Emily White comes crashing down around her when she loses her job. With no income, enormous debts and a broken-hearted five-year-old son she thinks that things can't get any worse. That is until a blast from the past threatens it all.

MERGERS & ACQUISITIONS

Kate Kennedy prides herself on running the very best advertising agency in Europe.

One day her top client asks her to work on a lucrative project with the notoriously fastidious Georgina Masters, of the American agency Mastery.

The temporary merger causes a fiery clash of cultures and personalities. Especially when Georgina sets her romantic sights on Kate's young intern, Sophie.

MERGERS & ACQUISITIONS

BY A.E. RADLEY

CHAPTER ONE

"A SPORTS CAR?" Kate repeated. She furrowed her brow at the idea.

"Yes, silver and red and really, really fast," Yannis said.

He stood up and paced excitedly around the meeting room. Yannis was tall, over six feet. His lanky frame seemed at odds with his constant need to bound around.

Kate suppressed a chuckle as she watched him pace. She appreciated his enthusiasm, no one wanted to work with a miserable client. But Yannis was almost too enthusiastic. He switched from one major project to another without stopping to catch his breath.

"Why a sports car?" Kate queried.

"We build engines, sports cars need engines. This is fantastic," he announced.

Kate suspected that Yannis felt his high-intensity enthusiasm would wear off on those around him. Bouncing around meeting rooms with excitement and informing people that things were fantastic were his way of injecting passion into a project.

Yannis was certainly a successful businessman, but he also was primarily an ideas man. Leaving the details to others. Like her.

"It's... different," Kate allowed.

"Different is good. Exciting." Yannis paused in front of the windows that overlooked the sprawling City of London. "We need to be different. We need to move, grow, change, adapt." He leaned closer to the glass and peered out of the window. "You can see my house from here."

Kate rolled her eyes good-naturedly. She stood up and walked around the meeting table to join him by the window. This wasn't the first meeting she had spent chasing after the excitable man, and it probably wouldn't be the last.

"This is east, yes?" He pointed out of the window. Before she could reply, he was staring intently into the distance, looking for landmarks.

"Yes," she replied. "Yannis, let me just get this straight in my mind. Atrom are going to build a sports car—"

"Ten," he corrected, still gazing over the city to get his bearings.

She felt her eyebrow raise. "Ten?"

"Ten," he repeated. "Selling for a million pounds. We'll only sell ten. I'm having one, of course."

Kate looked skywards. "Right, okay. Atrom are going to build ten sports cars, each priced at one million pounds, and you will buy one for yourself?"

Yannis looked at her. He smiled and nodded his head. "Yes, that's it. And this is big news, so I need my favourite marketing guru to tell the world for me."

"And we'll be more than happy to help," Kate assured. "I assume you want the works? Press releases, websites, viral campaigns, video campaigns, news slots?"

"Everything. International," Yannis said. He looked at her seriously. "It is very important to me that this is international news."

"That's definitely something we can do." Kate mentally put together a quick marketing brief. While she considered Yannis an idiot for investing in a project that was a glorified toy for himself, she welcomed the money the project would bring.

"It's a big job," he said.

"It is," Kate agreed. Huge, in fact. Atrom Engineering was by far their biggest client, in terms of size and profitability. The introduction of a new product, and all that went with it, meant a huge amount of income for Kate's agency, Red Door.

Yannis Papadakis was the kind of CEO that Kate adored. He was rich, eccentric, and didn't think twice about spending a small fortune marketing his already successful engineering company.

"I had lunch in New York last week," Yannis continued. "With Georgina Masters, you know her?"

Kate tried to control her grimace. "I've met her a couple of times. Award ceremonies, conferences. That kind of thing."

"Mastery is considered to be the best advertising agency in America." Yannis walked back to the meeting table. He sat down and opened his MacBook. He hunched over the small machine and typed in his password. "Georgina really knows her stuff."

Kate hummed noncommittally at his mention of the woman. If life were a cartoon, Georgina Masters would be her arch nemesis. The two women were constantly compared within the industry and by the media. They were both businesswomen in their forties, give or take, who had set up successful marketing companies in a male-dominated sector. Of course they were often compared. But comparisons are rarely kind; they certainly hadn't been between Kate and Georgina.

Kate had come to loathe the very mention of Georgina Masters. She was sure Georgina felt the same way about her.

"She is very interested in the sports car industry," Yannis was saying. He turned his MacBook around so Kate could see the screen.

She stepped away from the window and walked towards the table. She wasn't particularly interested in whatever Yannis was about to show her, but she knew she had to make an effort.

"This car was built by some guys in California, they are trying to go for the world land speed record. Georgina is representing them."

Kate picked her glasses up from the table and put them on. She peered at the website. It was garish. She had no doubt that many would think it was a fantastic example of modern web design. Flashing images, unclear navigation, lightboxes popping up. To Kate, it was gimmicky and crass. Just what she had come to expect from Mastery.

"It's a bit… flashy. Don't you think?"

Yannis grinned. "Yes," he agreed.

Kate removed her glasses and tapped the arm on her lip. "If this is the style you like, we can definitely follow this example. Maybe tweak it a little so there's not quite so much… visual noise."

Yannis spun the MacBook around to face him again and started to type. "I want you and Georgina to work together on this. Red Door and Mastery working together. Hand in hand. Then, this project would have the best marketing minds in America and in Europe. Together, the three of us can make something really exciting."

Kate blinked. She stared at Yannis, but he was again lost in his computer screen and oblivious to her reaction.

"You want us to work together?" Kate couldn't shake the shock from her tone. "Georgina and me? Working together?"

"Yes, isn't it perfect?" He didn't look up.

"Perfect isn't quite the word I'd use," Kate confessed. The last thing she wanted was for Georgina Masters to swoop in and take all the glory. And, potentially, the entire Atrom contract. "Yannis, we've worked together for years. I like to think we have a good working relationship?"

Yannis was focused on his screen. "Yes, yes, of course."

Kate knew he was only half-listening to her. "And Atrom and Red Door have always worked well together, haven't we? We can directly attribute the twelve-percent sales growth Atrom experienced last year to Red Door's advertising campaigns. Bringing in another voice, it could be tricky."

Yannis patted the seat next to him, still focused on his screen. "Look at this."

Kate rolled her eyes and shuffled around a couple of seats at the round meeting table. She put her glasses on again. Yannis gestured to a presentation chart on the screen.

"We need to get more social," he explained to her as if she were a child.

The presentation bore the Mastery logo. Kate pursed her lips. Clearly Georgina had presented this to Yannis and convinced him to take a new direction. Upon closer examination, it was clear that Yannis had been enticed by pie charts and line graphs that showed upward trends.

Competitor agencies pitching to existing clients wasn't a new thing. Any marketing director worth their wage would use any opportunity to speak to decision-makers. Subjectivity was not just the beauty of the marketing industry; it was also its curse.

In other businesses, a job may be a simple predefined product. The business makes widgets, a widget has set parameters. The business decides its success on widgets produced.

But marketing involves so much more. Marketing can be

good or bad, or good *and* bad at the same time. A logo can be loved and hated within one focus group.

The individuality of marketing allowed seeds of doubt to be planted by competitors. A magic formula could be proposed, fancy charts could be distributed and buzzwords deployed. All business owners want to recreate the success of other businesses, so a marketing agency promising such success was a potent thing.

Kate looked at the presentation with interest. As she thought, it contained all the generic statistics regarding social media success rates—the standard lure marketing agencies used to hook new prospective clients.

"Engineering firms can only benefit from social media to a point," Kate explained. It was a conversation they'd had several times before. Each time she explained it, Yannis agreed and understood. But within a few weeks, his flighty mind had forgotten and she was left to repeat herself. "The average person on the street doesn't care that the engine on a train is made by Atrom."

"We need to be a part of the conversation," Yannis insisted, clearly repeating the buzzwords he'd recently heard.

"There is no conversation about your sector, Yannis," Kate replied. She took off her glasses and let out a small sigh. Competitor interference in marketing was a common thing. One day a client would be happy, the next they would have read an article and would be explaining what they felt her agency needed to do.

Kate spent most of her days explaining to clients that she knew their market better than the competition. The difficulty was, this was Yannis. The phrase *bee in his bonnet* might have been created specifically with him in mind. Once he had an idea, nothing could make him let it go.

"Georgina has more information on this," Yannis explained. He gestured to the screen. "You understand all of this better than I do, anyway. But the thing to take away here is that this is exciting! We are going to build sports cars, and I want everyone to know about them. We can work together and make this the best campaign ever. Between us, I'm positive that we can make The Bolt something that everyone is talking about."

"The Bolt?"

"I'm thinking of calling it The Bolt." Yannis closed the MacBook and placed his fingers on top of it, protecting the secrets within. He leaned close to Kate. "I am still working out all of the details, but I can feel this is going to be a huge success." He smiled at her, willing her to join him in his excitement.

While his passion for the project radiated from him, Kate felt utterly unable to join in. She didn't want to work with Mastery. The whole point of running her own agency was that she didn't have to work with anyone.

"Yannis," Kate said carefully, "while working with Mastery would be wonderful, I'm not sure how we can work out the logistics. They are based in New York. You and I are based in London. Trying to split the workload, coordinate the teams, that would be very difficult."

"We're a modern world," Yannis told her. "We have video conferencing, Internet, and airplanes." He stood up and started to pack his belongings into his laptop bag. "I need the best, Kate. That's you in Europe. But I need the American market. Do you know how many millionaires are in America?"

"Not off the top of my head," Kate admitted.

"Me neither, but it's a huge country, so there must be a lot. Picture it, my Bolt driving down Sunset Boulevard, maybe driven by a movie star or a pop singer. Who knows?"

Kate knew when his mind was made up. In his head, he was already winning awards and being proclaimed the genius behind the sports car of the decade. Yannis had often explained that his success was borne entirely from his sheer willpower to make success happen. He was dogged in his approach, unwavering in his beliefs. If he wanted Kate and Georgina to work together, that is exactly what he would have.

Any further argument from Kate would just make her sound awkward. As much as she hated the idea, her best course of action now was to play along.

Georgina wasn't a fool, she didn't get to where she was by not spotting an opportunity. There was no way she'd just stumbled upon Yannis. She'd sought him out, presumably armed with enough statistical information on the car industry to put Jay Leno to shame.

It was clear to Kate that Georgina was after the Atrom Engineering account. Now it was up to Kate to do everything she could to hang onto it.

LIFE PUSHES YOU ALONG *by* EMMA STERNER-
RADLEY

The unchallenging and dull life of an assistant in a small
London bookshop is where Zoe Achidi feels safe.

Frequent customer, Rebecca Clare, makes Zoe's days a little
brighter. But the beautiful, and impressive businesswoman in
her forties seems unobtainable.

Zoe's brother and her best friend are convinced that she is
stuck in a rut. When they decide to meddle in Zoe's life, they
manage to bring Zoe and Rebecca together.

As they find the bravery and resolve to allow life to push them
along, the question soon becomes - will it push them together
or apart?

LIFE PUSHES YOU ALONG

BY EMMA STERNER-RADLEY

CHAPTER ONE

ZOE WATCHED as one of her favourite customers observed her with what seemed to be desperation. She felt her heart twinge with sympathy.

"So, do you have it?" he asked.

She knew she was going to disappoint him.

"I'm not sure, Mr. Evans. A book with a bird on the cover that was based somewhere with a big forest... that doesn't ring a bell, I'm afraid."

The bookshop's unpleasantly sharp fluorescent lights showed every crease on his wrinkled face as it took on an embarrassed look.

Zoe quickly added, "I know the feeling though. There's lots of books I have been looking for and I can't remember anything but the cover, or a piece of the plot, or half of the author's name. It's a pain."

He nodded. "Yes. Yes, my dear, it certainly is."

"Do you remember anything else about the book? Who was the main character?"

He looked up at the ceiling for a moment. "I suppose she was quite a bit like you, actually."

Zoe felt her brow furrowing. She didn't want to be rude but that didn't narrow it down much. Did he, perhaps, mean that the main character was someone who worked with customers, someone who dressed like her, or someone who was in their late twenties? She hoped he wasn't alluding to the fact that she wasn't white because she wasn't sure if a conversation with this elderly gentleman would stay politically correct if they got onto that subject. She liked Mr. Evans and wanted to continue liking him.

"I see. Um, how was she like me?"

"Young and likable," he answered simply.

Zoe was relieved. It was still just as impossible to find the book he was looking for, though.

"I'm afraid that doesn't give me much to go on. Tell you what, I'll keep an eye out for a book with a forest setting and a bird on the cover. We have your contact details on file, so I can call you if we get it in?"

His face lit up. "That would be splendid! Thank you ever so much for your help."

She smiled at him, happy to be able to help. Mr. Evans put his trilby hat back on, and she couldn't help but smile at his posh, old-fashioned sense of style which perfectly matched his way of speaking.

"Goodbye. I hope to hear from you but if I do not, I shall come in to purchase another book instead."

"You do that, Mr. Evans. Goodbye."

Just as he was leaving the bookshop, he turned around and shouted, "Oh, by the way, it might have been something other than a bird, now that I think about it. I think it was something that flew. So, maybe t'was a bat, a moth, or perhaps a ferret? Anyway, cheerio."

The door closed behind him and Zoe stared into space, puzzled.

Had he meant to say 'ferret'? How the hell was that categorized as something that flew?

Zoe's manager, and the owner of the bookshop, Darren, walked in with a small box under one arm.

He held out the box to her. "We've got a book delivery. Who was that?" He inclined his head towards the door.

"Oh, it was Mr. Evans."

Darren's bushy eyebrows met at the bridge of his nose. "Who?"

"Mr. Evans. You know, the retired bank manager who likes books about nature and sea journeys. Comes in here every week?"

Darren still looked like he was trying to do complicated arithmetic.

Zoe managed not to sigh. "The old guy with the big mole on his right cheek?"

"Oh, that crazy, posh old badger. Right. Anyway, here's the new batch. Put them on the system and then shelve them, will you?"

She gave a curt nod and took the box from him. There was no reason why he couldn't do this himself—well there was one reason and that was simply that he was lazy. He'd stand at the counter and watch her put the books out, and as soon as she was done he'd slink back into the breakroom, leaving her to man the counter as always, while he drank his bodyweight in sweet tea. *No wonder he always needs to use the loo*, she thought as she unpacked the books. She put them on the system and looked at the packing slip to check the details as she did so.

Her job wasn't the dream that most other book-nerds conjured up when she told them what she did. Yes, she worked in an independent bookshop. However, it was a lacklustre bookshop, where she was overworked, her boss didn't care much about the running of the place, and the clientele was dwindling.

As Zoe began to shelve the books, she looked around at the cheap birch bookcases, faded beige walls, and harsh fluorescent lights and thought about how she had ended up here.

She had been in dire straits when she applied for this job. She had been out on the street since her parents kicked her out. She didn't think she was focused enough for further education, she was down to her last twenty pounds and totally unqualified for any job.

Out of desperation, she had applied for this position and when Darren had asked her, in the interview, why he should hire her and not the other two applicants, who both had degrees and experience, she had broken down in tears. He had grumbled about not being able to stand seeing people cry and after a long chat about her situation, he had agreed to give her the job on a trial basis. She had never known how to thank him for that, and so she merely put up with him as a way of showing her gratitude.

She had just turned eighteen back then and she had stayed in the job for the following eight years out of loyalty, habit, and a feeling that there was no other job out there for her.

She sighed as she placed another book on the shelf. What was she qualified to do? Other bookshops were run a lot more professionally than Darren's Book Nook. Her quick foray into wanted-ads told her that they would demand that she "showed initiative" and "managed her own workload." She was sure she wasn't ready for that. She figured that a trained monkey could do the job she was doing right now and so that was what she would stick with, no matter how much it bored her.

The little bell above the door rang out. Before Zoe had time to turn to see who their new customer was, she heard Darren's sharp intake of breath. She knew immediately who must be at the door. Rebecca Clare.

Their favourite customer was shaking drops of water from her elegant brown coat and looked unfairly beautiful despite her red hair being wet and her glasses covered in little raindrops. Zoe stole as many glances as she dared while Rebecca rid herself of the worst of the rain. She admired the fancy high-heeled shoes, the black stockings, and what she could see of the knee-length black dress under her coat. And that was saying nothing about her face; those stunning eyes and the heart-shaped lips were truly mesmerizing. Especially this close up. Rebecca was near enough for Zoe to be able to reach out and brush her cheek. Not that she was daydreaming about that, of course.

Zoe knew she shouldn't be staring. Not only because it was rude, and borderline objectifying, but because Rebecca was way out of her league. And far too old for her. Zoe didn't know how old Rebecca was but she was certainly older than her own twenty-six years. Oh, and to make Rebecca even more of an impossible choice, she was Darren's huge crush too.

Just as Zoe was dragging her gaze away, she saw Rebecca quickly remove her drenched glasses. The water that had rested on them shot out in Zoe's direction, some hitting the side of her face.

Rebecca looked mortified. "Oh, I'm so sorry. Are you all right, there?"

"Yeah, sure! I'm, uh, waterproof," Zoe replied. She hoped her tone was light and jokey but worried that she sounded as terrified as she always felt when this woman spoke to her.

They had never had any long conversations, she realised. Zoe, and by extension, Darren, only knew Rebecca's name because she had ordered books and they always took contact information to be able to call or e-mail the customer when their book arrived.

Rebecca   Clare,   RebeccaClare@acacia-recruitment.com,   Zoe repeated in her head, stopping herself before she reeled off the memorized phone number too.

The contact information, which showed that she must work in recruitment considering the company's name, and Rebecca's fondness for crime-fiction was all Zoe knew about this woman. Well, that and the fact that she had the sort of presence that you couldn't miss. Despite Rebecca's feminine looks and apparel, there was almost a masculine air to her behaviour. Zoe realised that what she saw as masculine could probably be boiled down to confidence, calm, directness, and a sense of power. Rebecca was polite and friendly but in a way that spoke of a person who you couldn't take for granted.

Either way, Rebecca Clare demanded all the attention of her onlookers without having to fight for it. And that, combined with her obvious beauty, took Zoe's breath away. Just as it was doing right now as she stood with droplets of water running down her cheek and Rebecca smiling politely at her.

Zoe wiped away the water from her face with her sweater sleeve and watched Rebecca dry her glasses on a tissue she had taken out of her pocket. Then she put the glasses back on. Zoe struggled to find something to say. Something normal. Something witty.

She heard Darren clear his throat and come rushing over.

"Mrs. Clare, isn't it? Come to pick up your latest bloodcurdling chiller?" He grinned at Rebecca. Zoe realised that he probably thought it was a charming smirk. It wasn't.

"It's *Ms.* Clare," Rebecca replied casually. "And yes, please. I got an email a few days ago and haven't had time to pop in until today."

"Terrible weather for it, though. You should have waited until tomorrow," Darren said, his strange smile still fixed in place.

Zoe saw Rebecca raise an eyebrow for a brief moment.

"Well, it's meant to rain all week, so planning to only go

out when it's dry seems futile. We're Londoners, right? We're experts at dealing with rain."

Darren laughed, far too loudly and for far too long. Zoe wondered if Rebecca was suffering from second-hand embarrassment as much as she was right now. Deciding to rescue the other woman, Zoe put the books down and went behind the counter to pick up the book Rebecca had ordered and put it through the till.

When she was done, she handed Rebecca the thick tome. "Here's your book. I've never heard of this author. Is she any good?"

"Very good. Or, at least, her last three books have been. Here's hoping her latest doesn't disappoint." Rebecca looked down at the book and gave the front cover a quick pat. Then she looked back up at Zoe, with a smile.

Zoe felt herself freeze. She was meant to be telling Rebecca the total for the book, and asking if she wanted a bag but all she could do was stare. The charming smile was bad enough but Zoe had just ignored her own advice − never look this woman in the eye.

Rebecca Clare's eyes were a common blue-green colour, but what made them so dangerous was that they always seemed to glimmer. As if Rebecca was constantly happy. Or constantly flirting. It was insanely distracting and Zoe had to force herself to ignore those gorgeous eyes and just say the total sum. She barely remembered to offer a bag for the book.

When Rebecca had paid and thanked her, she turned on her high heels and click-clacked back out into the rain and out of Zoe's line of vision. Zoe sighed deeply and stopped herself when she realised that Darren could probably hear her.

It turned out that she didn't need to worry about that. Darren was busy staring after Rebecca, looking like an abandoned puppy. Zoe looked around at the shop which suddenly looked ten times duller and knew how he felt.

ABOUT THE AUTHOR

Having spent far too much time hopping from subject to subject at university, back in her native country of Sweden, Emma finally emerged with a degree in Library and Information Science.

She now lives with her wife and two cats in England. There is no point in saying which city, as they move about once a year. She spends her free time writing, reading, daydreaming, working out, and watching whichever television show has the most lesbian subtext at the time.

Her tastes in most things usually lean towards the quirky and she loves genres like urban fantasy, magic realism, and steampunk.

Emma is also a hopeless sap for any small chubby creature with tiny legs, and can often be found making heart-eyes at things like guinea pigs, wombats, marmots, and human toddlers.

You can connect with Emma on her website

Connect with Emma

www.writingradleys.com

THE LOUDEST SILENCE *by* OLIVIA JANAE

Kate, an up and coming cellist, is new to Chicago and the 'Windy City Chamber Ensemble'. During her first rehearsal, she is surprised and intrigued to meet Vivian Kensington, the formidable by reputation board president who also happens to be…deaf.

Slowly Kate develops a tentative friendship with the cold-hearted woman and as she does, she finds a kindness and a warmth that she never expected.

As their friendship begins to grow into something more, Kate wonders, is it possible for two women, one from a world of sound and one a world of silence, to truly understand one another?

THE LOUDEST SILENCE

BY OLIVIA JANAE

CHAPTER ONE

THE FIRST THING Kate noticed when she walked in was that it was quite an impressive hall for so small a chamber group.

Kate shrank back against the gold embossed doors, feeling tiny in the ocean of steep, red velvet seats, the stage looming in front of her in a grand half-circle. The hall was unnecessarily lavish, with its tall pillars, double-decked balconies, gold-leafed walls, and its huge chandelier of cloud diffusers. It was a lot, and it was intimidating. Then again, she reminded herself, this was the home of the Chicago Symphony Orchestra, one of the largest and best ensembles in the country, as well as the WCCE, so... there was that.

Built to comfortably hold the CSO, an orchestra of more than one hundred people, the measly group of twenty musicians that made up the Windy City Chamber Ensemble seemed comically small on the large stage.

She was grateful for that, though. It helped the nerves... a little bit.

She bounced her shoulders and rolled her neck.

Kate had spent the better part of her life with a cello strapped to her like a child's backpack, and while it only weighed thirty pounds, it left her shoulders and neck aching constantly. Stretching and popping had become as second nature to her as walking and talking – not to mention something of a nervous habit. She pushed her head to the side, waiting for the usual pop as she studied the crowd ahead of her, finding comfort in the routine of it. She was nervous, and no matter how much she told herself that it was fine, that she was fine, the flutter of butterflies wouldn't leave her stomach.

Stepping out of the way of a new arrival, she tensely checked her phone again, unsure if she felt better or worse that her screen had, thus far, remained blank. Tonight she had been forced to do something she hated, something she rarely did if she could help it. She had left Max with a stranger. She was pretty sure it won her a whole bundle of bad mom points, but they had only been in the city for forty-eight hours, so *anyone* she left him with would have been a stranger. There had simply been no other choice. She needed to get to work, so she hired a babysitter she had only just met that afternoon.

A horrible image flashed through her mind: Max alone and injured, her apartment empty of their few belongings, the fan still swinging haphazardly. The whole mental image was in black and white, just like old cops and robbers movies. Of course, the officer who responded to the 911 call would have his hat cocked, sounding very much like Humphrey Bogart as he explained that there was 'very little we can do, sweetheart.'

She gave a start, realizing she had let her mind drift. She knew she had to get her head in the game, that this was why they had moved to Chicago. This was why they had packed up and moved in a week, setting a new record for quickest and most finance-depleting relocation of their many relocations. This new job with the WCCE meant that she could stop freelancing for a few years, a reprieve she was thankful for. She didn't want to be thankful for the former cellist's tragic accident, of course not, but… it would also be a lie to say she wasn't, just a little bit. Her last contract had ended a few months ago, and she had been stuck. It felt like bad karma to be grateful, but this job, while not great, and with a small, local chamber group when she had grander dreams, was going to save their butts.

It also meant that she was going to have to deal with some awkwardness for a little bit, but that was a small sacrifice, assuming of course that her son wasn't hog-tied by the new babysitter or something.

She rolled her eyes, inwardly chastising herself for being an idiot.

Kate took a deep, shaky breath, clicked on her usual crooked half-smile, and started toward the stage, hands shoved deeply into her jeans pockets.

Common practice in the world of classical music was that all auditions were posted online, and then, once the job was won, photos and a bio of the new hire were posted as well. It was just one of those unspoken rules, like slapping a big red '*sold*' sticker over a property sign once it had been purchased. Because of this, few were all that interested in a newcomer, having already checked her out online. She didn't mind that. She had hated the times when she'd walked into the rehearsal space and everyone had turned to stare as if she were a new zoo exhibit.

It gave her uncomfortable PTSD flashbacks, reminding her of all the first days at new schools she had suffered as a child and teenager. Each time a new family thought that the blonde-haired, green-eyed little girl was the one they wanted to foster, Kate had been forced to relocate, to start a new school in a new area, new town, new city. The fact that said family would inevitably decide they didn't actually want her wasn't the worst part of the scenario; it was that first day of walking into a new school, feeling all of the new and curious eyes on her. She had hated it then, and she hated it now.

The problem this time was that Kate's photo hadn't been posted; the audition hadn't been listed. No one knew who she was. No one knew anything other than the fact that she had been the one out of ten cellists to win the last-minute audition to fill Hilary's place. She was there under extraordinary circumstances, and as she walked toward the stage the constant humming of talk died until the drop of a pin could be heard. Each and every head turned to stare, looking at her as though she were both a relief and a curse.

Kate was there to cover for someone who had been hurt. The very need for her scared them, and so they stared.

Kate flinched, hiking her cello up on her shoulder as she paused at the foot of the stairs. This wasn't her first rodeo, though, so she took a moment to steady herself and then, shoulders squared, she climbed onto the stage.

She spent a few minutes introducing herself to a number of officials in suits and ties, their lofty yet uninterested expressions all clear markers that they were board members. Once that was done, she turned to her fellow musicians, who looked a bit more like her in jeans and T-shirts.

The casual wear helped to settle Kate's nerves a bit more. She had been worried that the performers in a chamber group this prestigious would always be in professional wear, concert blacks even during rehearsals. It had happened to her before. She had shown up to a new orchestra job in her typical, comfortable clothes to find the lot in bow ties and cocktail dresses. The whole room had rolled their eyes as if to say, with an elitist groan, '*Freelancers.*' Kate had pretty thick skin, but it had been humiliating to sit beside the elegant, well-dressed people while wearing jeans, an 'I heart NY' shirt, and old, scuffed Converse.

Still, for the sake of looking her best and making good first impressions, she anxiously forced her fingers through her hair, trying to tame a few of the windblown curls. She wished she had thought to stop in the bathroom and brush it down. She got a few smiles back, but most just gave her a shifty-eyed nod and then turned back to their instruments and books of études. Nonplussed, she sat and released her cello from its confines to begin her usual warm-up routine.

"Katelyn? Are you Katelyn?" From the wings a woman floated onto the stage, her features small and sharp, her hair in a raven crop. A large, reddish-purple bruise on the side of her neck let Kate know she was a violinist. Which, if Kate recalled, also meant that this was the personnel manager she had spoken to on the phone.

She stood again, nervously running her hands over her thighs before giving her a half-smile. "Kate. Hi."

Obvious relief on her face, the woman dropped some papers into Kate's chair and shook Kate's hand with both of hers.

"Hi. It's so nice to meet you! Thank you again for doing this. I'm Mary."

Kate gave a nod. "Yeah, of course. It was the fastest move we've made, but it was nice and easy." Mary's face slackened into an open and wide look of pity that made Kate uncomfortable, so she added quickly, "Thank you for the opportunity."

"Of course. I'm just sorry it had to be under these circumstances. You come very highly recommended."

"Yeah, well …" Kate wasn't sure to say to that. Her hand was still trapped in Mary's, and starting to feel uncomfortably warm, but when she gave a small pull, Mary didn't seem to notice. "How is Hilary? Any updates?"

Hilary Ajam was, or had been, the Windy City Chamber Ensemble's resident cellist for the last five years, and as far as Kate had heard, no one had any complaints. However, just over a month before, Hilary had been crossing the street on her bike, safely in the bike lane, when a Nissan Altima blew through the crosswalk. The hit had fractured her leg cleanly, but in her forearm the radius had been shattered, ripping through one of the attached muscles. The ten-month WCCE season was about to begin, and Hilary would not be participating.

"From what I hear, she's good. They put some type of anchors in her." Mary's eyebrows drew together, trying to remember. "Extensor something or other. I don't know, but you're here!"

Kate chuckled, finally pulling her hand free.

There had been the audition, and Kate had won. She felt bad for Hilary. Everyone in the classical world dreaded an accidental, career-ending injury, but Kate knew she had gotten lucky as a result. The contract was for one year, and Mary had assured her that come next May, there would be another waiting for her, as Hilary would most likely need another year of rehab. Kate had never seen someone come back from that type of injury in even two years, and so she was elated for herself and for Max, sure that, for the time being, they could settle.

"Well," Mary sighed, reaching out and giving Kate's arm a caress, "I'll let you get warmed up. I'm so glad you're here. Thank you again."

Kate nodded and sat, doing her best to ignore the eyes on her.

The musicians around her brought out their instruments and began plucking or tooting away, warming their muscles like athletes stretching before a game. The scatting of the trumpet to her left made Kate's ears pop.

She pulled her cello to her, all at once comforted by its steady presence, but before she could begin her own warm-up, a voice spoke behind her.

"You look nervous."

She craned her neck a little as she turned to see who had spoken, cello supported firmly between her knees. For just a split second, her eyes widened as she took in the face of the attractive woman half hidden behind a huge, upright double bass.

Kate clicked on a polite smile. The fact that she had been staring dumbly for a few seconds made her cheeks go slightly pink.

Though a moment before her expression had been bland, on seeing Kate's pause, the bass player broke into a huge, smug grin. Kate had been gawking, and this gorgeous stranger knew it.

"I'm sorry?" Kate asked, thoroughly unimpressed with her malfunctioning brain.

The bass player's smile had melted again, expression matching her tone. Her aloof gaze twitched between Kate and the cell phone in her hand, as though she was talking to Kate to be kind and the text she was reading demanded her full attention. Kate cleared her throat a little awkwardly, and the stranger finally looked up, her piercing olive eyes holding Kate's gaze with intrigue and confidence. Her strong jaw, angled cheeks, and pale skin were as impressive as the long, dirty blonde dreadlocks tied in an effortless knot behind her head.

It was unusual to see a female bass player. The instrument was huge, so women usually had a harder time wrapping around it. This woman seemed to have no problem with that; her arms draped around the large instrument comfortably, her long, thin – and now phoneless – hand resting with ease across the strings.

"I said you seem a bit nervous, *chica*."

As a matter of fact, she was attractive enough that the horn player to her left kept shooting furtive glances her way, as if begging her to look over and notice him. The woman's expression gave Kate the distinct impression that she was aware that she was good-looking, just as she was fully aware of the hopeful glances of the horn player to her left, who kept shooting furtive glances her way, as if begging her to look over and notice him. The woman, however, was firmly ignoring him. That didn't surprise Kate. She didn't need her "gaydar" to know this woman was "Kinsey-six gay." It radiated from her like a Sapphic cologne.

"Uh, I'm not nervous exactly."

It was more that she wasn't entirely sure she was supposed to be there. She had won the job, yeah, but she still wasn't sure they had meant to pick her instead of some other thin blonde with her initials. It wasn't a new feeling, either. She was always somewhat convinced that someone somewhere had checked the wrong box, passing her forward in the audition instead of kicking her to the gutter where she truly belonged.

It was stupid – she had earned her place and she knew it, – but it always took her a little while in a new job to let go of the feeling. She hadn't gone to a prestigious school like most of her colleagues, she didn't come from money, and she didn't have a gaggle of parents or cheerleaders behind her. In fact, it had always been her, alone, until Max was born, and then it had been them, the Flynn duo out to get the world.

A large part of her imposter syndrome was habit; she knew that. Kate had never really felt like she would fit *anywhere*; that was just a fact of life.

Then again, she could still hear the small voice in the back of her head reminding her that this job didn't really count, that she had only gotten it because of an emergency, that they had been desperate. It warred with her logic, and though she tried to ignore it, the voice was persistent.

Of course, she wasn't going to tell this unfamiliar woman all of that. Instead, she cleared her throat and said, "It's more that if there're *any* mistakes, then it's all me. There's kind of no one else to blame when you're the only cello."

The bass player just shrugged one shoulder. "*Maaaan*," she said through her laugh, her words slow and casual, "we all make mistakes. It's whatever. No one is going to judge you for them, at least not yet." She gave her eyebrows a devilish and entirely charming waggle.

Kate's own eyebrows shot up in surprise. "Wow, talk about making the new girl feel welcome," she dryly muttered, running her hand over the comfortingly smooth wood of her cello. "Should I be expecting some type of initiation, too? Gonna make me run around the Loop in my underwear?"

"Not the first week." The stranger winked.

Kate gave an amused snort.

"Kay, just give me some warning, and I'll wear some cute underwear at least."

"You really talking to me about your underwear?" the bassist cried in mock concern, her hand placed reverently over her chest as she spoke in one of the worst Southern belle accents Kate had ever heard. "I *just* met you! I'll have you know that I am *not* that kind of girl!"

Kate gave a loud snort of a laugh.

She grinned back, her bright eyes twinkling. "Ash. Er, Campbell." She gave her a wide smile that was all teeth. "Ash Campbell. Is me. Hey."

A little charmed, Kate took her offered hand, noting the chipped black polish and the tattoos littered up and down her forearm. Kate turned her arm to get a better view of the largest tattoo, a poisonous-looking bite wound riddled with streaks of purple and green as though infected and bleeding. In the center were the words "Love Bites." It looked like the kind of tattoo you got when you were freshly eighteen and had just been dumped by your girlfriend for her ex-boyfriend.

Kate chuckled while fighting the urge to roll her eyes. "That's quite a tattoo."

"Yeah, well." Ash shrugged. 'It's a tattoo. I dunno. What can I say?"

Amused, she swallowed it down, and, willing enough to be friendly, Kate gave her hand a quick shake. It wasn't as though she had an abundance of friends or even acquaintances here. Besides, there was something intriguing about the bass player. "Kate Flynn."

"It's good to meet you, Katie."

"Kate," she corrected with a small shake of her head. She was definitely not a "Katie," never had been.

"Okay, guys!" Her attention was drawn back to the front of the stage as Mary called for silence and began running them through a few notices. "And of course, as you all can see, our new cellist has finally made it. Kate Flynn. Welcome! We're so excited to have you!"

Kate nodded with a plastic smile.

Mary spent a while going over the plans they had for the upcoming season, what they would play for the first concert, and explaining who would be playing with whom, something that *was* indeed new to Kate. Typically an orchestra played together, all working as one to produce something beautiful, but things were different in a chamber music organization. Unlike an orchestra, the ensemble employed a mere twenty people from specific instrument sections, often hiring a single trumpet, violin, cello, and so on. Those twenty rarely played together as a complete group. Instead, different pieces of music were programed for their concerts, and then those twenty people were divvied out into trios, quartets, quintets, or sextets, depending on the type of ensemble the piece required.

Kate was pleased to find that she was placed in several groups. She hated it when the new person was held back for a while to learn the ropes. She was very much a grab-life-by-the-balls, all-or-nothing girl.

Mary's lecture carried on forever; she was clearly a fan of her own voice. At first the length of the talk made Kate's skin itch. She hadn't warmed up, and she wished that she had come in earlier. This information wasn't new. Why go on and on about pieces that were already well known to the musicians? It wasn't as though they hadn't played the pieces before – ten or more times.

She was just slipping into another worried daydream about her son when a flurry of motion caught her eye to the side of the stage, snapping her back to her surroundings. At first she glanced around guiltily, hoping no one had noticed her inattention, this being her first day and all. When she saw that most around her had glazed, lost looks on their faces, too, she glanced back toward the motion, struggling to see past the stage lights.

She squinted and saw a brunette standing in the shadows off stage left, back perfectly straight, chin high as she glared into the face of the man she was speaking to. She looked as though she wanted to claw his eyes out. Kate winced for him as the woman snarled, saying something that made the man cower back a step or two. She couldn't blame him for being nervous; that woman looked fierce. Next to the angry woman stood a younger, sweet-faced Asian woman, her rich eyes sparkling as she gave a grin that didn't seem to go with the conversation they were all having. She stared in clear concentration at the man, her hands jumping and dancing as *he* spoke.

Kate frowned, the lecture from Mary forgotten. She didn't know much about it; only a few things she had seen on *Sesame Street* with Max, but that was the language deaf people spoke, right? Um, Sign Language; yeah, it was called Sign Language, a name she had always thought was beautiful, and perfectly described what it looked like.

This was definitely something that she had never seen before. Well, she had seen a deaf person or two in her life, someone walking down the street and talking with their partner, or perhaps on TV, but she had never seen a deaf person in a setting like this one. What was a person who couldn't *hear* doing in a chamber rehearsal? Both of the women were dressed too well, too perfectly, to be anything other than there on purpose. It wasn't like they had taken a wrong turn at Albuquerque.

The younger and taller of the two finally let her hands fall still to her stomach as if in rest position, her expression blank as she turned toward the other, expectantly waiting. The other woman's face had only grown ever more lethal, her deep red lips curling back in open fury. She pinned the man with her eyes, saying something that made him quake in his boots as she pointed, threatening to jab in him the chest. He was in the middle of a fast and nervous nod when he turned on his heels to escape, walking just a bit too quickly for him to keep a strong hold on his dignity. Kate had a moment to feel bad for the guy before her eyes were pulled back to the women. She watched the younger woman's eyebrows shoot into her hairline as her hands flew into beautiful, fluid motion again. The other rolled her flashing eyes in response, and with quick stabbing motions she answered in the same language.

Kate was intrigued by the mystery of deaf women in a classical music setting, but just then her attention was drawn back to Mary as she finally separated them to rehearse.

The rehearsal went as smoothly as she could have hoped. The group played beautifully, as she had known they would, and it was a confidence boost to be among them, which was great since the first gig was scheduled for only a few days later.

On occasion, as she played, her eye was drawn from her

sheet music to the wings, looking for the flying hands again, almost like a tic. Despite her interest, she hadn't been able to take a moment to watch as she wanted to. It was difficult not to keep glancing back; something about the language, something about the hand motions, about the flow – it was so intriguing.

ABOUT THE AUTHOR

While new to publishing, Olivia Janae is not new to writing. It has been her favorite pastime since she was young.

As a child growing up in California, it was always her dream to one day see her name on the cover of a book.

Olivia now lives in the Midwest with her classical musician wife, three cats and, soon, a baby will make six.

Outside of her love of writing, Olivia is an avid movie buff with an obsessive love of cooking, candy making, and *Buffy The Vampire Slayer*.

Connect with Olivia

www.oliviajanae.com

Made in the USA
Lexington, KY
15 July 2018